Corpse-Candle

Corpse-Candle

Margaret Duffy

PIATKUS
CRIME

Copyright © 1995 by Margaret Duffy

First published in Great Britain in 1995 by
Judy Piatkus (Publishers) Ltd of
5 Windmill Street, London W1

**The moral right of the author
has been asserted**

*A catalogue record for this book is available
from the British Library*

ISBN 0 7499 0281 7

Phototypeset in 11/12pt Compugraphic Times by
Action Typesetting Limited, Gloucester
Printed and bound in Great Britain by
Bookcraft (Bath) Ltd

Prologue

16 April, 11.07 p.m.
The murderer was driving without lights and very slowly. When the destination was almost reached, the engine of the vehicle was turned off, ensuring a virtually silent arrival. The sky was dark for there were no towns in the vicinity to light up the heavens, and the village too, straggling along the main road on the other side of a thick belt of trees, was in darkness. The murderer needed it to be so.

The dead body of the woman in the boot of the car was heavy and difficult to handle but after a short while, utter silence of paramount importance, it had been manoeuvred the final few yards towards the rear of the house from the car.

There were several very bad moments while the body was being moved to its resting place and the murderer was sweating heavily by the time it had been manhandled into place. It entailed accompanying the dead woman for a while on her journey down into the blackness and for one nightmare moment, etched like acid onto the murderer's memory for ever, those cold, dead lips had touched the cheek of the one carrying her.

There was only one small light that could be permitted and when that was kindled the murderer felt weak with relief that part of the task was completed, though it was not quite finished.

The only real worry now was that the faint sounds associated with what was taking place would be heard by those in the house. *If* there was anyone at home; nothing

1

was certain. But the woman who was now dead would be safely hidden for a while until other arrangements could be made. The murderer paused – surely she could stay here for ever? Who would know? Who came to this part of the house now?

When she started to rot, though ...

The murderer shuddered and positioned the heavy load carefully.

When it was all quite dark again, everything still, the corpse moved slightly, slumping until it leaned against the door of its tomb. The candle, forgotten, guttered and went out.

Chapter One

Almost exactly seventy-two hours before she found her very first corpse, Ginny Somerville let herself into her flat, picked up the post from the hall carpet, tossed it onto the sofa as she crossed the living room, kicked off her shoes in the kitchen and put the kettle on. After the day she had just been through, with London hot, dry and dusty, she really felt like downing a pint of iced Coke very well laced with rum. Common sense prevailed, however; she had work to do.

There had been another terrorist bomb in the City, and Ginny, an assistant television producer, had been working in the locality.

When helping to plan and research a series of programmes about the Metropolitan Police's Anti-Terrorist Branch, she had possibly ignored or not realised the risks attached to such a subject. Working on a fly-on-the-wall documentary meant that she would be right there as things happened, with her small team; Alvis, cameraman, and his assistant Ted; Pru, sound assistant, wired up to Alvis; and Sparky Harris, lighting. They had trailed Commander Fielding – with his somewhat grudging permission, 'On your ain heids be it' – as he strode around the cleared and cordoned-off area near Hanover Square in the West End. Fielding was a dyed-in-the-wool Scot from Lanark. A prophetic remark Ginny called it later, because on their own heads it almost had been.

Alvis had been ecstatic later with the action shot he had inadvertently obtained when he had dived to the pavement. The suspect van, together with every window within a quarter-mile radius, had at that moment ceased to exist. Instantly the air had been filled with scything death, glass and slivers of metal whistling above them as they lay on the ground.

For one shocked, desperate second there had been utter silence. Then every security alarm in the neighbourhood had gone off, this racket almost obliterated for a few moments by the crash as all the glass and other debris had landed.

Someone, somewhere in the distance, was screaming. Ginny had been aware of this but the main impression just then had been of a weight across her shoulders, pinning her. This had soon proved to be Commander Fielding, who had somehow turned and thrown himself protectively over her. She had instantly forgiven him his irascibility.

No one had been hurt. The woman screaming — an office worker being led to safety — had only been suffering from shock. It was the first time the team from Nimrod Productions had been exposed to such hazards, but they kept working, ending up with some very valuable material indeed.

'That was quite interesting,' Alvis had drawled in offhand fashion during the short debriefing before they had all gone home. He had then ruined the rather *soigné* effect by suddenly yawning like a horse. Yes, they were all exhausted.

Much later, Ginny had noted down the questions she wanted to ask Commander Fielding at the filmed interview they would be having with him in his office the following day, showered, and was sipping a glass of Chenin while her dinner cooked. Turning to the letters on the sofa, she postponed acquainting herself with the telephone and electricity bills and opened the letter from Scotland, the envelope made of heavy paper that crackled as she extracted what was within. She set aside her wineglass as she read.

Messrs Cromarty and Macduish, Solicitors, Notaries Public and Estate Agents of Bridge of Corran, Inverness-shire, begged to inform her, with deep regret, that her father, Alastair James Somerville, had died in hospital on 10 July, two days previously. If she contacted them she would learn something to her advantage.

'The old devil,' Ginny whispered. 'He's drunk himself to death at last.'

She could just, and only just, remember him. Her mother, alas now also deceased, a teacher who had been brought up in the south of England, had left him and Scotland when Ginny was six years old, swearing that she would never cross the border again. She had kept her vow, preferring Torquay and telling everyone she was a widow. Only Ginny had known that, somewhere, her father was still alive. Oddly, there had never been a divorce, but hearing her mother speak of him on very rare occasions Ginny had understood why she left him and had grown to hate him for the violence and drunken rages that her mother recounted. Her only memory of him was unhappy, albeit hazy: sitting on his knee when she was five while he extracted a large splinter from her finger, her small hand imprisoned in his strong brown one, no escape. It had hurt dreadfully and she had cried but he had told her not to be such a baby. Presumably a splinter had been very small beer for a doctor who was used, in those days, to lancing the boils that a bad diet induced in the local population.

Shuddering, her mother had recalled some of this. She had never settled in what she regarded as an alien country and the poor suburb of Edinburgh where they lived had been her idea of a nightmare. That and the rain, the cold and what she referred to the 'unrelenting greyness'.

Ginny had in her mind a picture of a big man with a loud voice — her mother had said that he would never speak quietly if a shout would do — the sort of man who was afraid of nothing and no one. What on earth, Ginny had sometimes wondered, had brought her parents together?

The phone call to the solicitors would have to wait until the next day; it was too late now.

As soon as she arrived for work at the company's headquarters, on the second floor of a one-time warehouse in Brock Street, just off Wardour Street, Soho, there was a summons from Jake. Jake Crawthorne was the managing director and executive producer of Nimrod Productions, mainly, it must be said, because of the two men who had

5

gone into partnership to set up the company, he was the one with the money.

Barry Chichester, on the other hand, for whom Ginny worked, possessed the reputation. Barry had been with the BBC for years and, as a producer of weighty, insightful documentaries with a hands-on, sensitive approach to his subjects, he had been one of the jewels in the crown of that organisation. There had been the BAFTA-award-winning investigation into false allegations of police corruption made by those involved in organised crime and terrorism. This had earned him the respect of many senior police officers and when a series of films about the Metropolitan Police was mooted, heavy pressure had been applied from New Scotland Yard that Chichester should make them.

At that point, the BBC was being restructured, and Chichester felt increasingly vexed at being, in his own words, 'always hampered by accountants and tyrants', so he resigned to start up on his own. Then he met Crawthorne, late of a small company producing, among other things, cosmetics-promotion films, who was seeking to find himself a new, more serious and artistic image. And Chichester, with his prestigious series waiting for a backer, was just the man he needed.

Ginny, with a degree in media studies and a little experience in radio, had joined the new company on a short contract in order to gain experience. She and Barry had taken to one another immediately and when Barry's wife had been injured in a car crash while on holiday in Greece, Ginny had been presented with an opportunity rarely given to young producers. They had already done most of the preparation work when Barry had to drop everything and fly out to Athens, so it was a question of carrying on, trying to remember everything he had taught her and trying out a few cherished ideas of her own.

Everyone liked Yasmin, Barry's beautiful wife, a researcher. For three days her life had hung in the balance, Barry at her bedside. When it had become apparent that she would recover, Barry had rented a flat so that he could stay close by her until she was strong enough to be flown home. This had taken place some three weeks after the

6

accident and after another long stay in hospital Yasmin was now at home being looked after by Barry. Ginny could at least contact him more easily by phone and she was very glad of this; he was a constantly patient, encouraging source of advice.

Perhaps unconsciously, to make up for his lack of reputation, Jake had bought himself a very large desk. There was an executive-style swivel chair to go with it. Both had the unfortunate effect of making Jake − whom no one, even in a charitable moment could describe as an imposing figure − look smaller.

'Ginny, my dear!' he exclaimed, arms wide, as though he had not seen her in months.

She thwarted his embrace by placing herself in close proximity to a tall, spineless yucca, one of several large plants that shared Jake's office with him. They were flourishing because he had green fingers, sponging their leaves, feeding them and even talking to them when he thought his desk intercom was switched off.

'And you're *quite* all right after yesterday?' he asked solicitously.

'Of course,' Ginny replied, giving him her best interviewing smile and sitting in the chair nearest the yucca.

'I'd have given anything to have been there with you,' Jake said, casting himself into his swivel chair with a skill born of long practice and revolving a few times, a big grin on his face.

'How was Plymouth?' she asked, ignoring the lie. He hated anything that went bang.

'Damned hot. As you know, it was a business trip, but the more I see of the West Country, the more I want to do a project there. Shipbuilding, sailors, copper mining and the tinners, china clay − loads of material.'

'Wreckers, press gangs, smugglers, the Armada, Drake's Drum, the legends of Dartmoor,' Ginny suggested eagerly.

'That aspect's okay for kids,' Jake said dismissively. He frowned, creasing a brow that already had a few lines in it, staring into space. He tended to look slightly worried these days, small darting eyes not detracting from this. He was slightly built and had narrow shoulders and long arms. In

7

colouring he was pale, his hair mousy and receding. This, together with thin, bloodless lips, meant that the overall effect was somewhat snaky.

'You wanted to see me?' Ginny reminded him.

He came out of his reverie, leaned back in his chair and beamed at her. 'I think you and I ought to have private little meetings like this. Now and again. While Barry's away.'

'Surely everything can be discussed at the weekly general meetings?'

Another beam. In a conspiratorial whisper he said, 'You and I ought to work much more closely together.'

Ginny decided to carry on playing dumb. 'You mean to involve yourself more deeply with day-to-day shooting?'

He took a deep breath, stared at the ceiling and said, 'Yeah.' He did not add 'sort of' but his tone did.

'So all at once I'm not capable of working on my own any more?'

Instantly, he was conciliatory. 'Now did I *say* that?'

You horrible little coward, Ginny thought. You haven't the guts to come out with what's really on your mind. She said, 'Barry and I are in very close touch − I'm really only carrying out his instructions.'

He made a play of placing all the pens and pencils on his desk in a large china mug marked ADMIRAL. 'Barry's had several months off to look after Yasmin but she's almost fit now. The question is, can Nimrod support two production teams?'

'I wasn't aware we had two production teams,' Ginny retorted. 'At the moment nothing happens like that − there aren't enough staff.'

'There has to be some restructuring,' Jake muttered. He suddenly smiled at her in a way that he presumably thought made him look winsome but succeeded only in resembling a lovesick anaconda. 'The real point, Ginny, my love, is, can this company support two producers? Your contract with us is almost up.'

'Times are hard, eh?' Ginny said sympathetically, knowing that she was listening to nothing more than blackmail. 'That's all right, Jake. I'm more than happy to be Barry's assistant.'

8

'I'm the one who makes that kind of decision,' he said quietly.

'And I make the decisions about my private life. The answer's no.'

'I've been very good to you, Ginny,' he said, tight-lipped.

'No, you just threw me in the deep end when Barry had to fly out to Athens.'

'That's not true. I gave you your big chance.'

'So you weren't scared stiff that if you showed your face to the boys in blue someone might remember all about you driving while disqualified a few years ago?'

There was rather a long silence.

'Is that all you wanted me for?' Ginny asked, finally. 'Only I'm rather busy right now.'

'Yes,' he replied, face like an Easter Island statue.

She was still seething when she picked up the phone in her own office and dialled Cromarty and Macduish's number. When a woman answered, she asked to speak to the man who had signed the letter, John Laird.

'I'm so sorry we had to break the news so boldly in a letter,' he said when he came on the line. 'But we were aware that you and your father were somewhat estranged.'

'For over twenty years,' Ginny said. 'I wasn't even aware that he'd moved to the west of Scotland. Is it necessary for me to come up?'

'Well, there's the funeral in two days' time,' Laird said, his careful lawyer's voice only slightly tinged with reproach.

She consulted her work schedule. With a little juggling around ... 'Yes, I should be able to make it if I fly up. Is there anything else?'

'No doubt you'll want to see the house. He left it to you.'

This was a real shock and Laird must have understood her silence for he continued, 'It's not in Bridge of Corran but a small village some five miles south. He had a surgery there two days a week and his main practice here. He moved there years ago − 1970, I think − when he left Edinburgh, after his wife ... He was fond of the place. The village is called Kinloch Ruthven, by the way.' He went on to spell

9

it, the second word being pronounced 'riven'.

'And the funeral's being held there?'

'Yes, at the High Kirk at ten fifteen. Would you like me to arrange accommodation for you?'

'That would be kind of you, Mr Laird. Thank you.' Ginny wrote down the directions he gave her to find the church, asked him to order a wreath for her and rang off. After making two more phone calls, everything seemed to be organised. It was a real blow, the realisation that the trip would take two very valuable days, but there was nothing she could do about that, the distance was too great. Her hand strayed towards the phone as she wondered if she could ask Laird to change the time of the funeral to the afternoon. No, perhaps that was not really good form.

'Respect the dead,' she said as Alvis came through the door, munching on a large Granny Smith. He never knocked, not that she particularly wanted him to.

'I'm not,' he whimpered in mock horror, his hands convulsively clutching the material of his baggy T-shirt.

'I didn't mean you, you daft turnip,' Ginny responded mildly. She thoroughly enjoyed Alvis's offbeat sense of humour.

He grinned at his reflection in a small mirror on the wall and raked his fingers through his untidy thatch of brown hair. 'But yesterday − for a second or two ...' ·

'Me too.'

He subsided into a chair. 'Who's dead then?'

'My father. The day before yesterday.'

This time his emotion was genuine. 'God, Ginny! I'm so sorry.'

'Don't be. I'm not. He was a beast to my mother and she got shot of him donkey's ages ago. Trouble is, I've let myself in for the funeral the day after tomorrow and it's in Scotland. With a bit of luck I'll only be away for − '

'But of *course* you must go. How could you not? He was your father, after all.'

'I suppose so,' she murmured.

'How come he was living up there?'

'He was the local sawbones. When my mother walked out he left Edinburgh and went to live in a village called

10

Kinloch Ruthven. I'd never even heard of it.'

Alvis's good-natured face screwed up into a scowl. It always did when he was thinking. 'They have Highland Games there so it must be quite a big village. Folk come from all over the place. I went there once when we were on holiday when I was a kid. Big hairy blokes in kilts heaving telephone poles around and people playing porridge guns.'

'*Porridge* guns?'

'Bagpipes.' He gazed at her with interest. 'He was a Scot?'

'Oh, yes.'

'So you're half Scottish. That accounts for it.'

'Accounts for *what?*' Ginny demanded to know, annoyed that it had not occurred to her before.

'The determination to get things done, courage in the face of bombs, peril and dragons,' he answered, resoundingly rolling all the 'Rs'.

She threw the wastepaper basket at him.

Ginny's mother had said that it had hardly stopped raining the entire time she had lived in Scotland, and Glasgow seemed to be carrying on the tradition with gritty resolution. A light but amazingly soaking drizzle blotted out all but the immediate environs of the airport. Thus, Ginny remained in total ignorance of the rolling Campsie Fells to the north of the city and the Kilsyth Hills slightly farther east; for that matter she had been oblivious of any landscape that Scotland might possess on account of the thick cloud that had materialised at Carlisle.

Two hours later she was driving along the shores of Loch Lomond, having stopped to buy a road map, some fudge – called 'tablet' here – and a golf umbrella. When, rather testily, she had informed the man in the car-hire office that a couple of weeks previously the Wimbledon tennis championships had finished having not had a drop of rain during the entire fortnight, he had merely grunted and wished her a good journey.

She knew that Alvis, the same age as she was, twenty-nine, had wished he had the courage to ask if he might accompany her. She would have put him off without offend-

11

ing him. He was what Pru called a real sweetie; fun, easy-going, pleasant to work with even when things became difficult. Although Ginny was aware that there was a gleam in his eye as far as she was concerned, and they had been for a drink together a couple of times, she felt that she wanted no part in the life of a man who just seemed to drift, smiling gently and relying on girlfriends who could cook and sew because he was always hungry and his toes apparently chewed holes in his socks.

Jake was the real problem. What he had in mind was by no means unusual in the trade, of course, and for all she knew he had decided to endeavour to wear her on his arm to boost his image. Which made it worse in a way. She would have almost preferred him to have admitted to driving lust than behave the way he had. Her colleagues, she knew, would recommend her to find a boyfriend, preferably one well over six foot in height, who would deter Jake for ever. But Ginny didn't want a boyfriend. Men did not really interest her, close relationships did not interest her; it all got in the way of what she liked best; making films.

Scotland continued to be a mystery. The loch was no more than occasional glimpses of steel-grey water through the curtains of rain, this no longer drizzle but a wholehearted downpour.

At Crianlarich she stopped for a late lunch, dashing through the rain to a café, the wind strong enough to make coping with a large umbrella difficult. The distance to the village now horrified her and she was angry with herself for not having planned her journey more thoroughly beforehand. Normally she was a very good organiser, her work depended on it.

As she went farther north and west, the terrain became wilder and more rugged and it was also misty − low cloud, she supposed. The road was quite a good one but it twisted and turned, and although she could not see she had an idea that there were steep drops at the sides of some of the bends. Sheep and lambs, apparently intent on suicide, would suddenly appear out of the mist, forcing her to brake sharply.

In Glencoe she parked and ate some fudge, feeling a

fool because she was so unnerved. It was distinctly eerie, the only sounds the rain pattering on the roof of the car and the distant roar of a waterfall. Water was streaming down the sides of the hills in white plumes. Anything, she felt, could loom out of the mist.

Past Ballachulish, she became slightly cheered by the sight of a transport café with its car park overflowing with cars and trucks – so that was what had happened to all the traffic. She left the shores of Loch Leven and turned northeast along Loch Linnhe. Half an hour later she rounded a bend and saw Kinloch Ruthven below her.

Alvis had been quite correct. Strung across the village street was a banner proclaiming that the annual games would take place on the Thursday of the following week, 22 July.

John Laird had not contacted her to let her know where she would be staying, but several cottages had Bed and Breakfast signs outside. She stopped at one that fronted directly onto the road and rang the doorbell.

'You poor wee soul!' exclaimed the woman who answered the door. 'And you having to drive all that way in this dreadful weather. There was a severe-weather warning – I hope you heard it on the radio. Hardly anyone's got through. Now don't you worry, my dear, John Laird's booked you in with Maggie Mossblown down at Langside House.'

Ginny stared at her in astonishment.

'You *are* Miss Somerville?' asked the woman anxiously.

'Yes,' Ginny replied faintly.

'I thought I was right. I met Maggie in the post office this morning and she said that if I saw a lass looking lost I was to send her *straight* down. Such a shame about your poor father! He was well thought of hereabouts and now everyone has to go to that dreadful modern clinic in Bridge of Corran. And we all know John Laird, of course, he was born and bred here and *his* father was the minister for eighteen years. Now, if it wasn't a bit late I'd ask you in for a cup of tea but Maggie will fret. She can't abide that road herself and won't go anywhere near Glencoe at night or in the winter. Haunted it is, she says, by all those poor souls who were murdered there. No, you'd best be off. It's the third house down on the left-hand side, not counting the farm.'

Bemused, Ginny thanked her and was opening the car door when the woman called, 'You're not thinking of staying here by any chance? All the young folk move away.'

'I can't,' Ginny told her. 'My job's in London.'

'That's a shame. It's a fine house.'

But in London, Ginny thought as she drove away, no one knows your business.

She drew up outside a cottage, realised she had counted in the farm and drove to the next gateway, where a drive led down to a detached house on the shores of the loch. It seemed a different world here, the air soft on her face as she alighted from the car, the rain now like a fine mist, what she would soon learn that the locals called 'smirr'. It was very quiet; all she could hear was a robin twittering in a hedge and the gentle splash of tiny waves on the shore.

Langside House looked as though its front step was scrubbed every morning. Certainly the brass knocker and letter box were polished regularly and there was not one dead bloom on the dripping-wet scarlet geraniums in the window boxes. Ginny rang the bell, wondering if her father's house was like this.

Maggie Mossblown was a lot younger than Ginny had imagined, a fair-haired woman of very generous proportions.

'There, you found me!' she cried before Ginny could say a word. 'Come in the warm and get dry. John was that worried about you, what with his phone being out of order yesterday. He said he'd call in later and introduce himself. He had an idea you'd not get to his office tonight.'

'That's very good of him,' Ginny said, resigning herself to the fact that the entire village knew all about her.

'Ach, he only lives a few minutes away up at Hillhead.'

Having taken her overnight bag up to a scrupulously clean but freezing-cold bedroom, Ginny gratefully accepted an invitation to take tea in Miss Mossblown's own sitting room. This, thankfully, had an open fire and she warmed her hands trying not to look frozen to the marrow.

'You'll not be tempted to live here with the summer so bad this year,' said Maggie, rings glinting as her podgy hands

14

deftly flitted around the bone-china teaware. 'They say the soft-fruit growers will be ruined. And it snowed at the end of May when the grouse were sitting on their eggs, causing the birds to leave their nests, so the big estates won't be able to hold shoots this year. I don't know what we're coming to. Not so long ago they were saying that it was going to get so hot that the poles would melt and we'd all be flooded. Well, we're flooded all right − with rain.'

'My job's in London,' Ginny said, not for the first time.

'Can you not transfer?'

'No. I'm sort of freelance but work for a small film company. Most of our projects are in the south.'

Miss Mossblown sighed. 'I thought it would be like that. But you're not to be blamed. What would a young girl be doing here on her own?' She brightened. 'I suppose you're not engaged?'

Ginny shook her head.

'That's a shame too. You know, I thought of going to London once. To work, I mean. But I was talked out of it. That's been the story of my life, really − other people have always known what's best for me.'

Ginny wondered if she had been talked out of boyfriends as well.

'Now, I don't usually cook for my guests in the evenings,' Maggie was saying. 'But I can't see you having to go out again tonight.' She cast a scornful look in the direction of the rain-streaked windows. 'I could make you a wee drop of soup later on if you wish.'

Ginny, who had been thinking along the lines of supper in a snug pub, assured her hostess that she would not put her to any bother and, since she had been travelling all day, would like to go for a short walk.

Later, when she had changed into the warmest garment that she had brought with her, a soft woollen jersey dress that still let in far too much shiver-inducing air, John Laird arrived. Ginny was sitting in the guests' TV lounge by this time − on her own; there appeared to be no other people staying − and Miss Mossblown ushered him in like royalty before discreetly withdrawing and closing the door.

Laird's appearance fitted in with his father having been

15

a man of the cloth. He was tall, grey-haired and attired in a sober business suit. He shook her hand gravely and, after they had seated themselves, extracted papers from a briefcase.

'I took the liberty of bringing this stuff with me,' he began, 'as there might not be enough time tomorrow and no doubt you'll want to return almost immediately. I'd also like to apologise for not ringing you with your bed-and-breakfast arrangements — our telephone system at the office was host to gremlins all day.'

'I have to go back tomorrow,' Ginny said. 'I've a lot on at work.'

'I understand. And there's no problem as far as your father's affairs are concerned. How long is it since your mother died?'

'Six years. She had cancer,' Ginny replied, suddenly feeling rather depressed.

Laird was reading. He glanced up and his eyes twinkled as he gazed at her over his half-moon reading glasses. 'Forgive me, but I know you'll have a long and healthy life. And there's no doubt that your father would have been alive today if it hadn't been for the serious illness he had in 1970 — just after he came here.'

'My mother never said anything about that.'

'Really? He contracted double pneumonia as a result of answering an emergency call one winter's night. He recovered but it affected his heart.' Laird carried on reading for a moment. 'I got the impression when I spoke to him in connection with drawing up the will that your parents' break-up was fairly acrimonious.'

'Yes, it was. As you probably know, he drank heavily.'

'He told me he had in the past. But he'd certainly moderated his drinking by the time he arrived in Kinloch Ruthven.' He looked up again and read her expression accurately for he added, 'You weren't aware of that?'

'I wasn't aware of anything,' Ginny replied, more sharply that she had intended. 'My mother gave me to understand that he was given to drunken rages. When you gave me the news I immediately assumed that he'd drunk himself to death.'

16

Laird laid his papers aside. 'Ah, no. I wouldn't want you to carry on thinking that. It was his heart. He'd been pretty ill for some time.'

'I see,' was all Ginny could say.

'And I wouldn't want you to think that he wasn't interested in his daughter. He knew about your chosen career and listened to several radio programmes you were involved with.'

'But how could he possibly know what I was doing?'

'I rather think,' Laird said slowly, 'now you come to mention it, that he was told about you by someone connected with the media in some way. He used to mention a friend living in London.' He scooped up the papers again. 'In the event of your predeceasing him, the entire settlement would have gone to charity. Thankfully that is not the case and you have the house plus a small bequest which, after the normal deductions, is just over ten thousand pounds. As to the house, he added a codicil just before he died. You cannot sell it for five years. But don't worry, I can easily find you a tenant and impose an improving lease − naturally with a low rent. Then − '

'But why? Why did he do that?'

'To be honest . . .'

'Yes?' Ginny prompted when Laird hesitated.

'I rather think he hoped you'd live in it. He was very fond of the place, you see.'

It sounded like a sick sort of joke to Ginny. 'But I can't come and live up here!' she exploded.

'No,' Laird acknowledged sadly. 'And it's hardly a holiday cottage.'

'What's it called?'

'It's just referred to as the Old Manse, for until about fifty years ago that's exactly what it was.'

'So your family never lived there, then?'

'No. A new and much smaller house had been built by the Church of Scotland then.' He smiled. 'Called, believe it or not, the New Manse.'

'We lived in a flat in Edinburgh. My mother hated it.'

'She might not have hated it here, marital problems notwithstanding. The property isn't as extensive as it used to be, though. A few years ago your father sold off the old stables and coach house – quite cheaply, I might add, on account of the very poor state of the buildings – and the new owner has converted them into a most pleasant house.'

'So who lives there?'

'A Mr McQuade is renting it at the moment. The owner lives abroad and I believe works in the oil industry.'

'And the Manse is quite separate?'

'Yes. A new drive and entrance was made and I understand a hedge has been planted. I know that the old house is still quite private,' he added wistfully.

'It's a good selling point,' Ginny said.

'Yes, I must be realistic,' Laird said sadly. 'It's not the sort of house to appeal to a young woman. I'll give you the bare details: there are six bedrooms, three public rooms, as we call them up here, a study, kitchen, scullery, and the bathroom is downstairs. There are also sundry storerooms, attics and cellars.'

'A house like that must cost a fortune to heat. I take it there's central heating?'

'Er, no. There's an Aga, though, in the kitchen. It provides hot water. I understand it burns logs or other solid fuel.'

'Please find a tenant for the place as soon as possible,' Ginny requested earnestly.

'Don't you even want to see it?'

'Mr Laird, perhaps it's because I'm cold right now but my teeth are chattering just talking about it.'

Chapter Two

As she walked into the bar of the Dog and Drover, the only public house in Kinloch Ruthven, Ginny's notions of spending the remainder of the evening in the warm with a hot meal and a couple of glasses of wine were utterly dashed. It was warm all right, the thick fog of cigarette and pipe smoke saw to that, the walls and ceiling so stained with years or decades of it that the room resembled a brown cave. Additional heat was provided by a bottled-gas heater that looked as though several pints of ale had been upended over it. An extractor fan, encrusted in grease and dust, in a window in one corner, groaned under the load.

The clientele, absolutely without exception, were men. Two or three had filthy, cringing collie dogs beneath their chairs; one, imprisoned by the legs of a bar stool and those of its owner, growled and bared its teeth at her as she approached and was deftly kicked into silence by a heel, the man not pausing in his conversation after one quick, incredulous glance in the incomer's direction. The barman, to whom he was talking, wiped the counter with a damp, grubby cloth, a wide smile revealing broken teeth as he listened to what might have been choice local gossip.

'I'd like a half of lager and lime, please,' Ginny said, having waited until the tale had been told and given up all ambitions as far as wine was concerned.

The man carried on wiping for a few moments before dropping the cloth into a bowl of greasy water behind the bar. He poured the drink, placed it before her, took the proffered money and tendered change, all this achieved

19

without once looking her in the eye or speaking.

'May I see the menu?' Ginny enquired, mindful of a hand-written notice on the door that had promised bar meals.

'Food's off,' he mumbled.

'In more than one way,' said the man with the collie under his breath. 'You had a lucky escape there.'

'On your own, then?' another voice asked.

She turned and faced them, thirty-two eyes stripping her naked. 'Yes, I'm here for my father's funeral.'

'You're Dr Somerville's lass?' the man with the dog enquired.

'That's right.'

Amazingly, everyone but the collie owner went back about their business.

'He was a good man. But you'll be knowing that, of course.'

'No, I didn't. My mother left him when I was small.'

The man took a mouthful of his beer. 'Ach, weel. And London's a long way away.' He glanced over to where the barman was serving someone else. 'Your faither hadna set foot in here for years. He threatened to have Jamie closed doon if he didna clean the place up a bit.'

'So where did he go for a drink?'

'Sometimes he went to the Glen Hotel. But that wasn't to his liking either. Too many bloody foreigners.'

Ginny had noticed it, a large house at the end of a tree-lined drive. It had been too far to walk in the rain that had returned without warning when she was halfway down the high street.

Suddenly there was a commotion in the other bar. There was a crash as though a chair had been flung over and then shouts, yelled insults in such a broad accent that Ginny could not understand a word. She guessed the gist of it, however.

'Well, aren't you going to sort it out?' she demanded of their host.

He scowled at her and moved hesitantly in the direction of the trouble.

The fight was coming closer. Then, and it was impossible to tell who was first or hindmost, two men burst through the connecting door and fell in a heap. The one to find himself on top, bearded and with long hair, proceeded to grab the other by the ears and pound his head on the bare boards of the floor.

'Phone the police!' Ginny shouted at the barman.

'Who needs them?' said the man with the dog and got to his feet.

This seemed to be the signal. The group sitting nearest to Ginny also rose and they all grabbed the bearded man, hoisted him up and propelled him violently out of the door and into the street. They returned to restore the other to an upright position and dust him off, whereupon, without a word, he returned to whence he had come.

'Who needs them?' said the instigator of this again, grinning at Ginny. 'Andy would only get himself arrested again. I wish I kenned what that was all aboot, though.'

'Which one was Andy?'

'The one with the hair,' he replied as though she was slow-witted and then left, saying he had to look to the sheep.

Shortly afterwards Ginny left too, not even remotely hungry now. It had stopped raining, and the clouds were breaking up. As she paused by a gate looking across a field towards the small loch that gave the village its name, the setting sun suddenly shone through a hole in the clouds like a huge spotlamp, the golden light illuminating a mountainside on the far shore. What had been a dull monochrome became bright greens and purples; granite glinting, the water sparkling with a hint of blue. Then, as quickly as it had come, the light went out.

'That was summer,' Ginny said and resumed her journey back to Langside House for an early night.

She had gone perhaps another hundred yards when a car approached from behind and slowed as it came alongside her.

'Can I give you a lift anywhere?' a young man asked.

'No, thanks,' Ginny said. 'I'm almost there.'

He was very fair, looked as though he had fitted his height into the small saloon car with difficulty and was almost certainly an American. 'If home's nearby, then you're a newcomer.'

'I'm staying at Langside House.'

Keeping up with her as she walked, he said, 'It's a great place. That Maggie's a real nice lady. I stayed there before they opened the accommodation wing at the institute.'

To be polite, for he was pleasant and seemed to offer no threat, Ginny said, 'Is that nearby?'

'Just up the hill,' he answered with a jerk of his head in the general direction of a mist-shrouded mountain. 'The Institute of Art. You must come and have a look round. Just ask for Murray.' And with that he waved and roared off.

By morning it was a lot colder, with heavy showers of rain. Occasionally one or other of the mountaintops would be revealed, lit by fleeting gleams of sunlight, the highest with a sprinkling of snow. It was as though, Ginny thought, watching from her bedroom window just before breakfast, the peaks were playing hide and seek in the clouds.

The High Kirk, set on a small hill at the northern end of the village, was grey within and without and seated about a hundred and fifty people. For the funeral of the local doctor the building was almost full, something that surprised Ginny greatly and equally relieved her, for she had had a ghastly dream the night before that she would be the only person present. She sat next to John Laird, still feeling that she might be in a dream, and found herself staring wonderingly at the coffin with her own wreath of white lilies and cream carnations placed upon it. Flowers for a dead stranger.

There were other wreaths and sprays of flowers outside and when the coffin had been lowered into the ground of that bleak, quiet hillside she went and looked at them, feeling strangely moved. Most of them were, she supposed, from grateful patients. One superb wreath of yellow roses had a card with a name that she recognised; McQuade. It was from her father's neighbour at the Coach House. She must remember to thank him.

'Well, my dear?' said John Laird when it was all over and people were drifting away.

'All these people,' Ginny murmured. 'I feel that I should have organised some kind of refreshment for them.'

'In the village hall,' he replied with a smile. 'No, you're not to thank me — he was by way of being an old friend as well as a client. And, speaking of business, if you should change your mind and want to look at the house, I have the keys and am free all day.'

'I'm not sure that I do, really. I mean, I don't feel that it's mine.'

He looked at her kindly. 'But it is. Every stick and stone of the place.'

'Perhaps it is on paper and perhaps I'm being silly but if I can't sell it and I can't live in it . . .' Shockingly, her eyes filled with tears that had nothing to do with a house. Right then she could not have put a name to her emotions. She blinked quickly. 'Please forgive me, but right now . . . I mean, after all my mother told me about him, I'm not sure I want to go just yet to where he *was.*'

'I understand,' Laird said softly. 'Believe me, I do. I shall be at home if you have second thoughts. Or perhaps you'd like me to give you the keys?'

'No,' Ginny said. 'But I'd be grateful if you'd let me have a list of those who sent flowers. I'll write and thank them.'

'Of course. And meantime, come and meet some of them.'

Ginny was never sure afterwards why she decided to go and thank Mr McQuade personally instead of merely adding his name to the list. Perhaps, subconsciously, she wanted to catch at least a quick glimpse of her father's house from a safe distance. She felt too remote from his life to want to go inside. Not once, not even after the death of her mother, had she tried to contact him. He had not come to the funeral either, even though informed through solicitors.

When she returned from the village hall, she changed from her slate-grey suit into slacks and the only sweater − a thin one − she had brought with her and paid a quick visit to Bridge of Corran, where she bought a thick, handknitted one made from local wool and a waxed jacket with a quilted lining and a hood. She donned both garments there and then in the shop, much to the amusement of the staff, who agreed that it was *rather* cold for July.

She had asked Miss Mossblown the whereabouts of the Coach House before she left.

'Up the lane with the pine trees on the corner, next to the

post office,' had been the reply. 'You can't miss it, there are only the two houses up there – that's unless you go all the way on up to the tripe factory.' Upon observing her guest looking a trifle thunderstruck, she had added, 'That's what we call the art place. Modern art. You know. They make pictures and things out of what most people would regard as rubbish. Young Murray – he stayed with me for a while – said there's a girl up there who makes sculptures out of bits of wood and old cowpats.' Maggie had cackled with immoderate laughter.

Definitely worth a visit, Ginny thought as she walked up the lane. Overhead, a buzzard mewed, heralding another squall.

She came to the Coach House first, the name neatly carved into a piece of slate at the end of the drive. She had to shelter beneath a large beech tree for a few minutes, such was the ferocity of the hail, and she gazed around hopefully but not so much as a chimney pot of the house next door was visible above a tall cypress hedge.

The conversion from stables and coach house to a dwelling had been very attractively carried out with a courtyard in the centre, living accommodation on two sides and an open-fronted barn on the third. The latter, presumably at one time a cart shed, now housed an old Land Rover. The drive continued around the side of the house suggesting to Ginny that what she was looking at was the rear of the building and the front door was around the other side. No matter; she knocked on a door that appeared to lead into a large kitchen.

Swallows wheeled around the roof and all was utterly silent. She knocked again, more loudly.

Still no one came.

The bonnet of the Land Rover was still warm, she discovered as she crossed the courtyard. Perhaps the man was in his front garden or whatever lay around the other side of the house.

There was a small area of garden and much more interestingly, there was also a gate in the hedge and it was open. Ginny went through it and immediately found herself in a Scottish version of a jungle, a garden of about half an acre where nature had been permitted to run riot for at least two years.

Then she saw the house.

Of course, this was it, her father's house. *Her* house with its peeling paint, cracked windows, slipping slates, knee-high grass, fallen rose arches, dried-up pond, weed-covered drive and paths ... Built of red sandstone, the house was like a miniature castle and actually had a small turret set with windows on the side that overlooked the loch. The turret even had a flagpole. And there was a huge Victorian conservatory.

It was a marvellous house.

It was the most wonderful, gorgeous, fantastic house she had ever seen in her life.

The front door was ajar and creaked a little as she pushed it open wider to allow her to enter. She thought of announcing herself, calling out, but was then struck dumb as she wandered from room to room, forgetting even to ask herself who had left the door open.

The place was like a film set for a period drama, the furniture heavy and dark, mostly made of oak and thick with dust. There were paintings on the panelled walls of the hall, some of misty Highland landscapes with cattle or deer, several on the staircase, portraits of worthies with their fat, contented wives. One portrait in particular took her attention, that of an elderly woman; the eyes looked somehow severe, yet kindly, her past beauty still apparent even in old age. She wore a lace cap and the collar and cuffs of her otherwise plain gown were also trimmed with lace; heavy and costly.

In a sitting room the paintings were seascapes. These were enormous in gilt frames, the largest sited on the wall above a grand piano. The grandfather clock in the same room had stopped.

'But John Laird never said a *word,*' Ginny whispered to herself.

Then she heard a sound in the next room.

It must have been her father's study; the walls were lined with bookshelves, more shelves housing a few stuffed birds, some oriental ginger jars and a carved wooden Buddha.

And, gazing at the books as though he was searching for one volume in particular, quite oblivious to her presence, was a man wearing a kilt. Then he turned and saw her.

Ginny grabbed the first useful-looking weapon to hand, a sword from the wall. It had a strange, basket-shaped hand guard and was extremely heavy, requiring both hands.

'Put that damned thing down before you chop your own feet off,' said the bearded man she had seen forcefully ejected from the Dog and Drover.

She walked forwards, the point of the sword raised in his direction. 'All I know about you is that your name's Andy. What are you doing here?'

'God, you're holding it properly too. That's right, Miss Somerville. My name's Andrew McQuade. I live next door and was about to borrow my last book.'

He was a good hand's breadth taller than Ginny, which made a change as she stood five foot ten without shoes. Because of the beard and long hair, it was difficult to guess how old he was or what he looked like, but his eyes were hazel, clear but tired-looking. Physically he appeared weak, standing slightly hunched over, and she could not help noticing that his hands were shaking a little. That was what happened to you when you drank too much and got into fights, she reasoned. One thing was certain, though, he was not shaking because he was scared.

'Do you have a key then?' she asked.

He smiled bleakly. 'Well, I didn't break in. Yes, I kept an eye on the place for Dr Somerville while he was in hospital. He thought he would be coming home, you see.' He dug in the pocket of his filthy jacket. 'Here, you'd better have it now.'

She took it, first hanging the sword back on its hooks.

'It's the Red Graham's sword,' McQuade said. 'A *claidheamh mór*. In English, a great sword.'

'A claymore.'

'That's right. Now, if you'll excuse me ...' He gave her a quaint little bow and turned to leave.

'Your book?'

He gestured to the shelves, which extended right up to the ceiling. '*Your* books.'

'Look, if my father said you could borrow them, then please ...'

He shook his head. 'Not now,' he replied quietly, glancing around the room sadly as if for the last time. 'Good day, Miss Somerville.'

'I came to thank you for sending the wreath.'

'He was very fond of yellow roses. There are quite a lot in the garden,' McQuade remarked as he left.

Hearing the front door close, Ginny hurriedly left the room and went upstairs.

The house had a smell all of its own, a musty, damp odour with a hint of mothballs and stale cooking. This seemed to be just as much in evidence on the first floor and Ginny opened a window on a wide landing and leaned out. The air was fresh and as cold as though it had blown straight off the Alps.

The main bedroom – not the one where her father had slept, she later discovered – had a four-poster bed in it, the bedcover and hangings heavy with damp. At the foot of the bed was an oak chest. She lifted the lid to behold blankets, the top layers all full of the moth. The wall near the bed was wet, the paper peeling off to reveal flaking plaster and patches of black mould.

'It's a nightmare,' she said to a small Italian marble figure of a child. 'I can't sell it, I can't live in it and it's all falling apart with neglect. *And* needs thousands spent on it.'

She did not particularly relish the thought of other people living in it either, poking around in her father's study and thumbing through the books, some of which looked as though they might be valuable.

Back at Langside House she uncharacteristically poured out her heart to Maggie Mossblown.

'You could auction off the pieces of furniture that you don't like, put the rest in store and let the house as John Laird suggested,' said that lady. 'And when the five years are up you can decide what you want to do with it. But one thing's for certain, my dear, you'll have to have some repairs done to the place before winter sets in or you'll be left with a ruin.'

'I had a visitor.' Ginny said, smiling wryly as she recollected the encounter. 'Andrew McQuade.'

27

'That must have come as a bit of a shock to you,' Maggie said meaningfully.

'What does he do?'

'Do? Andy? Not a lot.' Maggie sniffed. 'He does odd jobs when the mood takes him or perhaps when he runs out of whisky. People say that he's quite handy in his way but won't do heavy work. He does the garden up at the tripe factory two or three mornings a week. It's an all-organic sort of place. They grow all their own veg and stuff in the summer. There's no proper plumbing, so they say, so perhaps . . .' She broke off with a shudder.

'And yet he lives at the Coach House. That must have quite a high rent.'

'Only the good Lord knows how he affords it,' said Maggie piously. 'The local grapevine has it that a woman pays the rent. Frankly, seeing he's been in trouble with the police, it's anyone's guess where he gets his money. The man's not from round here so no one knows anything about him.'

'In trouble for doing what?' Ginny asked, intrigued.

'Oh, fighting when the pub closes. "Causing an affray" it said in the *Corran Echo*. And poaching from the Mackiver estate.' She chortled. 'A jointed deer was found in his freezer. *He* said he'd shot it to put it out of its misery when he saw it in his garden with a crossbow bolt in its shoulder, but the gamekeeper identified him as the man he'd seen running away.'

'With the dead animal over his shoulder?' Ginny asked innocently.

'I suppose so.'

'The man doesn't look strong enough to run with anything heavier than a coat over his arm.'

'Well, I don't know about that. All I know is he's a real bad lot. You stay away from him, my dear.'

Yet McQuade had been looking at a shelf devoted to books of poetry . . .

It was only much later, when she was thinking of going up to her room to pack her few things and perhaps have an early night, that Ginny remembered she had left the window open at the Old Manse. There was a short inner battle between her sense of responsibility and tiredness, the former winning easily when she recollected that the rain was beating in that way. She put on her new coat again and went out into the evening.

Ginny walked quickly, mulling over the telephone conversation she had had with John Laird a little earlier. If he had been amused by her confession that she had seen and quite liked the house, he had kept it well hidden. Yes, he had agreed, the better furniture and the pictures ought to go into store and certainly urgent repairs could be started immediately. If she wished he would arrange to meet a local builder at the property as soon as possible and decide what ought to be done. Ginny had immediately assented to this, it was a huge weight off her mind.

She had already stayed in Scotland longer than she had intended and this had necessitated a few phone calls, including one to Jake. He had not been pleased.

'Don't you go getting involved with any of those Scotsmen,' he had said, making a joke of it. 'They don't wear anything under their skirts, you know.'

'No chance,' Ginny had said, replying in the same vein while thinking how trite and boring he was. 'Besides, it's too cold for anything but three pairs of longjohns.'

The manse was locked and quiet; no visitors tonight. Ginny let herself in, ran up the stairs, shut the window and then noticed for the first time the narrow staircase tucked into a corner of the landing. In a tight spiral, it ascended some ten stairs to quite a large room above. It was the turret room she had seen from outside. There were three long windows and the view from them over the loch was like being in a mountain eyrie, an eagle's nest. She felt that she might be able to fly from it and soar over the water.

'You're a true silly romantic,' she said to herself, going down again.

There were still parts of the house that she had not explored and she was drawn to look into the kitchen, situated down a short passageway that led from the rear of the hall. This was another period piece with a very old Aga inside a huge fireplace that had certainly at one time housed a range. There was a large wicker basket at the side of it filled with logs.

Except for a little wood ash spilled on the floor, the

kitchen was remarkably clean, a few copper pots gleaming on their hooks on a beam, a ceramic sink with a wooden draining board looking as though they had both been recently scrubbed. She could not resist peeping into the fridge, which was plugged in and working. It was empty but for a bottle of white wine, rather a good one.

There were several doors off the kitchen. One proved to lead into a walk-in larder, the shelves loaded with salt-glaze jars, glass preserving jars and what looked like a ham wrapped in muslin hanging from a hook in the ceiling. Another opened up a real glory hole; boxes, empty bottles of all kinds, piles of yellowing newspapers and medical magazines. Obviously, nothing had ever been thrown away.

Ginny turned the key in the lock of the last door that looked as though it might be a cupboard – a fourth and fifth opened to the back garden and a scullery respectively – and blackness yawned in front of her. She switched on a light, a single low-wattage bulb that revealed a steep uncarpeted staircase leading downwards and around a bend. She went down.

The musty smell was stronger here, emanating, she thought, from a pile of mouldering lumber in one corner of the cellar she found herself in, a room some ten feet square. There was another lightbulb but it was so covered in grime that it gave out hardly any light at all. She turned, startled, as something rustled under a pile of sagging boxes; their contents, yet more newspapers and magazines, bursting from the disintegrating cardboard. There was evidence of mice.

One of the two doors in this room reluctantly opened on squealing hinges when she hauled on it to disclose nothing more exciting than a pile of coal. The trap doors above it had collapsed downwards, the coal soaking wet and sprinkled with soil. The other door was locked but rotten, the wood wet and spongy. Water actually dripped from a small shelf with an old candlestick on it, the short stub of red candle nibbled by mice.

'That's not rain coming in,' Ginny said out loud. 'There's something wrong with the plumbing.'

The means to break down the door was lying almost at her feet, a heap of rusting tools that included a crowbar. She used it, forcing it in near the lock, and the wood simply fell to pieces, the entire frame of the door loose in the wall. Another prod with the crowbar caused the whole thing to move. For the door was heavy, and there was a weight leaning against it on the other side. The entire frame gave way and Ginny leaped out of the way just in time as it all crashed to the floor in a wave of stench with its burden.

Bones pierced through rotting flesh and tattered clothing, this stained with dark fluids which now oozed and trickled across the floor. The eye sockets, where woodlice heaved and tumbled, seemed to stare at the finder accusingly.

Chapter Three

To be utterly overcome with panic was a shocking thing in itself. Ginny had no control over the way she backed until she hit a wall and then ran, blindly, knocking into furniture, the edges of open doors, clawing things out of her way and hearing them crash to the floor behind her. Then she was outside and vomiting helplessly, clinging to a tree for support, seeing nothing but that dead face, the lank black hair and the shrivelled scalp peeling away from the white bone of the skull beneath.

Not aware that she was crying from shock, she blundered through the gate in the boundary fence and ran towards the house next door. There was a light on in the porch at the front. She hammered on the door with a fist and then went straight in, the need to see another living human being overwhelming.

Andrew McQuade was sprawled in a chair in his arrestingly untidy living room, his feet up on a stool, an almost empty bottle of whisky at his elbow. The overall effect was of someone shipwrecked on a beach with sundry articles of flotsam and jetsam. At her sudden entry he floundered, knocking over the stool, completing the illusion.

Ginny sank into a chair, her knees giving way, and closing her eyes as another wave of nausea swept over her. When she opened them a few seconds later it was to discover that the whisky bottle was now a few inches from the end of her nose.

'That isn't the answer to everything,' she said, angry at the realisation that he probably wasn't going to be a lot of use.

'It tends to be hellish useful under the circumstances you appear to be in,' was the crisp and amazingly sober-sounding retort.

Gingerly, she took a sip, carefully wiping the neck of the bottle first.

'It's a single malt − Bruichladdich from Islay,' McQuade said. 'Take a good swallow, you have to really tackle the stuff if it's to help.'

The amber liquid went through her system like benevolent fire.

'See?' he said with a grin.

'I've just found a body,' Ginny said, handing him back the bottle. 'In the basement. It's been there for ages.'

He observed her carefully for a moment and then said, 'Rat, cat, dog or what? Not a spider?'

'God, you don't think I'd get this upset over − ' Ginny shrieked, then clamped her hands over her mouth until she had herself back under control. 'A *person,*' she managed to say through her fingers at last.

Without taking his eyes off her, McQuade swallowed a mouthful of whisky, then placed the bottle carefully back on the table and got to his feet. This was achieved with difficulty and involved his partly turning round so he could haul himself up by holding on to the back of the chair.

'Right,' he said. 'Show me.'

'I can't go back in there,' Ginny whispered.

He looked down at her with contempt. 'Come on, woman! You've got a scoop. Let the cameras roll!'

This spurred her to her feet. 'You know about me.'

'Too right.' He went in the direction of the door. 'You're lucky. I'm not usually mobile at this time of night.'

'You said you were keeping an eye on the place,' Ginny said to his back as they went down the hall. 'How come you never found it?'

He paused. 'You say it's in the cellar? The one off the kitchen?'

'Yes.'

'I can't remember the last time I went down there. There was no need.'

'What about my father, though?'

'Latterly he couldn't manage the stairs.'

The truly appalling thought hit her. 'You mean he could have lived in the house and not known there was a decomposing corpse down there?'

McQuade voiced a worse option. 'Well, surely you don't think he'd have known it was there and kept quiet about it?'

Ginny just shook her head.

'No, not through there,' she said when they were in the garden. 'I was sick.' She was fighting off a strong urge to take his arm, not just for her own reassurance but to prevent him from pitching headlong. He had already tripped over his own doormat.

'It's that bad?' he asked disbelievingly.

She stopped walking, having started to shake uncontrollably.

He came back and stood watching her. Then he said, 'So we're not talking about some old tramp who fell through the coal hatch looking for somewhere to sleep a couple of weeks ago and broke his neck?'

'Look, I know you've had a few drinks,' Ginny said. 'But I did say it had been there ages. *Ages.*'

He held out his hand. 'Come, wee sleekit, tim'rous beastie.'

'I did Burns at school as well, you know,' Ginny retorted. 'That was addressed to a mouse.' She scorned the hand and went into the house. Nevertheless she was glad that McQuade knew where the light switches were so that they did not have to grope their way to the kitchen, it being almost dark now. She had a horror that the thing in the basement had somehow come back to life and was oozing up the stairs to meet them.

Handkerchief clamped over her mouth and nose, Ginny followed him down. She stayed on the bottom step and he went forwards alone.

'As you say,' he said, his voice controlled, standing a couple of careful paces away. 'Bloody ages. And at a guess, it could be Jean Kirkpatrick. She's a local woman who went missing a while ago.'

'But how did she get *here?*'

34

'God knows.' McQuade came back, gathering Ginny up and pushing her up the stairs.

'I was beginning to like this house,' she mumbled as they left.

McQuade called the police. But not before they had shared the rest of the Bruichladdich.

Chief Inspector Ian Speir of the Highlands and Islands Police CID (South Division), a man of immeasurable dourness, picked up some files from a tray on his desk and bad-temperedly rammed them onto an already overflowing shelf on the wall. 'What do you know about this man McQuade?'

'Nothing,' Ginny said. 'I met him for the first time today – no, yesterday.' She decided not to mention the incident in the Dog and Drover.

'So you've no idea how a man whose only apparent source of income is doing odd jobs and gardening manages to live in what must be regarded in normal circumstances as a pleasant house.' This was no doubt a comment on the occupant's haphazard domestic arrangements.

'No,' Ginny replied, refusing to repeat gossip.

'He's been interviewed in connection with other offences,' Speir went on grimly. 'And until he's more forthcoming on certain matters, I have no choice but to regard him as a suspect.'

'You think he could be a *murderer?* Isn't that a bit drastic?'

Speir looked surprised. 'Miss Somerville, the victim did not get into a storeroom in your father's cellar by accident or design on her part. The lock, as you know, is on the outside of the door. Almost certainly she *was* murdered – I expect to get the pathologist's report to confirm it in a couple of hours' time.' He seated himself behind his desk. 'You've signed your statement?'

They were in Speir's office at the Bridge of Corran police station and it was a little after midnight.

'Yes. Can I go now?'

He ignored the question. 'I'm finding it hard to believe that your father was living in a house with the body of a woman in the cellar and knew nothing about it.'

35

'McQuade told me he'd been too ill to get up those steep stairs for some time. Had Jean Kirkpatrick been reported missing?'

'Yes. She was last seen on 16 April of this year. She worked in the kitchen at the Institute of Art and was working overtime on the night in question as there was a social gathering there. They have it in the spring of every year, a sort of open day, I believe, to show the local people the work they do.'

'And you are quite sure it is her?'

'Oh, yes. Her husband has identified the wedding and engagement rings on the body as those belonging to his wife. It's merely a matter of confirmation from her dental records. Miss Somerville, I do have to regard your father as a suspect too, I'm afraid, at this stage. The body was found in his house and at one time the woman was one of his patients. Can you throw no light on the matter at all?'

'No. I have had no contact with him since I was six years old.'

'So you're not even aware if he remarried?'

'My parents were never divorced. But what he did after my mother's death ...' Ginny shrugged. 'I can't see him having a secret wife, can you? Chief Inspector, I've a very long journey tomorrow. May I go now?'

'In a moment. What were the circumstances of your meeting with McQuade?'

'I went to the house to have a look at it. McQuade was in the study, my father had said he could borrow his books. He returned the key to me. It was as simple as that.'

'I must confess to being surprised. Your father allowed free access to a suspected thief?'

'Oh, you mean the deer in the freezer? I think that as far as that's concerned I'd tend to go along with McQuade's account of how he'd shot the beast in his garden because it was wounded. That isn't against the law. No one in their right mind would waste all that good food.'

'The gamekeeper positively identified the man who was running away as – '

'And the deer? Did you have an identity parade for that too?' Ginny stood up to leave. 'The one thing that my mother

36

would say in my father's favour was that he was a good judge of character. That's good enough for me and in view of the respect with which he appears to have been held in Kinloch Ruthven it ought to be good enough for you too.'

'And the business of McQuade being fined for being drunk and disorderly on several occasions recently and assaulting a German tourist who took his photograph without permission?'

'Everyone has bad days. Has he been charged with assault?'

'It didn't come to that,' Speir replied with a tinge of regret. 'Herr Schmidt withdrew the charge and McQuade apologised. But a policeman has to wonder about such things. A mere photograph ... What has the man to hide?'

Ginny returned to Langbank House, where she had to tell the story all over again to a sympathetic but totally riveted Maggie Mossblown. At a quarter to two she fell into bed.

Sleep was impossible, however. All she could see when she closed her eyes was yellowing teeth bared in a ghastly smile, and hands like claws. Was it true that the fingernails continued to grow after death?

Finally she opened a curtain and sat up in bed to watch the sunrise. It had been getting light when she had gone to bed, it did not seem to get really dark here at this time of the year. As she watched, beams blazed up like swords behind the mountain opposite and instantly all was jewel-bright colour as a wonderful golden light flooded the landscape, the loch a perfect pearl-grey mirror.

'That Jean Kirkpatrick was the sort of woman to come to a nasty end,' said Maggie when she brought Ginny's breakfast into the dining room. 'They say she would go with any man for the price of a drink.'

Despite everything, Ginny discovered that she was hungry. 'And yet she was married.'

'Oh, Kenneth wouldn't care. As long as his Giro cheque arrives every week and they don't make horseracing illegal, he's perfectly happy. He wasn't over upset when she disappeared, apparently. She'd done it before − went back to her mother in Greenock for four months once.'

'I understand she worked up at the institute.'

Maggie sat down at the table. 'I'll get your toast in a minute and then it won't be cold. Yes, she did. Not as a proper cook, you understand, I doubt if Jean could have cooked anything other than mince and tatties. No, Mrs Smith's the cook, Jean prepared the veg and cleared up. She cleaned the rooms too. Of course they got someone else after she went missing.'

'Chief Inspector Speir said that the last time anyone saw her was the evening of the institute's open day, 16 April. Did you go?'

'Me! To the tripe factory?' Maggie shrieked. 'Not on your life! You wouldn't catch me within a mile of the place.' She gave Ginny a hard look. 'You could be your father sitting there with that frown on your face — the face he wore when he thought people were giving him a load of havers. Well, I'll tell you straight, I've heard about the goings-on. Not at the official do, you understand, but the drinking that went on among the staff and some of the students.'

'Perhaps you ought to mention it to Speir.'

'No, not at all,' said Maggie, getting to her feet. 'He'd want to know how *I* know and it's only gossip. But I'll bet a pound to a penny that Jean would have been rolling in the hay with all the men up there — that McQuade included.' She went out and then put her head back round the door. 'Not speaking ill of the dead, of course.'

One could hardly go round and ask him.

If Ginny hadn't glanced quickly up the lane towards the Old Manse as she drove by she would not have seen the vehicles. She pulled up and reversed a short distance and as she did so another arrived and parked on the verge on the corner, beneath the pine trees. Ginny had been in the media business for long enough to know that the man who alighted from it was a reporter.

'I don't know your face,' he called across, grinning, when she got out of her car, 'but I bet you're on to our grisly murder as well.'

'*Worthing Herald,*' Ginny answered blithely and grinned

back when his eyes bulged slightly. Then she added, 'Only I'm on holiday.'

'Habit dies hard, eh?'

'Well, you never know! Someone from West Sussex might be involved.'

'You're out of luck, darlin'. The victim came from these parts, all the coppers are wearing tartan reach-me-downs and a little bird at the nick told me that they've come to turn over the house of the bloke who lives next door to where the body was found.'

'How interesting,' Ginny found herself calmly saying. 'Any idea why?'

'Well, according to my source he's the local ne'er-do-well and worked at the same place. Someone saw them together the night she disappeared.'

'Thanks,' Ginny said and hurried on ahead of him. 'Give my love to Wapping the next time you're down south.'

A police car and van were parked in the drive, the latter with an Alsatian dog barking inside. Farther up the lane, and blocking the entrance to the Manse, were several other vehicles and a motley collection of people including a television news team. As soon as they saw her they moved determinedly in her direction. Ginny ran past the police van and car and down the drive into the courtyard. There was a uniformed police constable by the back door and a lot of shouting coming from within.

Four men came out, one of whom was McQuade, struggling in the grasp of the others. Chief Inspector Speir then emerged, looking dishevelled, as though he had been up all night. The entire cavalcade shuddered to a halt at Ginny's yelled accusation.

'They're hurting him!'

Speir spoke quickly, under his breath, and McQuade ceased to writhe. There was a short silence broken only by the prisoner's agonised breathing.

Speir said, 'Miss Somerville, I must request you to leave.'

'Shall we have an action replay of the last scene for the benefit of Scottish Television over there?'

Someone carefully cleared his throat.

'Mr McQuade resisted arrest,' Speir said. 'He assaulted one of my officers inside the house. And we are now in possession of a very important piece of evidence, the details of which I have no intention of divulging.' He walked round Ginny and spoke directly to McQuade. 'Kirkpatrick was your mistress, wasn't she? And one night when she was here and you were blind drunk you killed her.'

McQuade shook his head and then made what seemed to be a supreme effort and stood up straight. 'No,' he said.

'Take him away,' Speir ordered.

'How was she killed?' Ginny asked when the car doors had slammed.

'Strangled.'

'That man's ill. He's not strong enough to − '

'You mustn't confuse debilitation following an excess of alcohol with physical weakness. Such folk have the strength of the Devil himself when they're under the influence of strong drink.'

'Have you interviewed the woman's husband?'

'Yes, and at the moment he is not a suspect.' Speir then wished her good morning and got into his car, parked in the courtyard.

There were people still in the house, Ginny could hear them tramping about. One of them, a man whom Ginny recognised as Speir's sergeant, appeared in the kitchen and paused to shout orders over his shoulder concerning the search of the property.

'Sergeant?'

'Yes, miss?'

'Which officer was assaulted by the man you've just arrested?'

He carefully felt his chin. 'Well, it was me actually. But I got in the way − he was aiming at the chief.'

'Really?'

The man gazed around quickly, saw that Speir was speaking into his radio and said quietly, 'It was unfortunate, really. Speir's all right when he's not pulpit-thumping about the dangers of demon drink. He's an elder of the Kirk and it goes to his head a bit. He knocked one of McQuade's pictures off the wall and the glass broke. I think McQuade

40

thought he'd done it on purpose. But as I said, Speir's all right. Just clumsy. He skleushes aboot, as my old auntie Agnes would say.'

'And I suppose it's more than your life's worth to tell me about your piece of evidence.'

'Everyone will find out soon enough. We found her watch under the bed in his room. The husband asked about it when we showed him the other jewellery that was found on the corpse. Apparently it had been her aunt's and was worth quite a bit. The aunt's initials are engraved on the back. And, as I said, we found it upstairs.'

'It could have been planted.'

'Speir's convinced he'll get a confession.'

'That's what bothers me, sergeant,' Ginny said.

The chief inspector bellowed out of the window of his car and his assistant departed at the run. In a squeal of tyres they were gone.

The search team appeared to be upstairs, judging by the noise they were making. Ginny went in, heading for the room where she had found McQuade the previous night. It was in an even worse mess now the police had been through it.

She soon found what she was looking for, a colour print of a golden eagle on the floor, the glass smashed, the frame broken. It was a very good photograph indeed, both technically – Ginny knew about such things – and the way the wild spirit of the bird had been perfectly captured as it perched on the branch of a dead tree, a hare it had just caught in its talons. There were other pictures in the room, some of wildlife, others of climbers clinging seemingly just with fingers and toes to utterly impossible-looking vertical rock faces. On impulse, Ginny extracted the picture of the eagle from the pieces of wood and glass and took it back outside. She had moved not a moment too soon, for heavy shoes could be heard clumping down the stairs.

Quickly, she went through the gate in the hedge, closing it behind her, and into the garden next door. No one could see her there, it was quite secluded. In the morning sunlight there were no echoes of the horrors of the night before, the old garden seeming to doze in the warmth – summer had suddenly arrived in Scotland. Bees were blundering in the

41

tasselled centres of the tumbledown yellow roses, a dragonfly hovered like a jewelled dart over the one-time pond, and one large, red water-lily flower thrust upwards through a tangle of weeds.

'He needs a solicitor,' Ginny said to the blue sky.

She made two phone calls and then got in her car for the long drive back to Glasgow and the airport.

Chapter Four

At about the same time that Chief Inspector Speir was approaching the Old Manse, a search warrant in his pocket, Ginny was attending a meeting in Jake's office that was supposed to be all about progress reports and work schedules. It soon developed into a debriefing session on her visit north of the border.

'Well, you know what Samuel Johnson said,' Jake stated importantly. 'Much may be made of a Scotchman if he be caught young enough.' He laughed. 'Obviously your Scot wasn't caught at all — until now, that is.'

Alvis stretched his long, lanky frame until everyone could hear the tendons creaking. 'Well, Ginny, if you ask me you're well shot of the place. It would give me the horrors to even think of living in a house that a body had been found in.'

Pru said, 'But Ginny doesn't look very glad to be back.'

'Nonsense!' Jake snapped. 'She's just worn out with all the travelling. Aren't you, Ginny?'

Ginny looked him right in the eye. 'I think McQuade's going to be stitched up.'

'Nonsense,' he said again. 'Justice will be done — we all know that. Now — '

'How the hell can you sit there and say that after listening to Barry talking about his researches into the police?' she burst out. 'They never make mistakes, eh? A suspect's face never fits the crime? This Speir is like nothing I've ever come across. He's all ready to put the man away because

43

he's fond of a dram and has been in trouble before. And McQuade doesn't seem to have anyone to stick by him. And I'm worried that if they lean on him he ...' She broke off, not sure in her own mind that McQuade would confess to something he had not done. She had an idea that he'd see Speir in hell first.

Kindly, Pru said, 'I don't really think you ought to worry. From what I've heard of the Scottish legal system it's better than ours.'

But Ginny was on her feet, a fierce glow burning inside her. She had never felt like this before, and it was the kind of feeling that took all before it, consuming reason, common sense and everything pertaining to level-headedness and sanity.

'I'm going back,' she said. 'I can't just walk away like this. My father's a suspect too and, well, I just want to be *around.*'

'You can't go now,' Jake said flatly.

'I'll ask Barry to take over from me.'

'I forbid it utterly.'

'Just who the hell do you think you *are*?' Ginny shouted at him. 'You sit there and pontificate. You heard me. I'm going back to Scotland. I'll ask Barry to take over from me for a couple of weeks or however long it takes.' She slammed the door on her way out.

'The woman's raving mad,' Jake blustered. 'She's not usually like this.'

'She's in love,' Pru said dreamily and so softly that only Jake heard her.

'Well, she can forget coming back and working for *me*,' he said viciously.

'In that case I reckon you'll be doing without the services of all of us,' Alvis said quietly and the ten or so people in the room all trooped out after him.

'Hey!' Jake bellowed. 'Come back here this minute!'

He couldn't remember a time when the building had been so silent.

Since Yasmin's accident, Barry had started to smoke again. He lit a cigarette now, drew on it and blew a large cloud of

44

smoke towards the ceiling. 'Yes, of course, honeychild. But will Jake go along with it?'

'Jake has no choice,' Ginny said. 'But is Yasmin well enough for you to leave her?'

'No problem there. In fact she's been nagging me to stop worrying about her and get back to work. The girl has the constitution of a horse.' He smiled. 'So, you've inherited your very own Hammer House of Horror. No one could keep me away from something like that. Tell you what – do some private sleuthing. The locals might tell you things they'd never let on to a cop.' It was one of Ginny's strong points, Barry knew, the ability to put people at their ease. Plus tenacity, of course.

'Yes, perhaps you're right. But only if I felt I could achieve something.'

'Clear your father's name?'

'Yes. Not that I think he's involved for one moment.'

'But this is the guy who your mother told you was some sort of ogre?'

'Faced with reality,' Ginny said, 'I'm beginning to wonder.'

'And there's the business of the bloke next door being pulled in over the watch.'

'I think it was planted.'

'But if he killed the woman it's possible her watch fell off during the struggle and – '

Ginny interrupted, 'I simply can't imagine him doing it.'

Faced with this feminine logic, Barry could only suggest, 'If he's broke he might have stolen it.'

'He wears a Rolex of his own.'

Barry smiled upon her broadly. He had fine fly-away hair, thinning rapidly, china-blue eyes and the kind of complexion that always looks tanned. He smiled a lot now Yasmin was getting better.

'You're laughing at me,' Ginny said.

'Not at all,' he assured her gravely. 'I don't think you mentioned this guy's name.'

'Andrew McQuade.' Ginny unwrapped the eagle photo-graph she had just collected from the framers. 'He's not just a local thug. He can't be. Look, the police broke this when they arrested him so I ...' She felt herself blushing under his scrutiny, feeling foolish. 'There are other pictures – of wildlife and climbers. Barry, I just don't think he's a murderer,' she finished in something approaching anguish.

Barry was frowning, staring hard at the picture. 'I know of *an* Andrew McQuade. In fact I've worked with him. He's from the Inverness area and specialises in filming mountain climbs and wildlife. He was almost killed earlier this year in a fall.'

'My God!' Ginny gasped. 'That would explain a lot.'

'He broke just about every bone in his body.'

'Everyone thinks he's just a drunk.'

'I've no doubt that after a drop or two of the golden gargle life might be more worth living when you're getting over something like that. But steady on, old china, it might not be the same bloke.'

'Would you have a photo of him in one of your reference books?'

'Better than that, I've a book of his in the study.'

Ginny paused fractionally before entering the room in his flat where Barry did all his research, for this really was his holy of holies. Then she went with him to a shelf and watched as he took down a large but slim volume. It was entitled *McQuade's Eagles* and contained, with only a little text, magnificent photographs of golden eagles in the Highlands of Scotland and other wildlife that had originally featured in a TV programme. On the back was a picture of the author.

Ginny shook her head. 'It *can't* be him. It says here he's twenty-nine.'

'Not the same man?' Barry asked sympathetically.

'He's got a beard and his hair's long.'

'Hair ... beard ...' Barry muttered, casting about the room. 'Ah!' He got his old retriever in a rugby tackle and, delighted, she rolled over to have her tummy scratched. Barry grabbed the book and arranged the long hair of her tail over the picture.

'I still don't know,' Ginny wailed. 'His hair's black.'

'Sorry, but she'd take a bloody dim view of being dyed

right now − it's her dinnertime.'

'It could be,' she agonised. 'But his eyes look so tired and old somehow.'

Barry got to his feet and opened the book at the front. 'This was published three years ago so he's thirty-two now. And believe me, honeybunch, falling several hundred feet off a chuck of rock onto another chuck of rock only slightly cushioned by heather would make you look a trifle strained around the eyes too.'

'I *must* go back,' Ginny whispered.

'Whoever the guy is? Even if he's only the local number-one shit? It might be a coincidence − he might have bought the pictures.'

'Whoever he is.'

Barry held out the book. 'A present for you then. And the best of luck.'

When he had let his visitor out − and they had both been as quiet as possible because Yasmin was having her rest − Barry went back into his study and was about to close the door when he saw a movement.

'Yasmin! I thought you were asleep.' He took her in his arms and gave her a big smacking kiss.

'Sometimes it's better for wives to be asleep,' she replied with a grin.

'Surely you don't think − '

She silenced him with a finger across his lips. 'Silly, lovely man. No, and besides, I like Ginny. I also know you very well by this time. What's this about her being in love with Andrew McQuade?'

'You were *listening.*'

She giggled.

'She doesn't know for sure that it's him.'

Yasmin seated herself elegantly in an armchair. 'I've been feeling very guilty about Andy. Perhaps we ought to contact him ourselves.'

Barry was feeling hellishly guilty. 'I heard a sort of trade rumour that he'd gone to pieces.'

'You didn't tell me that.'

'I was hardly going to worry you with someone else's troubles. At the time I thought I was going to lose *you.*'

47

'You worked with him on that thing about skiing and the environmental damage it does in the Highlands, didn't you?'

'Yes. He's a really nice guy. He liked a drink but not to excess. But I can understand it if he's going over the top now. He's a perfectionist and if he's lost his nerve a little after what happened to him and he's afraid that people will be badgering him to go back to the mountains ... I might do the same, in his shoes.'

Miss Mossblown was fully booked with tourists and visitors arriving for the Games but had promised over the phone to find Ginny accommodation somewhere in the locality. This proved to be the Glen Hotel, the news conveyed apologetically to Ginny when she called at Langbank House on her return. The reason for Maggie's regret was the establishment's charges, in her view little short of extortionate.

Close up, the hotel was a slightly forbidding stone edifice, the greyness of its exterior not alleviated by the single tub of purple petunias and blue trailing lobelia. The entrance-hall carpet was well worn and no one had yet cleaned the fingermarks off the glass-panelled inner door. Ginny had an idea that her mother would have said, as she did when describing anything or anyone mean, that you could expect the porridge to be well watered. It occurred to Ginny now that the saying had probably originated from her father.

'I'm sorry, Miss Somerville, but there seems to have been a mistake,' said the receptionist, a young woman clad in appropriate tartan but with a huge hole in her tights. 'Someone rang up a couple of hours ago and cancelled your booking.'

'Not at my request,' Ginny told her.

'I'm afraid we've no vacancies now at all. There's never enough accommodation during the Games.'

'Not even an emergency broom cupboard reserved for lost travellers in the snow?'

'Sorry, no. We're crammed full.'

'Did you take the call?'

'Yes, I did. He was quite clear in his meaning even though his voice did sound a bit strange as though there was something wrong with the line. I know I didn't get the name wrong – there's no one else with a similar name booked in.'

Ginny had a very strong disinclination to hawk herself and her suitcase around the district. Not when she had – she suddenly found herself thinking – a perfectly good house of her own in the village.

She had expected the police to have placed some kind of seals on the doors, but there was nothing to prevent her entry to the house. John Laird had informed her that Chief Inspector Speir had come to his office with a search warrant asking for the keys. The solicitor had also mentioned that he had been present while the house was thoroughly examined. What, if anything, had been discovered he was not permitted to say.

The first thing Ginny did, after she had put down her luggage, was to go into the kitchen and firmly lock the basement door with the large iron key hanging on a nail on the wall. After she had done this she felt very much better.

Gingerly, for she was not used to such things, she opened the fire door of the Aga. Astoundingly, the grate was clean and there was a pile of kindling with two firelighters lying across the top. A box of matches lay on the logs in the basket, which had been filled to overflowing.

She must remember to thank John Laird when she saw him.

Or had that man next door another key?

If he was responsible, he had been released from police custody.

She lit the Aga, for the house was like a fridge, learning very rapidly about things like draughts and dampers after the kitchen had filled with smoke and she had had to open a window. Soon a fire was roaring, the needle of the thermometer on the oven door moving off the stops. Ginny closed everything down a bit, mindful that the chimney probably hadn't been swept in years.

There was a heavy iron kettle on the draining board which was soon singing on the hottest hob while she warmed herself.

This domesticity was all very well but there was not a scrap of food in the house, the shops were closed and she was starving. The ham, wrapped in muslin in the larder, looked as though it had been there since the Crimea. Perhaps she would visit her neighbour, taking the bottle of wine that was in the fridge, and endeavour to engage in a little barter.

The house next door was in darkness, the Land Rover parked in the cart shed, cold. Which could only mean one thing; if McQuade was now a free man he was probably in the Dog and Drover.

The other bar in the pub was only slightly less disgusting that the one she had visited already and, either despite this or because of it, boasted a few female customers. The fug and chatter, smoglike and deafening respectively, was an assault upon the senses.

Ginny, who had driven all the way from London in order to have the use of her own car but had deliberately walked from the house she could still not think of as home, elbowed her way to the bar and ordered two doubles of the Macallan. She took them both to where a scarecrow leaned on a corner of the bar.

'I owe you a dram,' she said, placing it before him.

McQuade looked at her and then at the drink. Then he stared at the other item she had put in front of him, the re-framed photograph still in its wrapper.

'What is it?' he asked.

'Your picture. I hope you don't mind.'

Slowly, and in the manner of a man not inebriated but merely overwhelmingly tired, he removed it from the brown paper. Then, observing what she was drinking, he said, 'I'm pretty sure you don't normally touch the stuff.'

'No, but if I'm going to settle up here I'll need to get into training,' Ginny said, taking a stiff swallow and almost choking.

He took a sip of his. 'Are you now?' he muttered.

'Yes, I'm going to set myself up with a small company — *very* small, you understand — and make programmes about Scotland. I shall concentrate on ecological matters mostly but make sure that it appeals to a wide audience, an international one. Some of the home-produced stuff, frankly, is a little too

50

inward-looking. I want to cover wildlife, forests, fishing and recreational matters as well – mountaineering and mountain scrambling.' She beamed at him, the whisky like fire in her veins. 'Finance will be a problem, of course, and I'll probably have to spend the money my father left me on the house but, as you know, companies lease all the equipment they need.'

The man was looking at her as though he couldn't believe his ears.

'Alvis wouldn't be interested,' Ginny went on. 'He's far too urban. I can't see him trudging around the countryside getting shots of birds. And you really need people who know what they're doing, don't you?'

'Alvis?' McQuade said.

'He's Nimrod's most experienced cameraman. But as I said, a very urban animal. And I think he gets hay fever.'

McQuade appeared to want to settle something in his own mind. 'Would this Alvis want to work for you?'

Ginny got a little closer. 'Oh, yes. He's quite fond of me really.'

There was a short silence between them.

Slowly, as if his neck hurt, McQuade shook his head.

Ginny said, 'I was talking to Barry Chichester.'

The response was not at all what she had expected and utterly shocking. McQuade started to sob. Then he leaped to his feet and hurried from the bar. Ginny followed, grabbing the picture, which he had left behind.

'Look, I'm so sorry,' she gasped, running to catch up with him. 'I didn't mean – '

He rounded on her. 'Leave me alone! I don't want your charity.'

'Charity! Are you mad? You're the best there is.'

'*Was,*' he corrected savagely and started walking again, taking Ginny with him for she had grasped him by the arm.

'Please, listen,' she implored.

'It's over. Finished.'

By sheer strength she hauled him to a standstill. 'No. However much you drink or slum it you'll still be the same man.'

'That's what I have nightmares about,' he shouted in her face. 'So it's a coward you want working for you, is it? A man who breaks out in a cold sweat every time he has to get on the roof now to put back a slipped slate.' His eyes bored into hers. 'I *can't*. Do you understand? *Can't.*'

'Andrew, I don't want you to climb mountains.'

'You – don't – want,' he said, very slowly. Then roughly, 'Where are you staying? I'll take you there.'

'At the Manse – there's no room anywhere.'

'But there's nothing there! No heat, food ...' He groaned and hustled her along the street. 'You'd better have a bite to eat with me and then I'll light the – '

'I've done that. I was going to ask if I could swap a bottle of wine in the fridge for some bread and cheese.'

'He was saving that for his birthday,' McQuade said.

They did not speak again until they reached the Coach House.

'Surely someone could have booked you in for a few nights,' McQuade said, unlocking his back door.

'Miss Mossblown did, at the Glen Hotel. Someone cancelled the booking.'

He muttered something that Ginny could not hear and put on the lights. Then he swore vividly.

The blood was everywhere; in huge molten gouts on the floor, coagulating in runnels down the walls, sprayed in blobs across the worktops and sink unit, dripping slowing from its source. The sheep had had its throat cut and had been eviscerated, the entrails hanging down like a curtain, the body of the animal strung by the hind feet to the central light fitting, this a rather fetching thing with artificial candles on an iron ring supported by chains.

Neither of them spoke a word as they set to work. McQuade cut down the sheep, dragged it into the garden and buried it. Ginny found a bucket, cloths and a scrubbing brush and together they cleaned the room. In two hours it was finished and, staggering with weariness, they gazed at one another.

Ginny found a plastic rubbish sack. 'Your clothes,' she said, gesturing at the jeans stiff with sheep excrement and blood, torn shirt soaking with sweat and floor-scrubbing water.

He removed them there and then, shocked into it, Ginny thought, by catching sight of himself in a mirror, his beard and hair stiff with blood, face streaked with earth. She put the whole lot in the dustbin and went back to the Manse for a bath, her own clothes, a fine wool-and-silk-mixture suit, probably ruined.

It was very late when she warily returned, carrying the bottle of wine. She half expected McQuade to be in bed or drunk but he was in the kitchen, cooking. For a long moment she stared at him, speechless and utterly robbed of good manners. He was wearing a cream sweater and clean blue jeans and socks, no shoes. His hair, washed and glossy, was tied back. The beard had gone, revealing the same face as on the back of the book, only thinner. Ginny put the wine down before she dropped it.

'You like fried rice?' he asked.

'Anything but mutton chops tonight.'

He almost smiled.

There were mushrooms and prawns in the rice and a scattering of salted peanuts, McQuade apologising for a lack of proper ingredients. Ginny found a corkscrew but he took it from her with the air of a host who had failed in his duty. Ginny was grateful; for some reason she felt all fingers and thumbs.

They ate ravenously, without words. McQuade was the first to break the silence as they finished off the last of the wine.

'It was too much — that damned sheep.'

For a moment Ginny made no response. Then she said, 'Well, it wasn't intended as a joke.'

'No,' he agreed.

'Something to do with the murder?'

'God knows.'

'I presume Speir had to let you go for lack of evidence?'

'No. They found your father's diary.'

'Tell me,' Ginny whispered.

'Come and sit in the warm. I've lit the fire.'

Not only had he lit the fire, he had also gathered all the books, clothes and newspapers into one corner. The room was transformed.

'Your father wrote down everything he did in his diary,' McQuade began. 'On the day Jean disappeared he had asked a friend of his to drop in for a dram during the evening. He'd been up to the institute – we both had, I was there early as they'd asked me to help move chairs – and I brought him home at about eight thirty. His friend arrived at a little after nine. I was there too.'

'And the friend saw you both and has since corroborated your story?'

'Yes. And he happens to be a senior consultant at Inverness Infirmary.'

'I hope this means that you're no longer under suspicion.'

'No. By no means. Speir doesn't give up that easily. He reckons there was plenty of time for either of us to do away with the woman afterwards.'

'What about the watch?'

'That doesn't exactly help. It was under the bed and could have been there for months for all I know. My prints weren't on it, no useful ones were. That didn't please Speir at all.'

'Could someone have climbed up and thrown it through the window?'

'Easily. There's a creeper on the wall that can support the weight of a person – I know, I climbed in once when I'd locked myself out.' He gave her an angry look. 'You don't have to say it – you want to know if I was screwing the woman like everyone else. The answer's no. I haven't let myself go completely.'

'Someone got in tonight.'

'Well, I'm not exactly security conscious. The kitchen window was open and, as you've probably noticed, it's a large sash one. Whoever it was could have hoisted the animal in through that.'

'I think Speir ought to be told.'

'Do what you like – just leave me out of it.'

'That's difficult, seeing it was in your kitchen. And to

54

speak perfectly frankly, you can hardly blame the man for having his knife into you the way you've been behaving.'

'Look, this *is* me,' McQuade said, a long forefinger pointing at his breastbone. 'Whatever was in the past is over and done with – nothing can bring it back.' The same hand brushed over his newly shaven face. 'The beard, I admit, was getting to me.'

'And you can't wear a kilt with a ponytail,' Ginny pointed out gently. 'Too much like LA at Hogmanay.' She rose to her feet. 'Thank you for the supper.'

He also rose. 'I'd be really grateful if you'd keep quiet about me – especially to Speir.'

'On condition that you lay off the whisky a bit.'

'You're just like your father, you know that?' he said furiously.

'Those are my terms,' Ginny said regally.

He glowered at her.

'And I'll cook you dinner tomorrow night – tonight, I mean.'

'I'm beginning to think that he left you the house so you could keep an eye on me.'

'Good night, Andrew,' Ginny said.

'I have only a few minutes to spare,' Chief Inspector Speir said, ushering Ginny into his office.

'That's all right,' she said with a big smile. 'So have I.' She sat down without being invited to. 'As you'll probably understand, I'm deeply upset about this business of finding a murdered woman in my house. One of the things I'd like from you is an assurance that my father is no longer a suspect.'

'I can give you no such assurance, Miss Somerville,' the DCI replied. 'Not when I'm at such an early stage of the investigation. In fact, new evidence has come to light that makes it impossible for me to make any statements at all.'

Ginny was wishing that he would stop talking like a police-procedures manual. 'You mean the diary?'

'Who told you about that?'

'Andrew McQuade. I asked him why – '

Speir interrupted, 'The man is still a suspect. I have forbidden him to leave the area.'

'Someone slaughtered a sheep in his kitchen last night. As a warning, do you think? To drive him from the district?'

'I'm not surprised. Feelings must be running pretty high in the village.'

'Rubbish!'

'I beg your pardon?'

'Jean Kirkpatrick was hardly popular — not that I'm saying she deserved to die, but no one will miss her. It would appear that she was virtually a prostitute. And as far as McQuade's concerned, no one seems to be spitting on him in the street.'

'Well, it must be admitted that some witnesses intimated that she was known to — '

'Chief inspector, I think you owe me some kind of explanation for continuing to regard both of these men as suspects.'

'They were both seen talking to the Kirkpatrick woman at the institute on the evening that she disappeared.'

'That's hardly surprising. It was a social occasion. Then, I understand McQuade took my father home and then either stayed with him or returned later when a friend called. Are you actually working on the theory that they'd made some kind of arrangement with Jean that she'd visit them afterwards for sexual purposes?'

Speir shrugged. 'It's perfectly possible. They were both single men.'

'And then they *killed* her? That's utterly obscene.'

'Murder *is* obscene.'

'What followed then,' Ginny persisted, 'can only be described as rank stupidity. Instead of putting her body in McQuade's Land Rover — and I presume your forensic department have been over it with a fine-tooth-comb — and taking it up to the moors and burying it, they merely carried it down into the cellar and shut it in a storeroom. I'm sorry, Mr Speir, but that simply isn't good enough and you know as well as I do that a case presented along those lines would be laughed out of court.'

'I agree,' Speir said. 'But I'll repeat, the investigation has only just started. I have interviewed Dr Somerville's cleaning lady who assures me that he was of very uncertain temper. She was given the impression that he had very little time for women as *people* at all. And we all know that McQuade is short of money with which to keep himself in drink. Who knows what happened and what Dr Somerville paid him to do?'

Chapter Five

The main building of the Institute of Art, the studios, had at one time been a stone barn, most of the front of the original building having been removed and replaced by an extension with a large triangular window, the apex of which was slightly higher than the roof. At a distance, as one ascended the approach road, the all-pervading impression was of a massive, glittering, inverted V.

Ginny had walked, needing exercise and not wanting to risk the suspension of her car on the steep, deeply rutted track. Two of the vehicles parked outside the institute were of the four-wheel-drive variety, a Discovery and a Subaru. The third was Murray's little runabout, a little rusty and dented. Andrew's Land Rover was absent, however; perhaps he did not work on Wednesdays.

On each side of the main building further single-storey extensions had been built, all of local stone. The one on the left looked as though it was living accommodation, that on the right offices and a dining room; Ginny could see tables laid for lunch through an open window.

'Can I help you?' a man asked when they had almost walked into each other in the entrance lobby.

Ginny introduced herself. 'Is Murray around?'

'Murray Kenning? No, he's down at the show ground. They all are, I think.'

He freed a hand from the sheaf of papers he was carrying. 'I'm Malcolm Hurrell. Let me shove all this stuff in my car and we'll have coffee. Murray mentioned that he'd been talking to a young lady and we put two and two together.'

He was Dr Hurrell and the director of the institute, according to the metal nameplate on his office door.

'Do sit down,' Hurrell urged. 'And forgive the mess in here. I never seem to get organised. I've asked Peggy to bring us some coffee.'

'Jean's replacement?'

'Yes.' He smiled and then became very serious. 'God, of course! You found the body. How unbelievably nasty for you after having to come all this way for your poor father's funeral. We were all very fond of Alastair, you know. He always came to the open day and I made sure he had an invitation to the end-of-season party too − that's a private function.'

'So you're only open during the summer months?'

'For students, yes. The climate's the reason for that really. We're just above the snow line here and a bad winter makes life very difficult. I tend to go home to my flat in Edinburgh − either that or I work here if the weather's kind. I'm writing a book on Picasso. If you're interested I'll take you round the studio when we've had our coffee.'

He was an ungainly man, probably in his late thirties, with wispy, thinning hair and slightly protuberant, very pale-blue eyes. Of nervous manner, his movements jerky, and prone to finishing each sentence with a seemingly shy smile, he was nevertheless, inexplicably, charming.

'We have a tent with an exhibition of our work every year at the Games,' Hurrell went on. 'Very occasionally there are commissions but − ' he looked rueful − 'it's getting rarer and rarer, I'm afraid. The people in this part of the world are somewhat conservative in their tastes. I've heard that the inhabitants of the village call us the tripe factory.'

'I'm very curious as to why you're situated here.'

'It was as a result of a bequest by a Miss Agnes MacNaughton. Her father made his money in shipping and she was an only child. She never married and was, I suppose, what could be described as an eccentric; living very frugally and devoting herself to temperance and what she called Higher Thoughts.'

Probably a relation of Chief Inspector Speir, Ginny decided.

'She went for long walks over the hills, barefoot whenever possible, and bathed naked every morning in a burn in a field behind her house. Her will indicated her wish that everyone in the locality be able to share what she had enjoyed in the way of spiritual uplift. A trust was to be set up in her name to those ends. Apparently she told a friend just before she died that she wanted the village to be deluged – yes, she used that word – with artists who would gently lead the inhabitants to enlightenment. As you may imagine, Miss Somerville, to carry out her wishes to the letter is quite impossible. But at least I feel I can give young artists a chance to have their work seen. There's quite a nice arrangement now; paintings and so forth are sent to various galleries in Scotland and even farther afield.'

Their coffee was brought by a woman wearing a checked overall.

'I'm so glad Murray invited you to come here before you return to London,' Hurrell said, handing Ginny a plate of biscuits.

Ginny took a custard cream. 'There's more to it than that. I was hoping you'd help me. You see, the police suspect that either my father or Andrew McQuade, or even both of them, had something to do with the murder.'

'That's preposterous!' Hurrell exclaimed. 'I admit that Andy's a bit of a wild card and no one seems to know anything about him, but there's no way that Alastair would have been mixed up in anything like that. He was a respected man and for good reason. But I don't see how I can help.'

'Please tell me about your open day on 16 April.'

'There's not a lot to tell really – one open day is very much like another. I think – and not boasting or anything – that in the ten years we've been here we've got the public-relations side of it to a fine art.' He grinned self-consciously at the unintentional joke. 'The students arrive at the beginning of April, you see. Sometimes they bring some of their work with them and that's useful for then we have instant exhibits, so to speak. But the ones who haven't usually have something to show in a couple of weeks or so. We're not usually pushed for items to put on display. Frankly, what we're called in the village hurts and I suppose it drives me to try to prove that what we do here is of value. But not many of them climb the hill to see for themselves, I'm afraid.'

'Have you tried involving the local schools?'

Hurrell shook his head. 'No, that hadn't occurred to me.'

'You could try grabbing them young, starting with the tinies. Have painting and modelling competitions with the best on display here. They'd drag their parents along to admire their efforts.'

'I ... I hadn't thought of it quite like that,' Hurrell admitted.

'Unless in your heart of hearts you don't really want small children racing around on your lovely polished floors,' Ginny added, smiling.

'You're probably right,' Hurrell said with a sigh. 'I'm not very good with the wee ones.'

'And the open day?' Ginny prompted.

'Ah, yes. Well, I suppose about a hundred and fifty people visited us during the day with about sixty present for the buffet in the evening. We do make it very clear, you know, that all are welcome. Most of what one would call the local professional folk call in during the evening − I get the impression some of them are worried that if they didn't their friends would think them philistines.'

'What was Jean doing that evening?'

'She had been here all day helping the cook. In the evening she was serving drinks − we just offer wine, no spirits − and setting out the buffet. It's traditional that members of staff have a small gathering of their own when all the work is done. Some of the food and drink is set aside for them.'

'Where would that have been available?'

'This year I believe they had a table in the corner of the studio − some of the visitors joined them. Your father was one of them.' He added quickly, 'So did I, for a while.'

He did not want her to think him a snob, Ginny realised. 'When was the last time you saw Jean?'

'Then, I think. I suppose it was about eight o'clock. No, that's wrong. Andy took your father home shortly after that and then Jean had to get back to work and help to clear away — I saw her and Murray go in the direction of the kitchen carrying trays of glasses. Everyone was helping, of course. Even the minister was stacking chairs.'

'What time did it finish?'

'Not late. Some of the people had a fair distance to travel.'

'And you didn't see Jean after she went into the kitchen?'

'No.' Hurrell's hand jerked so that he slopped some of his coffee into the saucer. 'Poor woman!'

'I'm sorry if the police have asked you these questions already.'

'Yes, but I don't mind. I would feel just the same — needing to know the truth — if a close member of my family was under suspicion.'

'Did Jean get on with everyone here?'

'On an everyday basis, yes.'

'So, reading between the lines, she was one of those who would have agreed with the institute's alternative name?'

'Er, yes.'

'Was there any friction then?'

Hurrell finished his coffee, dripping it over his shirt front. Then he said, 'I think you must understand that there will always be friction in this kind of situation. A woman gets a job as a cleaner-cum-assistant-cook and sees young people with whom she has nothing in common getting free bed and board in return for what she regards as messing around with paints and bits of rock. Her own parents are probably struggling to make ends meet on unemployment benefit or a state pension. In Jean's case that applied to her own circumstances too — her husband is not the sort that anyone would want to employ. Yes, I'd be lying if I pretended that everything was sweetness and light. There were exchanges of words between her and the students sometimes, especially if one of them had been a bit thoughtless in making a mess after she'd cleared up. But that sort of thing must happen in any similar institution. I hope you don't think that *anyone* here might have had anything to do with her death.'

'She had a bit of a reputation, I understand.'

Hurrell frowned. 'Reputation?'

'It might be a little unfair to say, as one local woman did to me, that she would go with any man who would buy her a drink, but even Chief Inspector Speir confirmed that was what several people said.'

Hurrell was ineffectually mopping at his shirt with his handkerchief. 'I really can't help you on that, I'm afraid, but I can assure you that nothing like that went on on these premises.' He got to his feet. 'Perhaps you'd like to have a look round now.'

Ginny sat tight. 'Even the police must be working on the idea that she went with one, or several men, after the party that night and that one of them strangled her.'

Looking a bit desperate, Hurrell said, 'Well, it wasn't your father and I'm convinced, as I said, that nothing happened *here*. Now ...' He opened the door.

The studio was very expensively fitted out. The huge window extended right down to ground level. The floor, as Ginny had already noticed from outside, was of highly polished wood. Stainless steel and what looked like copper spot lamps were on fittings in the ceiling; other lights, medieval-style sconces made of wrought iron with large tinted glass shades, were set at intervals on the stone walls. Painted white, the walls could only be glimpsed in the spaces between richly colourful hangings made from the most sumptuous fabrics, made, Hurrell explained, by a woman who lived on the island of Mull.

As a living room it would have been glorious, as a backdrop to an art studio it was a disaster. The reason for this, Ginny thought, was the efforts of the institute's students.

Nearest to her, as she gazed around, was a large table piled with a jumble of different-sized pieces of expanded polystyrene and what she guessed was balsawood. Some of these had been slotted together, jigsaw-style, to form a structure not dissimilar to a North Sea oil rig. Or even a four-legged spider, Ginny decided, her head on one side.

'That's Murray's work,' Hurrell said. 'He's exploring the dynamics of jigsaw puzzles.' He led the way to a corner by the window. 'I'm not *quite* sure what Miss MacNaughton would have thought of Morag's work but it is in the spirit of the natural world that she so enjoyed. Don't you agree?'

On a table smaller that Murray's was a motley collection of stones, driftwood, moss, twigs and dried heather. It formed a sort of peak, the centrepiece of which was part of a dead branch of a tree crowned with a sheep's skull, askew. Black beetles had been glued in the otherwise empty eye sockets, the effect a penetrating stare at the onlooker. Between the teeth was a long bone.

'Fascinating,' Ginny said, hoping that he would not ask her for an honest opinion.

'She walks for miles, collecting her material,' Hurrell said. 'She says she's drawing in the spirit of the Highlands.'

'Did she find the fibula out in the hulls?'

Hurrell had walked on and came back. 'I beg your pardon?'

'The fibula. Or did she dig it up in the churchyard?'

'I'm sorry, I'm not with you.'

'That bone between the sheep's teeth. It's a human leg bone.'

He peered at it. 'Well, I never! Oh, that's Morag all right — she's enjoys a morbid joke. I expect she brought it back from abroad — most of the students are widely travelled. In fact, come to think of it, they're all foreigners this season but Morag.'

Ginny was looking at some cardboard boxes that had been painted black and suspended from the ceiling by different lengths of white rope. A separate group of boxes had been coloured every shade of the spectrum and stacked seemingly at random around a pole with ribbons hanging down from the top of it to the floor.

Hurrell said, 'That's Helmut's work. He's our star pupil, really — not that I regard myself as their tutor. I merely help to channel their ideas in the right directions. Helmut has a real future. He's already received commissions.'

'I've never seen anything like it,' Ginny said quite truthfully.

'He brought *The Maypole Dancers* with him from Germany. It had been exhibited at a show of young people's work in Hamburg.'

'And the black boxes?'

Hurrell beamed. 'That's just something he dashed off. It's meant to be a joke really. It's called *Life on the Ocean Grave.*'

'Utterly side-splitting,' Ginny murmured.

Earnestly, Hurrell continued, 'One of his better pieces is down at the show. You *must* visit our tent.'

'I will,' Ginny promised, wondering what she had let herself in for.

They left the building through a rear door, Ginny having expressed an interest in seeing the garden. Some ten yards from the door she stopped, enchanted.

'That's really *beautiful!*'

It was a garden seat, very rustic, with a wooden wheel at one end and handles at the other so it could be moved around like a wheelbarrow.

'You like it?' Hurrell said in offhand fashion. 'Pete did that. He's not one of our artists, just a friend of Murray's, they're both American. Because he works mostly with a chain saw I had to ask him to do it outside. The noise and fumes were upsetting the others.'

Then Ginny saw the giant. It stood some ten feet in height and seemed to be made, mostly, from the branches of dead trees. The huge man was leaning on an axe and staring inscrutably into the distance. His feet and toes were fashioned from tree roots, each toe gnarled but somehow perfect. He looked as though he had been standing there since the dawn of time and was the only creature in the whole universe to know a wonderful, aweinspiring secret.

'It's almost holy,' Ginny whispered.

'Your father liked it too,' Hurrell said, sounding bored. 'In fact, I was going to ask him if he wanted it at the end of the year. I'm afraid it rather detracts from what we're really trying to do here.'

Ginny tore her gaze from it to stare at the director in amazement.

'It would have saved it from ending up on McQuade's bonfire,' Hurrell finished by saying. 'As happened to a project of Helmut's. He still bears a grudge, but, I tell you, the boy's a real genius.'

*

65

Lochan Meadow, the show ground for the Highland Games, was a fifty-acre pasture field belonging to a farm on the Mackiver estate. It had been carefully mown and rolled and, on Kevin Mackiver's orders, a trench had been dug in an effort to divert, temporarily at least, the burn that the heavy rains had swollen to the extent of it bursting its normally modest banks. Despite these measures, however, there was a shallow lake right at the bottom of the field across the main entrance. The ground around it was a morass, churned up by the increasing number of vehicles that were arriving bringing people setting up stands, erecting tents and marquees, the public-address system and the stage for the dancing. It had already taken two tractors to haul from the mud a lorry delivering cabers for the tossing thereof. Somewhere, well in the distance, a piper was practising a lament.

'My God! He's like the side of a hoose!' exclaimed a woman's voice right behind Ginny.

She turned to see the speaker emerging from a tent with a notice on it intimating that on the morrow it would be reserved for the judges. Perhaps, Ginny thought unkindly, she lived there permanently; she looked judgemental enough with her severe hairstyle, sober tweeds and a certain pinched look about the nostrils indicating someone who would not tolerate the second-rate. She was looking in the direction of two young men, one of whom was Murray, the other obviously the subject of her comment — around six foot four in height with shoulders like a water buffalo.

'Hello again,' Murray shouted. 'Meet Pete,' he said when they were closer. 'Pete, this is the young lady I told you about, Ginny, Dr Somerville's daughter. I'm real sorry about your dad,' he said to Ginny. 'I got talking to Malcolm and we guessed who you were.'

Ginny rescued her wrung hand from Pete's grasp. 'You're the man with the chain saw!'

Pete's voice was amazingly quiet for a man of his size. 'I just kinda like making things out of trees that have died. You know — then they sort of live again.'

'I'd like to buy your giant that's up at the institute.'

'*Buy* it?' Pete exclaimed. 'You can have it for nothing.'

'No, that's not right. I couldn't possibly — '

'Of course you can,' he interrupted, grinning. 'But I tell you what, go and take a look in the tent. The one you saw was a prototype. Now I'm making them a bit smoother-looking and dunking the wood in preservative so they last longer.'

In a low voice Murray said, 'Malcolm isn't so keen on what Pete's doing. But I told him – Andy was with me actually and he agreed – that you can't expect country folk to appreciate the sort of work Helmut does. For a show like this there has to be a mixture of things on display.'

'Does Dr Hurrell take notice of what the gardener says?' Ginny asked, deliberately fishing.

'He's an educated artisan,' Murray said. 'You need opinions like his or otherwise everything gets far too academic and rarefied.'

Pete nudged his friend in the ribs, almost knocking him over. 'And Andy showed Malcolm how to use that new camera. Remember? He was so impressed he gave Andy a roll of film and let him loose with it. I've never seen such bloody fantastic pictures as that guy took of the sunset behind the mountains. Hurrell's going to get them blown up and put in the dining room.' He eyed up the pile of fir poles that had been dumped in a heap for the caber tossing. 'You know, I might just ...'

'Piece of cake,' Murray told him. 'You heave bigger chunks than that around all the time.'

'Yeah, but I don't throw them *end over end*,' Pete muttered, picking one up in experimental fashion.

The public-address system blared into life with a military march, the sound so distorted it was like listening to a hundred pianos being sawn in half.

'Tell me about the party you had at the institute on 16 April,' Ginny requested, having to shout.

Pete had readjusted his hold on the caber and was advancing purposefully with it towards the centre of the ring, the veins on his neck standing out like hawsers. Quite a few people seemed to have stopped working to watch.

'There wasn't anything special about it.'

'It was the last time anyone saw Jean Kirkpatrick alive.'

Murray actually blenched. 'God, yes, of course. You found her.'

'Who was she with when *you* last saw her?'

'She was with Andy, in the kitchen. But they weren't alone, we were all in and out. I didn't see her at all after the power cut.'

'What power cut? No one said anything about a power cut.'

'We have them all the time,' Murray said into a sudden silence, the racket having ceased as abruptly as it had begun.

Against all odds Pete accelerated and in one graceful movement heaved the pole into the air. It flew upwards and then down onto its other end, remained poised while half of Inverness-shire held its breath and pitched over in the opposite direction, demolishing the stage built for the Highland dancing. Moments later, when the sound of splintering wood had almost ceased, a yell of triumph fit to freeze the blood rang around the peaks, the like of which had probably not been heard since Bannockburn.

'Oh, God!' Murray moaned. 'Why do I stay on the same planet as this man? He felled one of the apple trees in the studio garden the other day, not concentrating.' He ducked under the ropes. 'You must excuse me while I placate the natives.'

Ginny soon found the tent devoted to the MacNaughton Institute of Art and went in. Pete, obviously not worried that someone might steal his work, had already set up a display. If Malcolm Hurrell had had a say in the fact that it was sited in the darkest corner of the tent with a view to giving full prominence to Helmut's work, set right in the middle, then he had failed. For this new giant reared above all, its implacable gaze meeting that of the visitors as they entered and imparting a silent, mystic invitation.

This one was also better made, stripped of all bark, and the preservation process had left it a pale-golden colour. There was another garden seat but this was statuary rather than utilitarian as two carved figures were already seated upon it; rotund, bearlike trolls. There were a few smaller items; a simple seat for one made from the stump of a huge tree, another troll with massive genitals that somehow managed not to be obscene and an oversized shepherd's crook, a snail with a smile carved into the top.

'Crap, isn't it?' said someone at the back of the tent.

Ginny guessed that this must be Helmut. 'No, I was thinking how utterly charming and unpretentious it all was.'

Just over five foot tall, probably in his thirties, he was dressed all in black, his hair of the same colour, short and tightly curled. His eyes were small, dark brown and right now were regarding her scornfully. 'Oh, yes, I'll give you both of those. I suppose you're one of those people who collect garden gnomes.' His English was perfect and without the slightest accent.

'No, but the giant would look wonderful in a woodland garden setting.'

'Perhaps,' he conceded. 'Personally, I prefer cerebral art. Something to which the mind of the intellectual can relate. Real art has to move away from the simple forms that any dolt can perceive.'

'Oh, you've lost me there,' Ginny said gaily. 'I'm not one of those serious people who can read meaningful messages into a pile of bricks.' She gazed around. 'Neither Murray nor Morag seem to have done anything yet.'

'Morag is out collecting her material now. It loses its vibrations very quickly so everything must be left until the last possible moment. Murray I don't know about. His jigsaw dynamics are not for me.'

While he had been speaking, Ginny was examining his own offering, a filing cabinet with each drawer open to a different extent and various articles spilling out of them; T-shirts soiled with mud and oil, a broken umbrella, a small roll of old-fashioned lino, very worn, and sundry other items, all damaged in some way.

'That lino must have been a real find,' Ginny said admiringly, going closer, 'It's the real thing too,' she enthused. 'Cork-backed.'

'It represents the orbit of the planet Neptune,' Helmut said stiffly.

'So this is the universe then?' Ginny said. 'Chaos out of order, order out of chaos.'

He stared at her unwaveringly for several long moments. 'No.'

'No?'

'I have called it *The Planets After the Ending of Time*.'

Ginny beamed at him. 'Well, you know what they say — no two minds think alike.'

'It's true,' Helmut said, pacing up and down agitatedly. 'And of course that is the beauty of something like this. Every mind sees it differently.' He gave her a look that, had the light been better, might have seemed more like a smile. 'Now, if you don't mind, I want to think. This is not yet finished.'

'Not at all. Perhaps when you're free you'll give me a few minutes on mundane matters?'

'And that is?'

'Murder.'

'You're a reporter?' he snapped.

'No, merely trying to make sure the police don't get the wrong man.'

'McQuade?' The name was almost spat out.

'You don't like him?'

'He's a peasant.'

'Ah,' Ginny said understandingly. 'He doesn't appreciate your interpretation of art?'

'He burned *The Last Bouquet to Lenin*.'

'Not all Scots are raging lefties,' she pointed out.

'No, no. You don't understand. The materials. He started a bonfire with them. I had to abandon completely.'

'So you decided to teach him a lesson with the slaughtered sheep in his kitchen?'

Helmut shook his head. 'What sheep? I never touch meat and renounced eating it many years ago. It pollutes the body.'

'And Jean? What did you think of her?'

She was quite unprepared for the venomous reply.

'The promiscuous cow deserved to die,' Helmut whispered. 'Women like that get what's coming to them. The Americans and other filth . . .' Here he spat copiously on the grass near Ginny's feet. 'Copulating with her like animals, cattle . . .' He broke off and turned away.

70

'Did she turn you down, Helmut?' Ginny asked.

She ducked as he snatched up one of the components of *The Planets After the Ending of Time,* a garden fork with one of the prongs missing, and hurled it at her like a spear. It impaled itself in the ground behind her.

Ginny left the tent, not running.

Chapter Six

Dr Somerville's one-time cleaner, Annie Dreghorn, known throughout the village as Bletherin' Annie on account of her fondness for gossip, declined, politely, Ginny's offer of her job back. Nothing, said Annie afterwards to female friends, would get her in to that house again. She had maintained for quite a while that the doctor – cantankerous with slovenly women like Annie – had 'done something' to the vacuum cleaner so that it gave her electric shocks.

Ginny, hauling the offending article from a cupboard that afternoon, having acquired the services of a young woman recommended by Maggie Mossblown, eyed it up suspiciously. It looked as though it had set sail in the Ark with Noah. And, having switched it on and observed the blue sparks fizzing around the plug in quite attractive fashion, she put it straight out the back for the dustman.

She had resigned herself to the fact that Andrew would either forget the invitation to dinner or simply wouldn't turn up. As the day wore on with Helen, the hired help, performing miracles with a new cleaner, a mountain of dusters and tins of polish of various sorts, Ginny became more depressed. All the silly old clichés seemed to fit what she was doing – burning her boats, putting all her eggs in one basket ...

Forcing herself to think positively, she lit a log fire in the study. Helen had started in this room, at Ginny's request, and in the light from a single table lamp it was very cosy. The old wood of the furniture gleamed in the firelight, the leaping flames reflected in the jars and the gilt frames of the pictures. With slight trepidation Ginny sat at the desk and opened the top drawer.

The first thing she saw was a small photograph mounted on card. It was of a man about fifty years old, standing formal and unsmiling by a tree in a garden. A black Labrador lay at his feet. The man was dressed as if he was going shooting, in a tweed jacket, breeches and leggings, and he had a shotgun crooked over his arm.

He did not look a pleasant man; the face was somehow closed and cruel.

Ginny replaced the photograph and slammed the drawer, all at once feeling that there might not be room in her own life for this man whom she had never known but who had left her a legacy of violence and mystery.

Restlessly, later, Ginny roamed the house. Helen had returned to her family, promising that she would work at least two mornings a week until the years of neglect — and, although this wasn't mentioned, Bletherin' Annie's laziness — had been eradicated, and after that, as and when Ginny wanted her to.

'I'm making all these arrangements,' Ginny said to herself. 'But I'm still not sure I can stay.'

She had not set foot in the conservatory until this moment and half wished she hadn't when she felt how cold it was and saw the rows of dying plants. Most were in pots; geraniums, ferns, a palm of some kind and several other things she didn't know the names of. There was an old oil heater but it was empty. A metal watering can was also empty and when she tried to fill it from a tap set low in the wall it was too stiff for her to move.

Ginny flung down the can and burst into tears, great sobs that seemed to tear her apart.

Suddenly, he was there, right in front of her, and she jumped up with a little scream, thinking for a moment he was a ghost. But ghosts were not dishevelled like this, their hair uncombed, nor out of breath.

'Did you fall?' Andrew demanded to know. 'I heard a clatter and — '

'I can't cope with this,' Ginny wailed, weeping afresh.

'Everywhere I go in this house it's either wonderful or horrible.'

Andrew was trying to tuck in his shirt. 'Scotland's a bit like that,' he said. 'You'll soon get used to it if you decide to live here.' He gave up, turned his back to her, unbuckled the straps of his kilt so that the shirt went where it was supposed to be and fastened it up again.

'That is a beautiful shirt,' Ginny gulped, trying to find the tissue that was up her sleeve. It was made of fine white cambric with full sleeves and ruffles down the front. Frankly, she didn't know what to say to him. Anything really, to stop herself running into his arms and telling him how much she loved him.

He had taken her previous night's comment to heart too and his hair was now fairly short, though thick and wavy. Ginny knew that she would faint from emotion if she ran her fingers through it.

'Well, if you're sure you're all right ...' he said, turning to leave.

'But – but you are *coming?*' Ginny blurted out.

He looked at his watch. 'Yes, but it's only six thirty and there's one or two things I'd like to do first.'

Ginny blew her nose. 'Of course.'

'Seven thirty?'

'Fine.' When he was crossing the living room she said, 'I'm really sorry I upset you last night. I had no right to try to bulldoze you into something like that.'

For a moment he had looked a little puzzled as she was speaking. 'Oh, no. It wasn't that, it was when you mentioned Barry Chichester. I worked for him at one time on a documentary about the damage skiing does to the mountains. It brought it all back to me really ... what I used to be, what I've lost.' His voice was a little husky as he spoke the last words and then he turned and went away.

Ginny wept afresh. For him.

A lot of cold water on her face, make-up and a stiff tot from the bottle of whisky she had brought for socialising purposes went only part of the way to restoring Ginny's composure before her guest arrived. Letting her own emotions run away

74

with her was having the effect of driving a coach and horses through his. And he was far more vulnerable. No, she would have to tackle the task of rescuing Andrew McQuade from his pit of despair as though it were part of her job. Perhaps, in a way, it was.

She placed the whisky glass on the draining board, on second thoughts rinsed and dried it, endeavoured to banish all thoughts of those wonderful hazel eyes and surveyed her culinary arrangements. There was a quiet tap on the back door.

'Come in,' Ginny called.

He still looked as though he had come straight off the set of *Rob Roy*.

'Is that the McQuade tartan?' she asked for the sake of something to say.

He had brought a bottle of wine 'No. McQuade's an Irish name. It's green MacLeod, my mother's clan.'

'And the little knife tucked into the top of your sock? Is it ...?'

'Skene dhu,' he filled in, with the patience displayed by most Scotsmen in the face of such questions. 'In Gaelic *sgian dubh*. They're really only for decoration these days − or for peeling apples.'

Stirring the carbonara sauce, Ginny said, 'Tell me about the power cut on the night of the party.'

'Shall I open the wine first?'

Mortified, Ginny realised she had not asked him what he'd like to drink or even to sit down. 'Oh, I'm so sorry,' she gasped. 'There's one in the fridge. Would you mind?'

'We're always having power cuts at the institute,' Andrew said when he had poured them both some wine. 'Branches get blown off trees and short out the wires.'

'Please think. Was it just at the institute or more general? Where were you?'

'Is it important?'

'I don't know,' she confessed.

'I was here,' he answered after due thought. 'I've remembered now. Alastair and I both were. And Colin Staverton.'

'The friend of my father's − the consultant?'

'Yes. The two of them were having a good blether, I was

75

just listening really. Then the lights went out. It didn't really matter, though — all the oil lamps in this house always have oil in them as a precaution. It was just a matter of lighting a couple until the power came back on.'

'Just lamps? No candles?'

'No, Alastair thought candles were dangerous because of the naked flames.'

'So if anyone had wanted to go anywhere in the house they'd have simply picked up one of the lamps and taken it with them.'

'Yes.'

'And up at the institute?'

'There are camping lamps. And candles — white household ones.'

'No red ones?'

'Yes, but only for evening functions after dark. We put them on the tables — ' He broke off impatiently. 'What the hell is all this about?'

'Do you think you could go down into the cellar?'

'With a candle?' he asked sardonically.

'There's a candlestick down there I'd like you to fetch,' Ginny went on doggedly.

'Look, the police went over everything.'

'Please.'

In an effort to counteract any lingering trace of the macabre, Ginny busied herself with placing a bowl of salad on the table — they were going to eat in the kitchen — together with garlic bread hot from the oven and some heavy damask napkins she had found in a drawer in the dining room. Nevertheless, when Andrew returned from his mission and placed the candlestick on the draining board, she repressed an involuntary shudder.

He picked up his wineglass and toasted her. 'To Ginny, who has a brain.'

Trying to remain calm, she served the meal and they both sat down. There was an unspoken decision to defer further discussion on the subject until after they had eaten and it was due to either their strong-mindedness or Ginny's cooking, or both, that this was adhered to. Then, Andrew in possession of the coffee pot and the whisky, Ginny with

76

a tray of crockery and a chocolate mousse she had made, they went into the study.

'Is that him?' Ginny said, taking the photo from the drawer.

Andrew had a look. 'No, that's Willie Tawse, a retired schoolmaster. The picture was of the dog really, it was one of the pups of a bitch Alastair used to have.' He stared at her, horrified. 'You mean you don't know what your own father looked like?'

'No, my mother burned all her wedding photos.'

'I've a couple of snaps somewhere,' Andrew said and, before Ginny could stop him, went away. When he returned he brought the candlestick with him.

Wordlessly, Ginny stared at the photographs that had been thrust into her hands. Measuring some ten inches by seven, they were colour portraits of a man seated on a boulder on a hillside overlooking a wooded glen. A thin blue line, a sea loch, could be seen in the distance. The only difference between the two pictures was that in one her father was looking at the camera, smiling, and in the other he was gazing at the view, his face serious and thoughtful.

'You took these?' Ginny asked.

A trifle roughly Andrew said, 'We drove up in the Land Rover. If you go on past the institute to Ruthven Loan you get a good view of Ben Nevis — that's the rounded peak in the distance.'

'I didn't know you went in for portrait photography.'

'It's a sort of hobby of mine — that is, it used to be.' He paused and then added, 'I had to sell my camera and everything that went with it.'

'Why?'

'For the same reason that I'm gardening up at the institute and giving Malcolm Hurrell a hand with the day-to-day running of the place — only for God's sake keep that to yourself as it's unofficial. Money. It's not that easy to get insurance when you're engaged in the sort of work I was. And now they're arguing about the payout. I might get a bit more if I stayed at home and just collected unemployment benefit but I'd go right off my head with nothing to do.' He glanced down at his watch. 'But I'm not selling this until I really have to.'

The man who had obeyed the photographer's request to smile — with an ironic lift of one black eyebrow — had the sort of face, Ginny thought, that could not be anything but Scottish. The chin was jutting and determined, the eyes wide apart and, like her own, blue. His hair, although greying, was thick, the hands clasped around the knees strong and capable, the same hands which had removed the splinter all those years ago.

'I simply don't understand,' Ginny whispered. 'He looks so *nice.*'

'He was a good man,' Andrew said.

'My mother said he was a monster.'

'He did mention once or twice that he'd had a bit of a drink problem in the past. But he'd had to lay off as his health got worse. I believe he'd been pretty ill and it had affected his heart.'

Sadly, Ginny laid the photos aside.

'Keep them, if you want to.'

She smiled her thanks. 'I was slightly perturbed, though, when Chief Inspector Speir informed me that Annie, who used to clean this house, had told him that my father had no time for women as people and was bad-tempered. That doesn't quite fit what other folk are saying.'

'Bletherin' Annie!' Andrew exclaimed. 'She's the most spiteful *cailleach* this side of Skye. I don't know why he put up with her. It would be the sort of thing she would say — it was probably revenge for his insistence that unless the house was reasonably clean she wouldn't get her money.'

A memory had just stirred in Ginny's mind. Several memories. They all pointed to the conclusion that her mother had not had a lot of time for men. What if her father's drink problem had not been as serious as she had been led to believe? Had it been merely her mother's excuse for leaving a country she hated and a man she no longer loved? Suppose he had turned to alcohol to help him cope with the stress and long hours that his profession demanded, because he was getting no support from his wife?

'Tell me,' Ginny said as she gave Andrew some chocolate

78

mousse, 'why would some bastard dump the body of a woman he'd murdered in a good man's house?'

He gestured towards the candlestick. 'Under cover of a power cut?'

'Yes.'

'Well, for a start, this came from the institute. I know, because I dug it up in the garden. According to Malcolm it's Victorian — I hate to argue with someone who knows about these things, but I think it's older than that. There are some in my family that go back to the time of Charles Stewart that aren't all that different. Still, that's hardly important now. Yes, you're right — it's quite possible that the murderer used this to light his way in the basement. He brought it with him for that purpose.'

'And gained entry through the coal thing? The doors have fallen in.'

'Have they? It's ages since I was down there.' He gazed at her for a moment and then said, 'You seem very sure that I'm not involved.'

'Just call me Miss Marple. Andrew, I meant every word of what I said last night. I don't know when I'll actually have my own business but there will be work for you and I don't mean the kind of thing that involves dangling from rock faces.'

He shook his head. 'But thank you. You've done me a great service. I can look at myself in the mirror now and I'm not afraid of saying no.'

'I don't quite understand.'

Softly, Andrew said, 'As I said last night, this is *me*. The past is gone. I knew that as soon as I was out of hospital people would start hounding me with jobs. But I can't. And when you've lost your nerve as I have, it's suicide to try again. If I can't do the jobs I used to, I'm going to leave it *all* alone. Suppose I'm filming a thousand miles from mountains and the producer suddenly decides he wants a shot from the top of a tall tree! You can do it, Andy, he'll say, you're good at that sort of thing. No. Never again. But at least you showed me that I can say no.'

Hoping she was successfully concealing her disappointment,

Ginny said, 'In any case there's no need to grow another beard and live like a tramp now.'

'You're very polite. What I was doing was hiding behind my own whiskers.'

'Nor to drink too much in order to forget?'

He gave her a wry smile. 'I can't afford to really. No, I'll probably tell my mother she needn't pay the rent any more and move back home and work for my father's company.'

This was uttered in such bitter fashion that it took Ginny's breath away. Then she boiled over. 'That's utter crap!' she shouted at him.

He looked a little shaken.

'You've your whole life in front of you. How can you talk like that?'

'Would you like some coffee?' he asked stonily. In other words, telling her to mind her own business.

'Helmut threw a garden fork at me this afternoon.'

'You must have upset him.'

'I asked him if Jean turned him down.'

Calmly, he gave her a cup of coffee. 'Woman, if you go round asking questions like that you'll get all kinds of things thrown at you.'

'Did she?' Ginny persevered.

'Yes, she told him she didn't care to be screwed by a dirty Jew.'

'But he isn't a — '

'No, but you can appreciate the insult to someone who probably carries a picture of the Führer next to his heart.'

'I'm liking the pair of them less and less. How much did Jean charge?'

He replied without hesitating. 'A tenner for straight sex, more for what she called "fancy goods".'

'So, after the party one assumes she and several males went off somewhere and she earned quite a bit of money. Then one of them strangled her.'

'I should imagine it's fairly safe to assume that.'

'Do the police know about it?'

'I've no idea. I didn't tell them. I wasn't feeling particularly helpful just then.'

'Who told *you*?'

'Murray. I didn't want to drop him in it either.'

'I wonder what happened to the money. It can't have been the motive for murder, surely?'

'God knows. If you take my advice you'll leave the police to get on with it.'

Ginny retorted, 'Perhaps I'm finding it obscene that someone is trying to pin this murder on a retired doctor and the police are going along with it'. She put down her coffee, untasted. 'Perhaps I'll do as Barry suggested and conduct my own investigation. I'll start by having a good look in the cellar at those broken-down doors above the coal store.'

Ginny was shivering as she took the key from its hook and unlocked the cellar door. Fusty, dank air wafted into her face as she descended the stairs.

'Look, you don't have to do this,' said Andrew's voice somewhere behind her.

'I can't just stand by and do nothing.'

He followed her down. 'Those damned doors are probably dangerous.'

'As dangerous as a terrorist bomb? That's what I was dealing with down in London.'

She was fully aware that the forensic people had been over every inch of the cellar and the garden and that any evidence, footprints and so forth, would have been destroyed during the period of time that had elapsed between the body's concealment and its discovery. Perhaps she was being stupid, doing something for the sake of it. On the other hand, she had never come to grief taking Barry's advice.

His thoughts obviously partly akin to her own, Andrew said, 'Some bullocks got into the garden a couple of months back and churned everything up at the rear of the house — somehow a gate was left open.'

Ginny had tugged open the coal-store door and they both stood looking at what was within.

'This was opened from the outside when it was functioning?' she asked.

'Yes, but there was a bolt on the inside as well,' he replied, hefting up one of the doors for her to see. 'Folk didn't trust one another *that* much.'

Ginny bent down to examine the interior more closely.

Everything was very wet where the rain had continued to pour in, the doors in an even worse state than when Ginny had first seen them. The one that Andrew had moved was hanging by just one hinge, the other had broken away completely, together with part of the frame, and lay in a corner. The coal, which had originally been covered by a thin layer of earth, showed every sign of having been carefully sorted through, the earth sifted. Speir's team had been thorough.

'I still think the body was brought in this way,' Ginny said. 'While the three of you were chatting during the power cut. What time did it come on again?'

'I can't help you with that. I went home in the dark and left them yarning. The power had been restored when I got up in the morning.'

'So there's just the candlestick to go on. Where was it kept?'

'The last time I saw it it was in Hurrell's office. He said he was going to show it to the curator of the museum at Bridge of Corran.'

'What about the red candles?'

'They're kept in a stationery store next to his office, along with all the stuff used for the social events − paper napkins, tablecloths and so forth. Oh, and the cases of wine. He likes to keep everything under lock and key.'

Ginny firmly closed the door again. 'What can you tell me about Hurrell as far as Jean was concerned?'

'Nothing. If he had any kind of arrangement with her, no one at the institute got to hear of it. And he's not married, if that's what you were going to ask me.'

Ginny was thinking back to her conversation with him. 'He said he had a flat in Edinburgh that he went to when the weather was bad in the winter. Otherwise, I suppose, he just stays at the institute. That seems a very lonely sort of life.'

'Hurrell doesn't actually live at the institute. He has a room there he uses sometimes but for the rest of the time he stays at the Glen Hotel.'

Thoughtfully, Ginny started to go back up the stairs. 'It's an expensive place,' she observed. 'I wonder ...'

'You're not the first to wonder,' Andrew said. 'I'm not so sure that Aggie MacNaughton left *that* much money.'

Turning to face him, Ginny said. 'Are you saying that you think something a bit dodgy might be going on?'

'What the police might call an irregularity? Yes.'

'And to whom, if anyone, have you voiced your concerns?'

'To your father. And in a roundabout way to Hurrell. But I didn't make it sound as though I was accusing him of anything, of course. It's not really any of my business. Why?'

'Someone put Jean's watch in your bedroom, didn't they?'

Chapter Seven

The stage for the Highland dancing had been repaired and the sides draped with red, green and white tartan taffeta caught up here and there with rosettes made from the same material. But this early, at a little after nine fifteen, it stood quite deserted, the first class timed for ten after Kevin Mackiver had carried out the official opening. The judges, meanwhile, were in their tent fortifying themselves with hot drinks or the contents of discreet hip flasks, depending on sex and inclination. For the morning, although bright and sunny, was chilly, a breeze from the surrounding peaks playing mischievous games with kilts and whipping the regal lions and blue and white saltires on their poles.

'The Crown and the Kirk,' said a grizzled old man to Ginny, observing the direction of her gaze. 'The auld rulers of the Scots.'

'I'm sure they made a much better job of it than Westminster does today,' Ginny said.

'Aye, lass,' he said sadly, wandering away. 'Better than that bunch of ...' The rest was lost, possibly mercifully, to the wind.

The show ground was filling up quickly, most of the people having come from the village and farms and other houses close by. Special buses had been laid on from Bridge of Corran and Fort William and these were arriving more quickly than the muddy entrance to the ground would allow, causing added problems for the lone policeman directing the traffic on the main road. Then, a very new and shiny Japanese four-wheel-drive vehicle became bogged down. It

84

was hauled free by someone's battered Series II Land Rover, to sardonic cheers from bystanders, and then went on to block a cattle truck that was bringing sheep for the sheepdog demonstration, and that also became stuck.

At the various stands, tents, trailers and caravans one could buy anything from heather plants to tartan trews, fishing flies to spare parts for bagpipes. Litters of Border-collie pups romped and tumbled in the backs of Range Rovers — not for sale, just brought along for the ride — steaming cups of soup were passed around poured from vacuum flasks; all this watched over by a small herd of Highland ponies in an adjacent field.

Ginny brought some homemade shortbread to post to Alvis and some smoked salmon for dinner and headed for the refreshment tent for coffee. Then she saw Pete. He had risen to the occasion with a 'kilt' made from what looked like a travel rug, complete with fringing, folded in half, wrapped around his waist and secured with a wide leather belt. For a sporran he had substituted a sheep's skull — it looked to Ginny very much like the one from Morag's masterpieces at the institute — with a large hunk of wool he had probably found in a thorn hedge. Another plaid rug was folded across his left shoulder, secured by what appeared to be a genuine brooch. Long woollen socks, with what might have been a small kitchen knife tucked into the top of one of them, and training shoes completed the outfit.

The overall effect was utterly superb.

'Couldn't afford the real thing,' he said, striding over.

'You look ferocious,' she told him. 'I take it you've decided to enter the caber tossing.'

He smiled self-consciously. 'I hope none of the purists will object.'

'Three of them have died of shock already,' said a voice at Ginny's elbow.

Pete stared at the speaker for several long seconds. 'Andy!' he exclaimed. 'For a moment there I didn't recognise you without the beard.'

'More importantly, what have you got on *underneath?*' Andrew asked.

Pete drew himself up proudly and after shooting an

apologetic look at Ginny said, 'Nuthin'. I'm really correct in that direction.'

Gently, Andrew said, 'But for violent activity it's polite not to risk offending the ladies. Put something on — swimming trunks will do.'

'Gee,' Pete said. 'Thanks. Perhaps Murray'll lend me his car.' He jogged away.

'It's almost a *breacan feile*,' Andrew said with a smile, eyes on Pete's back.

'Breck'n fail?' Ginny repeated.

'It means "kilted tartan". A sort of old-style way of wearing the blanket you'd slept in in the days of Highland skirmishes.'

'Will people laugh at him?'

'No, we tend to be quite polite. Besides, he has a real chance of being placed. A couple of the best men are out because of injuries.'

Ginny said, 'I was just about to have coffee. How about you?'

'I can't. I'm sort of security man at the institute tent for a couple of hours and I'm late already.'

The first person Ginny saw in the refreshment tent was Chief Inspector Speir.

'Oh, I'm not working, Miss Somerville,' was his response to the question. 'No, not at all. This is my day off.'

'May I join you?'

'Please do.'

She decided to take advantage of the fact that he seemed to be in a good mood. After fetching herself some coffee, she said, 'How are you getting on with the murder investigation?'

'Progressing slowly but surely,' he replied with one of his bleak smiles.

She had already decided to keep quiet about the candlestick, the man would only drag in Andrew for more questioning when he learned where it had come from.

'What about the husband? Is he really in the clear?'

'We've completely eliminated him from our enquiries. He has a very good alibi for the night his wife went missing.'

'But she only *disappeared* that evening — she might have been killed later.'

'Nevertheless — '

'Chief Inspector, have you endeavoured to reconstruct the night of the party at the institute?'

'As yet, it hasn't really been necessary to — '

'I'm only asking because there was a power cut. It's perfectly possible that the woman's body was placed at the Old Manse then. Under cover of darkness, as they say in corny detective stories.'

'But in a country district like this, Miss Somerville, where there are only a few streetlights in the main road, a power cut doesn't make much difference when it comes to moving anything.'

'I disagree. The body could have been removed very late from the institute and placed in a car. Presumably there are outside lights there which also would have been out just then. The same applies at the Manse where there's one light over the porch — which might well have been switched on as my father had visitors — and one at the rear over the back door which one must assume was not. Those indoors were relying on the light from oil lamps. Anyone breaking into the basement through that coal hatch would know that they could not be taken unawares by someone suddenly switching on the lights. The power failure helped them.'

'But the electricity could have come on again at any time,' Speir said somewhat scoffingly. 'It would have been an enormous risk to take.'

'Whoever it was might have made sure it would be off for quite a while. They might have inflicted deliberate damage. It would be interesting to find out from the electricity board the reason for the break in supply. Another thing I'd like to ask you is about the students or whatever they're called. Have any of them been to the institute before?'

Speir clearly pondered for a moment whether he would be infringing any rules and regulations by divulging the information; then he said, 'Morag Galloway was here last summer, together with Murray Kenning, and I seem to remember him saying that this was his third visit. As to the other American and the German, it's the first time they've been here.'

Further conversation was made impossible by the Boys' Brigade band bursting into life right outside. This was augmented by a pipe band playing something else and the whole lot journeyed, in an aura of mixed sharps and flats, to take their places for the opening parade. As she quickly drank her coffee and took her leave of Speir to go and watch, Ginny noticed Malcolm Hurrell at a nearby table. Staring sightlessly into space, smoking, he appeared to be in a state of high nervous tension.

On the rostrum Kevin Mackiver stood out sharply, mainly because of his dark pin-striped City suit, in slightly strange contrast to the tweeds and keepers' jackets around him. At his side was a woman also attired more suitably for Park Lane, and when Mackiver announced that the show was open, she waved like the Queen. The pair immediately left the group they were with, Mackiver giving a curt nod to the local provost, and disappeared into a tent devoted to the work of the Corran and Highlands Development Board.

Ginny followed, deciding it might be a good moment to wear her television producer's hat.

'May I see your invitation?' a young man requested at the entrance.

There was a notice on a stand informing visitors that there was a private function in progress and the exhibition would be open to the public at noon.

Ginny gave him her card. 'I'm not trying to gate-crash. Please give this to Mr Mackiver and tell him I'd like to talk to him.' She had never known it to fail.

The landowner had donned his reading glasses to peruse the card but snatched them off when he saw her approaching. His lady frowned.

'Well, Miss Somerville — it is Miss, is it? — what can I do for you? Oh, this is my wife, Fiona.'

'Pleased to meet you,' Fiona said, none too convincingly. Close up, and in spite of the suit, she was surprisingly plain, her make-up dated and unflattering with heavy use of bright-blue eyeliner. No such flaws marred her husband, who was polished, scented and exuded an air of well-fed success.

Ginny said, 'I was wondering, as you're obviously one of the leading figures in the community, if you'd be interested in appearing in a television documentary I hope to make.'

Mackiver gave her a cold, calculating stare. Then he took a glass of champagne from the loaded tray carried by a passing waitress, gave it to Ginny and said, having first cleared his throat, 'I'd be moderately interested.'

Ginny beamed at him. 'I specialise in fly-on-the-wall films where a crew keep in close contact with people over a period of time. I'd like to show the world how life is lived in villages such as Kinloch Ruthven in the Highlands — you know, what makes Scotland *tick*.'

Fiona said, 'They'd have to live in the house, though.'

'Only for a short while,' Ginny explained breezily. 'And I don't think you'd find it *too* intrusive. And of course other folk would be featured too — shepherds, gamekeepers, shopkeepers, the minister and so forth. I'd also be keen on showing aspects of life here that might be unexpected. Like the work of the Institute of Art, for example. That's *really* interesting.'

'Not my scene at all, I'm afraid,' Mackiver said.

'But part of the fabric of the place, surely? I mean, you must have been present at the opening this season — on 16 April?'

'Oh, yes. Well, I can hardly cold-shoulder them, can I? Yes, I popped in for a while during the evening. Showed my face, sort of thing. Fiona didn't, did you, sweetie?'

'I was in Edinburgh,' Fiona said. 'But I wouldn't have gone anyway. The people who work there give me the shudders.'

'Pity about the power cut,' Ginny said. 'It must have spoiled things rather.'

Mackiver frowned deeply and then garnered a plate of canapés from a nearby table and pressed Ginny to take some. His wife wrinkled her nose and shook her head when offered the plate.

'You can't live in Scotland and not like smoked salmon, sweetie,' he said, a fond smile not hiding his irritation. 'Besides, it's from our salmon farm. I made sure of that.'

'It's still *fish,*' she hissed. 'You know I can't stand the stuff in any shape or form.'

'You've obviously been talking to Hurrell.' Mackiver decided to ignore his other half. 'Yes, you've reminded me, but it didn't really put a damper on things. By the time it happened, people were thinking of leaving anyway. I'd arrived late as I'd been out that day on business. No, you have to get used to power cuts in this part of the world, I'm afraid, especially in the winter.'

Ginny said, 'I know this sounds a silly question but did you notice an antique candlestick while you were there? It had a red candle in it and probably came into use when the lights went out.'

'No, I can't say that I did. Why?'

'It disappeared and then turned up at my house. I like mysteries, don't you?'

Mackiver laughed. 'Well, don't look at me. I drove straight home and went to bed. And we've quite a few antique candlesticks of our own. Now tell me, Miss Somerville, when do you propose to start work on this film?'

'When I've set everything up and assembled a camera crew. But first you and I will have to sit down together and decide what we're going to do. I'm sure there are many aspects of work on your estate that merit our attention.'

'No doubt. Tell you what, come to our gathering tonight. We always have a bit of a do on the night of the show. Then you can meet just the sort of people you need to get in contact with. I don't suppose that there will be time for you and me to have our tête-à-tête tonight but perhaps we could do some of the groundwork.'

'May I bring a colleague?' Ginny asked smoothly.

'I've no real objection to that. But it's black tie so, if your friend is male, will he have time to hire something? It's early closing day in Bridge of Corran. Most of us will be in Highland dress, you see.'

'Oh, he's a true Scot, Mr Mackiver. I've no doubt that he'll wear his kilt and all that goes with it for the evening.'

A series of scarlet-cheeked tots, cherubic and otherwise, had skipped and hopped to the relentless urgency of a piper, urged on silently by mothers pale with tension. These had given way to older children and these in turn to adults, the sets of crossed swords miraculously remaining untouched by the delicate footwork. The crowds then moved on to watch frowning collies browbeat sheep into performing manoeuvres that puzzled the latter greatly but earned thunderous applause. There were more pipe bands, more music and then a display of dancing given by pupils from a girls' school. The heavyweights then appeared in the main arena to put the shot and toss the caber. After this there was to be a tug-of-war, this being, for some, the highlight of the day.

The contest was a tradition that went back many years, the teams from the Dog and Drover in Kinloch Ruthven on the one hand and the Stag in Bridge of Corran on the other. The latter were favourites and had more wins to their credit, the general view being that the local stalwarts were always debilitated by food poisoning contracted at their watering hole.

In the Institute of Art's tent several people were clustered around Pete's sculptures. One or two wandered around aimlessly looking at the rest of the exhibits, giving a wide berth to the stand where Morag stood scowling at nothing in particular.

In an unsettling way she complemented the array of articles she had gathered together. Perhaps in her late twenties or early thirties, she was wearing several layers of tattered clothing. When Ginny entered the tent she was contemplating some empty drinks cans, dented, piled at the foot of a piece of old fence post that had been set upright. On the top of this, where Ginny had expected to see another skull, was an inverted rusty bucket. Hanging by the tail from the handle in front was a decomposing dead rat. From this wafted a stench that made the stomach heave.

'Cat got your tongue?' the woman snapped unpleasantly.

'I'm sorry, I hadn't realised that you'd spoken,' Ginny said.

'I asked you if you liked it.'

'No, as a matter of fact it makes me want to throw up.'

'It's meant to. It's called *Youth Under Siege*. Go on, throw up if you want to. Most of the young people in this bloody country feel like doing just that, the way we're treated.'

'In Scotland, you mean?'

'It's worst up here. The bloody English hate us more.'

'More than what?'

'You're one of them. How can you understand?'

'I would have said you came from Liverpool with that accent.'

'Perhaps your ears are too big,' Morag whispered.

'They may well be. But I know a load of crap when I'm hearing it.'

'Piss off,' the woman snarled.

Helmut was fussing with his filing cabinet. Ginny walked past him and made no comment on the fact that his efforts were now entitled *Chaos out of Order, Order out of Chaos*. He did not even glance in her direction.

Murray's stand was stacked with his foam and wooden shapes, some interlocking, others standing on their own, on edge. The centrepiece, mostly constructed of jigsaw-shaped pieces of wood, was painted bright red.

'Show me an honest-to-God photograph of a golden eagle,' Ginny said at the entrance to a curtained-off corner. She added, when the person therein had appeared, 'Aren't you supposed to be guarding all this stuff so that no one makes off with it?'

Andrew was eating a sandwich, a rather doorsteppish affair with what looked like slices of tinned ham trailing from all sides. Swallowing a mouthful, he said, 'Three people want to buy Pete's giant even after I'd told them it was five hundred quid.'

'That's fantastic!'

'But strictly speaking he can't sell anything while he's with Hurrell — only take commissions.'

'That's no problem, surely?'

'No, I don't think Hurrell cares.'

Ginny changed the subject. 'We're going out tonight.'

He looked bored. 'Really?'

'To the Mackivers' place. I've been invited and can bring a friend.'

92

Andrew swore under his breath — in Gaelic, Ginny thought.
'No,' he said.

'He won't know who you are now you've shaved off your beard.'

'I said no and I mean no.'

'I want to find out about him and what he does. He was at the party at the institute in April. So for better or for worse I've offered to make a film with him in it about the locality. It should be quite easy — you and I can turn up with clipboards, wander around waving our arms and tell him we're planning the shooting script.'

Andrew shook his head. 'No.'

'I also want to find out why the gamekeeper lied about you and the deer.'

'I know the answer to that already. He'd lost the poacher he'd been chasing who had shot the animal with a crossbow and decided I'd make a good scapegoat.'

Ginny sighed. 'All right. I'll go on my own then.'

'It's a proper ball so you'll need a long dress.'

'And a coach that turns back into a haggis at midnight?'

He merely stuffed the rest of the sandwich into his mouth.

'His wife has the look of a woman whose husband is unfaithful a lot of the time.'

'Och, aye, he's a grand eye for the ladies. You'd better watch yourself.'

Just then Malcolm Hurrell came into the tent.

'Good man, Andy. You can finish now if you like — I'll hold the fort.'

Andrew collected his jacket. 'Do you want me later? To help pack up the stuff and take it back?'

'No, I think we can manage. Murray and Helmut's work is being collected by courier for the exhibition in Glasgow. I think they can pack it up themselves and I've borrowed a van again for the others to remove theirs. Pete will be here and, let's face it, he has the strength of three.'

Pete, in fact, had just proved it, winning fourth place in the caber tossing. And, a man having injured his shoulder putting the shot, Pete was asked to take his place in the Dog and Drover's tug-of-war team. That young man's delight was now boundless.

'Hurrell's like a cat on hot bricks,' Ginny commented when they were outside the tent.

'Yes, as you say, he appears to have something on his mind.' Andrew's attention was on the commencement of the tug-of-war. 'We should win this. We've a new anchorman who's ex-navy and who used to be in Devonport's field-gun team.'

'And I suppose there's betting on the result?'

'Lots and lots of money. The folk around here will bet on anything, even the number of puppies a bitch'll produce in a litter.'

Kinloch Ruthven were definitely winning, hauling the other team inexorably towards the line. The leader's toes were a matter of inches from it when disaster struck; the new anchorman fell, letting go of the rope. A dreadful howl of dismay rang around the show ground as Bridge of Corran took immediate advantage and in a matter of moments it was over.

'The man's injured,' Andrew announced, ducking under the ropes.

Members of both teams were clustered around the fallen man. A St John's Ambulance unit ran over.

The truth, that a dart had been thrown from the ringside, hitting the man in the leg, travelled as fast as only scandal and outrage can and started what amounted to a small war. The fighting started among the teams, spread to supporters and then to some of the bystanders. It was entered into with a fierce enthusiasm and ruthlessness that only those taking part and students of Scottish history could understand. The MacDonalds fought the Campbells, the Comyns the Bruces. Everyone else fled as the public-address system burst into life with a series of pleas for calm, only to expire in an explosion of sparks and shattered decibels. A group of men had ploughed across the cable, at the same time demolishing a stand selling hot doughnuts, thereby spilling cooking fat and washing-up water on a badly insulated junction box.

Ginny decided that her allegiance lay firmly with Kinloch

Ruthven when she saw Andrew being surrounded by three burly men wielding wooden staves. As she ran up to them, Pete felled one from the rear, whirling the end of the tug-of-war rope like a flail. Andrew grasped the man's stave and there was a brief encounter before a third hit him and he staggered.

Grabbing the third man, Ginny spun him round in Pete's direction, thus lining him up for something that ensured he took no further interest in the proceedings. She then collided heavily with someone running up behind her and was bowled right over, all the breath knocked out of her lungs. The same person tripped and fell on top of her and she was engulfed in bony limbs and whisky fumes. Police sirens could be heard in the distance.

Somehow, she regained her feet, leaving the inebriated one, an old man carrying a shepherd's crook, to croon into the grass. Buffeted by various warring factions, she sought her next-door neighbour. She found him eventually, standing at bay with a long-haired thug about to smash him in the face with a raised fist. The punch failed to connect when she yanked on the greasy locks and as he turned with a howl of rage she kicked him in the groin.

Really warming up now, she was dismayed when she was seized by the hand by Andrew and taken at a very fast pace from the arena. Their problems did not end there, though, for people were running in all directions, some young hot-heads making for the affray to reinforce their friends. Finally, bruised and battered, she and Andrew tripped over a tent rope and crashed into the mud. Seconds later he had rolled them both beneath the canvas and they found themselves in almost total darkness.

Their prison, or sanctuary, measured some eight feet by five and was about two feet high. It was constructed of wood and smelled of something similar to creosote.

Andrew, who got his breath back first, moved carefully so that he was no longer lying on top of her — for that is how they had come to rest — and became still. He was so still, but for a slight movement of his shoulders, that fleetingly Ginny was very worried. Then he lifted his head

95

and looked at her through the thick lock of hair that had fallen over his eyes.

He was helpless with laughter.

Furiously, Ginny whispered, 'If you now say something really shitty like I'm a bonny wee lassie, I'll kick you so hard in the sporran when we're vertical that — ' She stopped speaking for he had come really close, looking down at her, still laughing.

'What?'

There was a lot of yelling and shouting going on outside the tent. Unmistakably, not too far away, Chief Inspector Speir could be heard bellowing orders. More police sirens blared in the distance.

Ginny's mouth had gone dry and she could not reply to the question.

'We're under Pete's display stand,' Andrew breathed into Ginny's ear. 'I think we should stay here for a while.'

'Kiss me,' Ginny said.

To stay where they were for a while seemed an eminently sensible idea, a supremely excellent one, in fact, in view of what was happening only a matter of feet from where they lay; utter confusion as the police tried to restore order and arrest those responsible for the affray. The noise and shouting went on for quite a while and then it became quiet but for a radio chattering in what must be a police car parked nearby and dogs barking, these too probably accompanying those enforcing the peace.

Andrew lifted up the tent canvas and peered out. 'I think we can get back in circulation,' he said. 'Mind that broken bottle.'

It was uncannily quiet now and when they rounded the corner of the institute's tent they saw the reason for it. All those suspected of fighting had been herded into the arena by the police and kept there for questioning, their womenfolk standing watching disconsolately.

'You'll be grabbed,' Ginny said. 'You have red marks on your face, they'll know you've been fighting.' She hustled him through the entrance to the tent.

'Welcome to the exhibition,' Helmut said.

He was sitting on the edge of his own stand, his face grey

and drawn. At his feet lay Malcolm Hurrell, the three prongs of the broken garden fork uncompromisingly through his neck, pinning him to the grass. Very slowly, a bloody foam was bubbling from his gaping mouth.

Chapter Eight

To console himself for being forced to deal with a riot, Chief Inspector Speir had gleefully confiscated eight hip flasks, three quarter-sized bottles of whisky, fifteen cans of Tennants lager and four partly consumed bottles of Irn Bru, the last on the grounds that he suspected they contained hidden additives. When Ginny came upon him, presiding over his haul, he had just been told that the real perpetrators — strangers, a few of whom had been armed with pickaxe handles — had vanished without trace. The detained locals were clamouring that these men had set about everybody at random, having shouted that the Kinloch Ruthven team had been nobbled. Which of course was perfectly true.

'So were they from Bridge of Corran?' Speir enquired of his informant.

'No idea, sir. But they weren't regulars at the Stag. They're swearing on their mothers' graves about *that.'*

Speir caught sight of Ginny. 'This is not a suitable place for a young lady.'

'Nor is the Institute of Art's tent,' she told him.

The scene was exactly as she had left it, with Andrew keeping Helmut company. The German seemed shocked but calm, insisting that he had been listening to rock music in the back, using his personal stereo, and had neither heard nor seen anything in connection with the murder. He had not even been aware of the trouble in the show ground.

Ginny did not repeat her comment, that he had thrown the same fork at her the previous day.

'I didn't kill him!' Helmut had shouted. 'I didn't even see Hurrell. As far as I knew I was on my own. Sometimes I looked round the curtain but the tent was always empty — everyone was watching the sports.'

'You found him?' Speir snapped at Helmut.

Helmut nodded. 'As I said to these people, I was listening to music. My tape finished and I came out here to see if anyone from the institute was around so I could go for something to eat. He was here — just like this. I think it had only just happened.'

'What makes you think that?' Speir asked.

'He was still alive, just. His hand moved. Then he became still.'

'Did you touch him?'

'No.'

Appalled, Ginny said, 'Didn't you even bend down to see if you could help him in any way?'

Helmut seemed puzzled. 'What was the point? He was finished.'

'I'll ask the questions, Miss Somerville,' Speir said. 'Perhaps you'd wait outside until I want to question you. You too, sir,' he said to Andrew.

'Another time I might have laughed,' Andrew said when they were outside, a full murder enquiry unleashed around them.

'He'll have to find out who you are pretty soon. I can't see him believing us if we say we were under the display stand, do you?'

'There's no point in mentioning it, surely? We heard and saw nothing.'

'Suppose someone saw us crawling out from beneath the canvas?'

He groaned. 'I wonder if the Foreign Legion would have me?'

Morag marched up to them. 'What the hell's been going on?'

'Hurrell's dead,' Andrew said before Ginny could answer. 'Someone spitted him with Helmut's garden fork. Where have *you* been, flower?'

Clearly staggered, but judging by what she then did, for

99

the wrong reasons, Morag crowed, 'Christ! It's the bloody gardener without his whiskers. Putting on airs then, are we, Andy, with a real posh Sassenach tart on our arm?'

Ginny had never slapped anyone's face before. She did so now and her hand stung for hours.

As it was, they both decided to tell the truth, the matter was of such great importance that to conceal information, however crazy-sounding, was folly. Speir listened to them, impassively, separately, and then sent someone to look under the staging to check on the possibility of such a tale being true. The constable emerged carefully holding in his handkerchief an earring, one of Ginny's, that neither she nor Andrew had noticed was missing. This was returned to her without further questions or comment.

Andrew had feared an ordeal but soon discovered that he had nothing to worry about. For the chief inspector had already interviewed several people, including the provost, who had seen him come under attack in the arena and the way 'yon plucky lassie, chust like her da' had gone to his aid. Getting an impartial hearing, Andrew mentioned his concerns about the institute's finances. To this Speir merely made notes. Then, admitting to a crushing workload and intense pressure from the superintendent for quick results, Speir apologised for his previous heavy-handedness. Andrew, for his part, promised not to get into any more fights at the Dog and Drover.

The chief inspector could do little more than arrange for an incident caravan to be set up at the show ground and his team continued to take statements from the hundreds of people who had been present − those who had not melted away over the walls and fences into the surrounding countryside, that is. And when a van arrived from Glasgow to take away some of the objects of art from the scene of the crime, after the items had been eliminated from the enquiry, everyone was glad to see them go. A fastidious member of the CID team had already consigned Morag's rat to a waste bin.

Helmut Beyer was taken to Bridge of Corran police station for further questioning when it was discovered that the prongs of the murder weapon had been sharpened. This was despite his protests that he had used the fork before in one of his 'cerebral art experiences' when it had been thrust into a log of wood, necessitating the sharpening.

After a lot of heart-searching Ginny had decided to accept Kevin Mackiver's invitation. She had made discreet enquiries about whether the function would still take place. Almost certainly, according to Maggie Mossblown, the source of the information. For one thing some guests, business associates of Mackiver's, were travelling long distances, from the Perth area, Inverness and even farther north. Muirpark, situated some eight miles from the village, was far enough away, Maggie was sure, for the occupants not to feel obliged to go into deep mourning. Maggie did, however, telephone the housekeeper, a friend of hers, to check and reported that yes indeed, the Highland ball would take place.

Ginny was eyeing herself in a long mirror, wondering whether the white silk blouse and long, plum-coloured velvet skirt would be deemed suitable when she heard a knock on the front door, more a beating of fists than a knock.

'Didn't you hear me?' Andrew McQuade said, having practically fallen into the hallway when she opened the door, such was his state of agitation. 'I thought you'd already left.'

With his Prince Charlie coatee — the correct sort of evening jacket to wear with a kilt — he was wearing a white shirt and black bow tie. His black patent-leather shoes had silver buckles, as did his belt. The sporran was silver-mounted white fur and had small fur tassels.

Oddly, even after what had taken place that afternoon, there was still a shy formality between them.

'I'm glad you've changed your mind,' Ginny said.

'I just hope he doesn't have his twelve-bore handy.'

'Now you've shaved off your beard and had your hair cut, he won't have a clue who you are. Even if we introduce you by your real name he'll think he's heard wrongly or it's a coincidence.'

'No. Perhaps I should have explained. He's known me for a long time and at one time he and my father Rory were business partners. There was a lot of bad feeling when the partnership broke up.'

'Which you've inherited?'

'He'll do anything to get back at my father.'

'Look, you don't have to come with me.'

'He won't shoot me in public,' Andrew said with a grin.

'But are you sure you're well enough?'

Still smiling, he said, 'I tend to be fine when I haven't been drinking or undergone two solid hours of physiotherapy. Both of those things usually happen on Mondays, Wednesdays and Fridays.'

'And the Thursday when I first met you?' Ginny asked, unabashed.

'That was one of the *un*usual days,' he replied, equally shamelessly.

They went out.

Muirpark, a grey stone house about a hundred and fifty years old, was situated at the head of a small glen in the hills which rose from the eastern shore of Loch Linnhe. The location admirably suited Mackiver — who had initially made his money as a whisky broker — because it meant he could combine the interests of a country estate with cruising the sea lochs in his yacht *Seawitch*. This was moored at a jetty on the lochside directly below a ruined tower built on a crag jutting from the hillside.

The approach to the house, by a private drive that joined the main Fort William road about five miles north of Bridge of Corran, was magnificently scenic. Curving to the contours of the glen, it topped a ridge and then swung downhill in a southerly direction for a couple of miles before reaching the floor of the valley. There it turned sharply northwest and was thereafter almost dead straight. This was the old carriage drive that dated back to the days when a house built in the sixteenth century had stood on the site. Nearer to the house, where it was more sheltered, the drive was lined by oak trees. At one time there had been a steep, and in winter highly dangerous, track from the shores of the loch, a legacy from the days when easy access had been only by sea.

Ginny, who was driving, was in no mood to enjoy the scenery. 'I keep thinking about Malcolm Hurrell.'

'Difficult not to,' Andrew muttered.

'Helmut might have killed him. And Jean, for that matter.'

'But it wouldn't have occurred to him to put that dead sheep in my kitchen. Too much like hard work. The idea of him setting off across Ruthven Loan to run down a ewe, lug it into my house and butcher it just to give me a nasty shock, is ludicrous.'

'He *did* throw the fork at me.'

'The fork hadn't been thrown at Hurrell, though. He had been knocked down – there was a large red mark on the side of his jaw – and then the fork had been shoved through his neck.'

'Were Helmut's knuckles bruised?'

'No, I made a point of looking. But he could have hit him with the handle of the fork first.'

'And there might be no connection between the sheep and the murders.'

'No, none whatsoever.'

'We're not very good detectives, are we?'

Highland cattle grazed in the fields of the valley, more, Ginny felt, for their decorative value than anything else. It was eight fifteen in the evening, the sun was high in the sky and it was still unseasonably cold, they discovered, when they had rattled over a cattle grid, parked and got out of the car. A Rolls-Royce that had been following them all the way down the private drive pulled up alongside.

Andrew seized Ginny by the hand and towed her quickly in the direction of the house.

'What's wrong?'

'I know that man. He's one of the senior executives of Grampian Television.'

Ginny stopped, forcing him to stop too. 'Andrew, you can't keep running away.'

'You're right,' he said after a couple of moments. 'I'd forgotten. All I have to do is say no.'

She wanted to point out that if he said yes to her he could say no to all the others.

He changed the subject. 'It's a strange time of year for this kind of thing. Most socialising takes place during the winter months, but a summer ball is a tradition at Muirpark.'

Memories came flooding back to Andrew of other Muirpark summer balls: yet another facet of his life that he had thought was past, over and done with for ever. And standing in the massive entrance hall of this house, as he had done so many times before, he noticed again the panelled walls arrayed with the dirks, swords and pikes of the Jacobites, and two Lochaber axes over the doorway. The utter squalor and futility of his recent behaviour suddenly hit him like a hammer blow.

Ginny misread the appalled look on his face and squeezed his hand reassuringly. When he gazed at her for a moment she smiled, unaware that her father had looked at him with the same penetrating blue gaze. Andrew, she was never to know, felt that he was being haunted by the ghost of his dead friend.

'I'm okay,' he said. 'I don't suppose anyone will expect me to climb trees or rescue a cat off the roof tonight.'

Murray made his way towards them, pushing through the crowd. 'Do you know what that *bitch* has done?' the American said to him after giving Ginny the briefest of smiles. 'She rang up the gallery in Glasgow, pretended she was Hurrell's secretary and asked if her stuff could be taken along for the show as well. Hurrell had already said no to her because Helmut was so damned awkward about it – said he'd withdraw if his work was next to a pile of rotting corpses. And now it's gone, that abortion of a thing she had at the show *plus* the one at the studio. What do you think about that?'

'She must have telephoned before Hurrell was murdered,' Ginny said before Andrew could reply.

'Yes, I guess so,' Murray said. 'The transport would have left Glasgow pretty early this morning. She hitched a lift with it, apparently, saying she wanted to set out her work herself.'

'Are *you* going?' Andrew asked.

'No, I'll send them a diagram. Mine's mostly about maths.'

'And Helmut?' Andrew persisted.

'I guess he'll go tomorrow if the cops let him loose. He doesn't trust anyone with his efforts. Anyway, see you guys later.' And with that he turned and went from sight in a crowd who had just arrived by coach.

Standing each side of a doorway beneath the Lochaber axes, Kevin and Fiona Mackiver were greeting their guests. There was no real awkwardness when it was Ginny and Andrew's turn but Ginny noticed that the men did not shake hands.

'I wasn't really expecting to see Murray,' Ginny said, steering Andrew around a waiter bearing a tray loaded with glasses of whisky and presenting him with sherry from another. 'Have you any idea why he was invited?'

Meekly, Andrew sipped his sherry. 'I think Mackiver bought one of his works.'

In direct contrast to the exterior of the house, the room they were in was highly ornate. The six long windows had been given the grand-opera treatment; swags, tie-backs in heavy, draped crimson and gold brocade. The embossed ceiling, from which hung a crystal chandelier, was painted red, white and gold, and mirrored by the carpet with its swirls of the same colours. The armchairs in red velvet, fringed, and the matching sofa were not genuine antiques but very good reproduction, the only nod, Ginny thought, to cost-cutting. She also thought that the room would make an excellent film set for a first-class gambling saloon on a Mississippi showboat, circa 1895.

In the next room a fiddle-and-accordion band was warming up with a lively tune, but, as yet, no one seemed to be interested in dancing, all talking at the tops of their voices.

'Well, it's a relief that you probably won't know any of the dances,' said Andrew.

'Sorry,' Ginny countered, 'but I can do a positively devastating eightsome reel. Who's that man over there in the doublet and ruffles?'

'Ninian Effric of Effric. He's the nearest thing to the nobility round here and, as you can see, he takes himself rather seriously.'

In spite of what Mackiver had said, only a minority of

105

the guests were in Highland dress and Ginny guessed, from overhearing snatches of conversation, that the rest were from England or Glasgow.

'You can't always tell,' Andrew told her when she voiced these conclusions. 'I was sent to school in Carlisle when I was eleven. Just because you hear what you think is an English accent it doesn't mean they're from down south.'

Leaving Andrew staring pensively at the mountain peaks through a window, Ginny left the room, ostensibly in search of the ladies' but primarily bent on having a look round.

There was a tremendous crush in the entrance hall. Women stood on tiptoe to shriek questions about family welfare to their friends and the talk was of kith, kin, dogs, shoots, salmon, poachers, bairns, weans, the weather, holidays, gardens and the secretary of state for Scotland. Through it all the Mackivers continued to stand like a couple of mandarins, nodding and shaking hands. Then there was a shout from the rear of the house and a pack of gundogs — labradors, retrievers and setters — burst into the room and tried to make friends with everyone.

'Get rid of these damned animals!' Mackiver yelled as a man panted into view on the trail of the miscreants.

There were a few moments of utter pandemonium, the dogs making the most of their freedom — hoovering up the nuts and cocktail biscuits from the upended dishes that their tails had swept from low tables, leaping up and leaving trails of saliva down the fronts of women's dresses — before they were rounded up and sent packing.

Ginny found all this utterly fascinating. For the man in charge of the dogs was the one she had kicked in the groin that afternoon.

A downstairs cloakroom along a narrow passageway was being utilised as the ladies' for the evening, a useful sanctuary for a few minutes for someone who was not sure if her antagonist of some hours previously had recognised her.

'Fiona looks as world-weary as ever,' said a tall, slender woman who was tucking a few stray wisps of black hair into an otherwise neat bun.

'I hadn't met her until today,' Ginny said.

'There. I thought you were Gavin Logan's niece. My

106

apologies.' She held out a hand. 'I'm never sure if women shake hands. I'm Kirsten MacLeod.'

Ginny introduced herself.

Kirsten said, 'I'm afraid I don't really know who's who in Kinloch Ruthven as I live near Inverness. And I'm not at all sure why I accept these invitations now that my husband's taken himself back to Ireland. But you can't cut yourself off completely.'

'So you don't see the Mackivers very often?'

'Not as a couple, no. We went with them on a short cruise on their yacht some years ago − just round the islands − which was fun. And then the recession started and put paid to that kind of thing. I'm glad, though, that they're keeping up the summer balls. The Kerrs, who lived here before, started them off and they've become a fixture in the social calendar.' She lowered her voice and said in mock seriousness, 'You can say you've arrived when you've been asked to Muirpark.'

'Or you've offered to make a film with them in it,' Ginny said with a grin.

'Oh, what *fun!* Is there a small part for hangers-on?'

'I don't see why not.'

Kirsten burst into peals of laughter. 'My dear girl, I was joking. Unless you want some old biddy who stumps around in green wellies feeding the chickens.'

'Ah, but it's not fiction. Think of it as a fly-on-the-wall documentary.' With no stretch of the imagination could Kirsten be described as an 'old biddy'. She was probably in her late forties, her complexion perfect and there were only a few grey hairs among the glossy black. She was wearing a white blouse that had lace sleeves and ruffles with a long tartan skirt and matching sash, the latter worn diagonally across her right shoulder and tied in a bow above the left hip. The fabric, as Ginny might have expected after hearing her name, was the same tartan as Andrew's kilt, green MacLeod.

Kevin Mackiver came upon them as they were crossing the hall and took Ginny by the arm. 'I've a few moments spare if you want to talk business. Hello, Kirsten, I didn't expect to see you this year.'

'It's just as well that Fiona sends the invitations,' Kirsten countered coolly.

'Perhaps I'll relieve her of that chore next time,' he snapped.

'What, and make a contribution to the arrangements?' she said before walking away.

'I'd like to see her face when she bumps into her son,' Mackiver said with satisfaction. 'The last time she clapped eyes on him the police had just released him from custody on a drunk-and-disorderly charge. His hair was down to his shoulders and he hadn't shaved for weeks. They probably got rid of him because he was full of lice.' Here he gave Ginny a grim smile. 'And now, lo and behold, he turns up with you looking quite the reformed man. But he isn't, you know, he's as rotten as his father. Rory McQuade did the dirty on me in business. I bet he didn't tell you about that, did he?'

Almost spitting out these short, angry sentences, he was scanning the room as he spoke as though if he caught sight of the man he was speaking about he would rend him limb from limb. He went on talking.

'Did he tell you that yarn about the deer he found injured by a crossbow bolt in his garden so he put it out of its misery? All lies. That fool Speir didn't think of asking him what he'd finished it off *with*. Rushed out and cut its throat with the kitchen scissors, I suppose. No, he has a hunting rifle that his old man gave him for the express purpose. It's not licensed either. It's hidden somewhere and I intend to find it. Then with a bit of luck he'll go to prison for a while. I wonder what dear Rory will make of that?'

'Are you saying that Andrew McQuade is shooting your deer on the instructions of his father because of some feud?'

'Yes, that's precisely what I'm saying.'

'Mr Mackiver, the man's famed for filming wildlife.'

'And I know all about his hobby of stills photography. So he's had plenty of practice sighting deer through a telephoto lens. That's exactly the same principle as using telescopic sights. Now, are we going to talk about this film or not?'

'As long as you understand that I've offered him a job and that when work starts he'll be here too.'

Mackiver shook his head. 'No. Besides, he's chickened out now. It's obvious — otherwise he wouldn't be skulking around in Kinloch Ruthven drinking himself to death.'

The grip on Ginny's arm was very tight. She said, 'I think you'll find that any loss of nerve he's suffering is only in connection with mountaineering.'

'It probably is. But that's been his main source of income and once you've shown you can do it people won't leave you alone. There aren't many in that line of business as they tend to get killed or end up raving mad, ignoring the risks. It'll pay to stay a coward — he knows that and he'll keep his head right down and go on the dole.'

In the large room that was being used for the dancing that Ginny had not yet entered the band burst into life with the Gay Gordons. The guests began to move through into that room, where also a buffet had been laid out, no one taking any particular notice of their host escorting an attractive girl towards the room he used as an office.

Mackiver's grasp was hurting Ginny's arm.

He said, 'I did check up on you, of course. I spoke to a man by the name of Crawthorne who said he was the executive producer. He didn't know anything about your working up here.'

'That's because I haven't told him yet.'

'Oh, was that indiscreet of me? I'm so sorry.' He didn't look very apologetic, smiling from ear to ear. 'Never mind, you can tell me all about it in my office.'

Ginny endeavoured to wrench herself free. 'The pair of you would get on like a house on fire — you seem to have the same outlook on life.'

Propelling her towards a closed door, he said, 'Then he must be a successful man.'

'Actually, he's an utter toad.'

They were through the doorway by now and only then did Mackiver release her. Shock, probably, then kept him rooted to the spot as he saw that they were not alone.

'Fiona told me where the office was,' said Andrew, sitting at the desk. Despite his seeming nonchalance, he was as white as the blotting paper in front of him. 'And I reckoned that if there were going to be any meetings about making films, in view of the fact that I'm the cameraman, I ought to be present.'

Chapter Nine

'It occurred to me earlier that you were starting work a little late,' Mackiver said, pointedly not addressing Andrew. 'For, after all, any film of this area is not complete without footage of the Games.' He opened a cupboard and poured himself a drink. 'Especially this year. We don't get *that* kind of thing happening very often. Wouldn't you say that was a wasted opportunity?'

'Flinders Cochran was there,' Andrew said, also addressing Ginny. 'From the Edinburgh agency. I had a word with him and said you'd be interested in good subject matter. I also gave him a list of names of a few people you'd want on film doing their own thing. You included,' he told Mackiver. 'So don't worry, you're recorded for posterity holding forth on the rostrum and wherever Cochran glimpsed you afterwards. He got some pretty good stuff on the battle too, from what I hear. The police have it at the moment to see if they can piece together what happened. But he should get it all back eventually.'

'We came straight back here after lunch,' Mackiver said. 'There was a lot to do. But I wish that I'd been informed of what you intended doing. I resent being filmed when I'm not aware of it.'

'So you could pose?' Andrew asked sweetly. 'Not on your life. That makes lousy films.'

Ginny was experiencing a huge golden glow inside. 'We'll leave out poor Dr Hurrell's murder. It'll be all sub judice anyway and I'm not particularly interested in making a real-life whodunnit. That's a thought,' she said, gazing at them both wide-eyed. 'Cochran might even have filmed the murderer coming out of the tent!'

'Knowing Flinders, he was right in the middle of the war,' Andrew remarked.

Ginny said, 'It would be useful if we could walk round the estate so we could get an idea of what we want to use. Would Sunday be all right?'

Mackiver seemed to come out of a trance. 'What? Oh — yes, if you want to. But I insist on being kept informed of your intentions. And no other people poking around, mind. Otherwise the arrangement's off. Do you understand?'

'Perfectly,' Ginny said.

'And on condition that your cameraman is sober,' Mackiver continued unpleasantly. 'I don't want the place to get a bad name.'

Observing that a rather wild light had come into Andrew's eyes, Ginny took his elbow and steered him from the room. Outside in the corridor he took a deep breath.

'I suppose I asked for that,' he said.

'Thank you,' Ginny said.

'For what?' he asked dully.

'For being there and supporting me.'

'I had an idea he'd want to get you alone so he could give you the third degree about why you wanted to make the film. Do you really intend to go ahead with it?'

'Yes, if I can get the finance. But it's probably not going to be a Highlands idyll so much as "two murders at wacky art institute" kind of thing.'

'And you think Mackiver's involved?'

'He seems to me to be the sort of man likely to be mixed up in anything dodgy. But I get the impression you know far more about that than I do. Why did your father pull the rug from under him?' She grabbed him as he swayed slightly. 'Andrew, have you eaten anything today other than that sandwich?'

He shook his head.

Ginny took him into the red room and had just pointed him in the direction of a chair in a quiet corner when he was spotted by the man from Grampian Television.

'Andrew McQuade!' He wrung Andrew's hand. 'Man,

I'm that pleased to see you're back in circulation. I'm not ashamed to say that I shed a tear or two when I heard about your dreadful accident. And here you are on your own two feet the same as ever you were.'

Andrew was smiling in slightly mechanical fashion.

The man went on, 'Now, it's vital that you don't rush things. Tell everyone who badgers you to work for them to sod off until you've really recovered. It'll take a year, I warn you. I know, I broke just about every bone I possessed skiing a few years back and I remember how I felt. Scared silly every time I saw a flake of snow in case someone wanted to hurtle off down some slope or other.' He brayed with laughter. 'Now I must go. The wife sent me to fetch some nosh.' He marched off, keeping in time to the music.

'He always was a bit of a prat,' Andrew said absently but looking rather pleased.

Ginny left him and fought her way through the crowd to the buffet in the next room, loaded a plate for him and returned, only to find that Kirsten had arrived.

'He shouldn't be here, Ginny,' she agonised. 'He's a sick man.'

Ginny handed over her hoard.

'It's the trauma really,' Kirsten said, lowering her voice. 'Mountains have always terrified me. I hope he never sets foot on one again.'

Ginny said, 'Forgive me for asking but if things are difficult between you and Kevin Mackiver, why *do* you come?' She had no intention of taking part in a conversation about someone who was present.

'For Fiona's sake really. She'd never see any of her family otherwise. Oh, didn't I mention it? We're sisters.'

Andrew, who was eating like a man starved, swallowed a mouthful and said, 'Meet my mother. She can always be relied upon to miss out the most significant piece of information, the thing that makes the rest of what she's telling you hang together.'

Kirsten flashed him a vague smile. 'We'd already met, dear. Well, I don't know about you, Ginny, but I'm going to get something to eat before it all disappears.'

112

'You might have mentioned that there was a family connection,' Ginny said when she had gone.

'It doesn't really exist any more,' Andrew said. 'I'm supposed to be a big boy now so I've been tossed from the nest. Mother's only renting the Coach House for me to get back at Rory. There's a lot of acrimony between them at the moment – she's even stopped using her married name. He wanted me to go and work for him in Ireland.'

'That doesn't sound at all like being tossed from the nest.'

'It's difficult to understand until you see the two of them together. All they're really doing is fighting over the bits.'

'Of you?'

'Yes.' He shrugged. 'Perhaps on the other hand I'm just a stubborn Scot after all.'

'Tell me how you killed that deer in your garden.'

He looked surprised and then smiled tiredly. 'I didn't. I'd had a visitor that day – Rory – who'd come over for a day's stalking and called in on his way home. He shot it. But being as Kevin has said on more than one occasion that he'd shoot *him* if he showed his face around here again, we decided to keep quiet about it. Rory took a haunch with him – he's not the sort who would pass up that kind of opportunity.'

'I'm really grateful for what you did just now.'

What he was eating was bringing him alive by the minute. 'Perhaps I owed Alastair a favour.'

'The man looking after the dogs here was one of those who started the trouble at the games.'

'It wouldn't surprise me.'

'Mackiver's involved with the murders somehow, I'm sure of it. He looked really shifty when you were talking about Flinders Cochran.'

'I noticed that too.'

'How did he and your father fall out?'

'They were in the whisky business together and Kevin fancied owning his own distillery. The one he wanted was very small, had been in existence since the late seventeen hundreds and was situated on one of the islands. It produced one of the best single malts in Scotland. Not surprisingly, the owners, descendants of the family who had started it up, wouldn't sell it to him. So he waited until there was a vacancy in the bottling plant and paid an ex-con who had worked in the trade to take the job and adulterate a few bottles with weedkiller. Quite a number of people were taken ill. I don't suppose much was made of it in the English press but it certainly rocked the boat up here and their sales dropped to nothing.'

'I remember reading something about a fire.'

'That was the one. The owners smelled a rat and still refused to sell. So he got his man to burn the place to the ground to destroy any evidence.'

'How was Rory involved?'

'Well, he wasn't. He got to hear about it somehow and warned the owners. But it was too late by then and if it confirmed their suspicions it didn't save the distillery, which went up in flames two days later. He had nothing to take to the police. Then some fool who had worked there told Kevin that one of his associates had warned them.'

'And he was forced to flee to Ireland? But why didn't your mother go with him? Why does she even speak to Mackiver?'

'Oh, their marriage has been on the rocks for years. Foundering but not sunk perhaps — sometimes I wonder if she's keeping an eye on things for him this side of the Irish Sea. She's very close to Fiona too, keeps trying to persuade her to leave Kevin before his past catches up with him.'

Ginny sat back, arms akimbo and gazed at him soberly. 'Do you think you could dance now?'

'No,' he stated emphatically.

'How about a trip to Glasgow tomorrow?'

'To the art show?'

'Yes.'

'What's on your mind?'

'There must be something odd going on. More than odd — criminal. People aren't killed over nothing.'

'Morag's a nasty piece of work but I can't see her killing Hurrell just to get her pile of garbage to Glasgow.'

'No, it must be something more complicated than that. And we mustn't forget about Jean either. There must be a connection.' Ginny was listening. 'I learned that dance at school too. What's it called?'

Andrew sighed. 'The Duke of Perth.'

Ninian Effric of Effric appeared at her side as if by magic and smiled his rather oily smile.

'Delighted!' Ginny exclaimed, leaping to her feet.

The dance was an energetic one and neither of them had the breath to talk. Her partner was, Ginny guessed, in his forties. Although he was beautifully dressed he was not an elegant man and tended to make up for grace, as far as the dancing went, with bouncing energy. Impassive of face, except for his eyebrows, which tended to fly upwards into his hair every few moments, he hardly glanced at her until the dance finished.

'I regret that your stay in Scotland has so far been distressful,' he said somewhat formally. 'Miss Somerville, please forgive me if this sounds inquisitive and impertinent but our host informs me that you intend to make a film. Do you propose to place us all under the pitiless glare of arc lights?'

While he was talking he had manoeuvred them both away from the dance floor and into a corner.

'No,' Ginny said.

'Oh, I rather gathered ...' He broke off and started again. 'So you're not one of those rather unpleasant investigative journalists?'

'No, but I think I'm on their side. They tend to expose people who deserve to be exposed.'

He gazed at her urbanely. 'You're not nervous about upsetting a few Scots, I can see that.'

'I'm half Scottish myself.'

'And you're not in the least tempted to play the amateur sleuth after the amazing number of dead bodies that have come your way since you arrived?'

There was more to this man than met the eye, Ginny decided. 'Oh, yes,' she said. 'When you find a dead body in your own house and someone seems to be trying to blame your late father for the crime, you're immediately very involved.'

'With young McQuade over there as Watson?'

'I don't regard myself as Holmes,' she answered shortly.

He smiled faintly and then said, 'I urge you to be careful.'

'Were you at the show this afternoon?'

'For a very short time; I left when the trouble started. In any case I had only gone in order to meet someone who had a shotgun for sale.'

'Was it Kevin Mackiver?'

'No, by no means.' This was uttered in very dismissive tones.

'Did you see him?'

'Mackiver? Yes, as a matter of fact I did. But he didn't see me, we were some distance from one another. He was leaving a tent, probably on his way home. I can't say that I blame him — it was getting out of hand by then.'

'Which tent?'

Effric narrowed his eyes, thinking. 'Well, it can't have been far from the car park for that was where I was heading. It might have been the one with the art show but I can't be sure. I'm not even a hundred per cent sure it was him.'

'He was wearing a dark suit.'

'Yes, so was this man. It certainly looked like him. Can I fetch you a drink?'

'No, but thank you. Did you see anyone else whom you knew?'

'Many. But just then, you mean?'

'Yes.'

'There were almost certainly people I knew in the vicinity but I saw no one to speak to. I was rather keen to reach the car as I'd bought the shotgun and was carrying it wrapped in an old coat. I was a bit anxious that it might be taken from me by the very last sort of people who ought to have it.' He suddenly looked alarmed. 'But that poor man was found in that tent, wasn't he? Look, I don't want to say anything that will incriminate anyone.'

Ginny decided to take a risk. 'I saw one of the trouble-makers here, this evening.'

'Surely not among the guests?'

'No, he works for Mackiver — the man with the dogs.'

'Ah,' said Effric quietly. 'I don't think you ought to read too much into that.'

'The way it looks at the moment, a diversion was created so that all attention was away from the Institute of Art's tent.'

'I feel I ought to tell you that a lot of money was at stake. Mackiver, I know, put a thousand pound bet on Bridge of Corran winning.'

'Who with? Anyone in particular?'

'Alas, with me. The man who was hit with the dart is my new gillie.'

'I'm rather surprised you came tonight,' Ginny said, astounded at the calm way he was telling her all this.

His eyebrows disappeared into his floppy hair again. 'Grown-ups aren't supposed to sulk, you know.'

'I'd be furious.'

'I am. But don't worry, chickens always come home to roost.'

A whole barn full of them, Ginny thought.

'There's a long list of things I want to know,' Ginny said to her next-door neighbour the following morning.

Andrew, sitting slouched at his kitchen table, groaned. Against his better judgement he had danced the rest of the night away and now ached in every sinew. That he had been told by his doctor to take a lot more exercise or be forced to undergo an extended course of physiotherapy if he did not want his body to stiffen up for ever was of no consolation right now. He was also wishing that he had kept his mouth shut about certain business propositions; even thinking about what he had let himself in for was tying his stomach in knots.

'First,' Ginny said, 'you said that you thought Murray had sold one of his works to Mackiver. And yet you also said that the students weren't really supposed to sell things, only take commissions.'

Andrew took a large mouthful of coffee. 'I get the impression that they can sell things that have been exhibited, otherwise the studio gets very cluttered. Why don't you ask Murray?'

117

'I intend to. Another thing I want to find out is what Hurrell was up to at the institute: the dates of past exhibitions, whose work was sent, who bought stuff in the past and so on.' She fixed him with her bright gaze. 'Are you free today or do you have to – '

He interrupted with, 'Strictly speaking I'm supposed to be up at the institute this morning to hoe the veg but – '

'That's all right, I'll give you a hand. No, I was really thinking of your stints with your physiotherapist. Mondays, Wednesdays and Fridays, you said.'

'Only for two weeks. Today's the last session and it doesn't matter.'

'Of course it does! I'll drive you there and then we can set off.'

There was a rebellious silence.

'I'm not trying to organise you,' Ginny said. 'Believe me, I'm not. I just want to get to the bottom of this ghastly business. And if we're going to have a look around the Mackiver estate on Sunday – that was your suggestion, if you remember ...'

'All right, all right,' he responded wearily.

'Bacon and eggs?'

'I don't have any.'

'I do.'

He was forced to smile at himself. Right then he would have done *anything* for a hot breakfast.

All the same it was pleasant to have someone to plant out a row of leek seedlings for him and earth up the potatoes. She had never done any gardening before, but between them there was a shared understanding that even though the director of the institute was now dead and the gardener had another job – well, sort of – there was the box of leeks waiting to be transplanted and if the potatoes weren't earthed up the light might get to them and they would go green. Andrew explained this last fact to Ginny and she was fascinated.

'How long would it take to sort out the garden at the Manse?' she wanted to know.

'It would depend on how much money you threw at it.'

'No, I mean – ' Ginny stopped speaking and went red.

118

'If you did it with perhaps someone helping you?' Andrew said tactfully.

'Yes.'

'At least a year. But if you got blokes in first to do the rough work with machinery, it would save time.'

Ginny had been about to talk of them tackling it together. The problem was, she was not even thinking about a future without him. 'But they might dig up the wrong things. There must be bulbs in the ground.'

'Hundreds.'

The whole place seemed deserted. Even Peggy, Jean's replacement, was nowhere to be seen. Morag, they knew was in Glasgow, Helmut might still be with the police but Pete and Murray should have been around. They weren't.

It was an excellent opportunity to have a look in Hurrell's office.

The door to the room was not locked but all the files had gone from the shelves together with Hurrell's personal computer, some notebooks that Ginny remembered had been on his desk and his appointments diary.

'The police have taken them,' Andrew said. 'We should have thought of that. I wonder who's handling the financial affairs of the place now so I can get my wages?'

'How much are you owed?' Ginny asked, peering at the items that remained on the shelves to see if anything would provide useful informatioin. But there were only a few art reference books, a *Shorter Oxford Dictionary* and a copy of *Roget's Thesaurus*. Sitting down at the desk and opening a drawer, she said, 'I'd be interested to know if they thought to search his room at the hotel.'

'Thirty-six pounds,' Andrew muttered.

Ginny sighed, closing the drawer, which was empty but for pens and a few sheets of writing paper. 'This is so difficult. If I offer to lend you some money you'll be offended. If I write you out a cheque for a month's salary in advance for when we work together, that's just as bad, and if I suggest giving you some it'll be a slap in the face to your independent Scottish spirit. Any ideas on how I can help you out?'

He drew up a chair and sat down. 'No,' he said unhelpfully.

Ginny opened another drawer. 'You know, I keep thinking back to when my booking at the Glen Hotel was cancelled by someone. A possible reason for that might have been that they didn't want me talking to Malcolm Hurrell. How could we get into the hotel and take a look at his room without anyone knowing?'

'The police *must* know he lived there.'

'They might not − not yet, anyway.'

'We don't even know which was his room.'

Ginny picked up the phone. 'I'll ask them − pretend I'm CID.'

He frowned. 'I'm sure Miss Marple never impersonated a police officer.'

There was a longish pause.

'No, perhaps you're right,' Ginny sighed, replacing the receiver.

'But I could go and chat up the receptionist − tell her that the envelope with my wages in might be in his room.'

'She's not really your sort,' Ginny pointed out.

Andrew quirked an eyebrow at her in the most infuriating fashion.

Chapter Ten

When Andrew returned Ginny was in the hall, looking at the portrait of the elderly woman.

'Waste of time,' he reported. 'The police were there going over a room on the first floor. There was a girl I've never seen before on the desk who knew nothing about anyone cancelling your booking and the other receptionist is on holiday in Spain. I only just missed bumping into Speir by going out the back way.'

'Never mind,' Ginny said soothingly. 'At the time the receptionist said that it was a man who rang and that the line was bad – his voice sounded strange. That might have been because whoever it was muffled the mouthpiece to prevent being recognised. Have you any idea who this lady in the picture was?'

Andrew realised that he had left the door open and closed it. 'She was your great-great-great-grandmother, Margaret Fraser-Somerville.'

'I can't remember *any* of these pictures.'

'That's quite likely. They came from your aunt Polly's house when she died some time ago.'

Ginny turned a startled face to him, then wandered away from him towards the kitchen.

'What's the matter?' he asked, following her.

'I didn't even know I had an aunt Polly,' Ginny whispered. 'And she's dead too.'

'You've cousins – she had several children. Alastair used to talk about them.'

Ginny's mother had never mentioned any of them. 'Your

121

appointment,' she said, 'what time is it?'

He looked at his watch. 'In three quarters of an hour.'

'Have you had lunch?'

'No, but – '

'I'll make us a sandwich and then I'll take you.'

'No. Look – '

'No, *you* look,' Ginny cried. 'I can't do anything about your pride. I understand, I really do, but I'm utterly helpless in the face of it. You've no money, not even to put petrol in the Land Rover. Not even to eat properly. Not even to *live*. So what are you going to do? Just walk away out of the village because you're a stubborn Scot and Scotsmen don't accept the help of mere women when they suffer a personal crisis?'

'I don't want to offend you,' he said softly.

'*Offend* me!' Ginny said and then her own pride forced her not to utter the words that had been on the tip of her tongue: that if he left now she would probably go back to London.

He spread his hands in a gesture of peace. 'Okay. But I can fix a snack – I've some ham left over from yesterday.'

He might be broke but he certainly wasn't mean, Ginny decided a short while afterwards, having to ask for a knife to cut the cliff of a sandwhich he gave her into more manageable pieces, meat overflowing from it everywhere. And if she still was angry with him on account of his stubbornness and pride, it evaporated a couple of hours later when he rejoined her in the car after his physiotherapy session, very pale.

'I think we ought to leave driving to Glasgow until tomorrow morning,' she said, turning the key in the ignition. 'You don't look too good.'

'I'll be all right in a sack in the boot,' Andrew muttered.

'Have you packed?'

He just stared at her.

'We'll have to stay the night – it's too far to go there and back *and* have any time to learn anything useful in what's left of today.'

'I'll take my tent.'

Ginny made no reply to this, driving them back to Kinloch Ruthven. There, she left the car outside the Old Manse and went indoors and up to the bathroom, where she had previously noticed some beefy-looking painkillers in the cabinet. There were no instructions on dosage on the bottle so she gave two, together with some water, to Andrew, who had remained sitting in the car. He took the pills meekly and she went back indoors to pack her own overnight bag. When she returned, her passenger was sound asleep. It was the sort of sleep that suggested she should have given him only one pill.

He slept while she drove round to next door, where she packed a bag for him, after much difficulty, having had to climb through the kitchen window and fruitlessly rummage in his bedroom for clean clothes, only to find some in an untidy pile on the living-room floor.

'Silly of me,' Ginny said to herself. 'It's where every other bloody thing is.'

He slept like something dead all the way to Glasgow.

The Grove Gallery, in a side street near Blytheswood Square, was situated on the ground and first floors of one of the houses of a terrace, the rest given over to offices, two antique shops and the Scottish headquarters of an international art auctioneer's company. There was none of the bustle in the street that Ginny had expected, despite the fact that it was only four in the afternoon: she had driven much faster than she did normally.

The gallery looked closed − was closed, said a notice on the door − but there was a light within, a table lamp set on a desk at which was seated a young woman. Ginny tapped on the glass of the door and the girl languidly rose, unlocking the door when the visitor held up her business card for her to read.

'There's no one here now, I'm afraid. They've done their display and gone for the night. But they'll be back in the morning when the show opens.'

'Might one have a peep?' Ginny asked winningly.

'Well, I'm not sure ...'

'I'm actually interested in taking a few photographs of the exhibits.'

'Really?'

'And I'd be prepared to let you have them if you could use them for future publicity.'

Thirty seconds later she was on the first floor.

'And who was here?' Ginny asked. 'Clearly Helmut was — and I see that Morag Galloway has set up her work.'

The room was a much more suitable setting than the studio at the institute, being very plain and lit carefully by concealed spot lamps. Helmut's *Chaos out of Order, Order out of Chaos,* the colours of the items spilling from the drawers of the filing cabinet bright and stark under the lights, actually looked quite striking. The garden fork was missing, however, presumably destined to be an exhibit in the courtroom rather than the art gallery.

'The usual robust stuff, isn't it? By the way, were you aware that Dr Hurrell, the director of the MacNaughton Institute, had refused her permission to come here? And now he's been murdered? Oh, dear, that *was* an unfortunate way to put it.'

The woman was looking at her open-mouthed.

'Was anyone else here?'

'No — but — '

'So who set up Murray Kenning's display?' Ginny had walked over to it; the same set of shapes that had been at the games, but differently arranged.

'I did. You're not from the police, are you?'

'No, I'm what it says on my card. Did he send a diagram with this?'

'No, that was the trouble. I rang the Institute, but he wasn't there. Then he rang me and apologised about it. He told me to arrange it just as I fancied — that was the point of it, it doesn't matter.'

'And yet he told me it was all about maths,' Ginny said, mostly to herself. 'And I thought maths was governed by strict rules.'

'I don't suppose ...' the woman started to say. 'Oh, my name's Sally Barnes. I run the gallery with my husband. I don't suppose you've seen this as Mr Kenning designed it.'

'Yes, as a matter of fact I have.'

'You couldn't give me a few leads, could you?'

'Would you like me to try to set it out as I remember it?'

Sally clasped her hands with joy. 'Oh, would you? That would be wonderful.'

Which was easier said than done, Ginny mused, surveying the pile of blocks in dismay. Maths, Murray had said. But perhaps he was being a little grand and nothing more complicated that arithmetic was involved. Some of the shapes had flat sides so must belong on the bottom row. When she had fitted those together the rest was easy. It was, in fact, a free-standing jigsaw puzzle.

'That's *much* better,' Sally enthused. 'I can't thank you enough.'

'I liked the way you had it,' Ginny said. 'All of a heap — the way it deserves to be.'

'So you're not an enthusiast then?' said Sally, sounding very disappointed.

'No, I think the whole lot's the most amazing, pretentious piffle.'

'I like your honesty. And frankly Morag Galloway terrified me. She actually asked me if I knew where she could get a rat for her display. I told her that the Health Department would never allow it. But did you say just now that Dr Hurrell had been *murdered?* How absolutely dreadful!' She shuddered. 'That sort of thing always makes me feel really creepy.'

Ginny was making good use of her time by examining the displays from every angle, trying to commit everything to memory. Works by artists other than those from the MacNaughton Institute were there: a sculpture made from driftwood supposed to represent a shark that was very inferior to Pete's giant in both conception and execution, some galvanised buckets painted to look like mushrooms inverted over broomsticks and a somewhat confusing edifice consisting of stacked blocks of toffee, its sole mitigating factor being that it smelled wonderful.

'I keep looking to see if any bits have fallen off,' Sally admitted. 'It's Thornton's, too.'

'I don't suppose a few pieces would be missed,' Ginny said and they both giggled like a couple of schoolgirls.

*

'Where am I?' Andrew asked, with no originality what-soever.

'In room 143 at the Glasgow Hilton,' Ginny told him briskly.

Blinking in the bright morning light, he sat up slowly.

'I think I owe you an apology,' Ginny continued. 'I shouldn't have given you two of those pills. They must have been very strong.'

'Where did you get them from?'

'They were in the bathroom cabinet at the Manse. It said "For Pain" on the label but there were no dosage instructions.'

He groaned. 'Handwritten in red ballpoint?'

'Yes.'

'They were Alastair's sleeping tablets. He always kept a few handy.' He put his head in his hands. 'God, I feel as though I've been sandbagged.'

'I'm really sorry.'

'What time is it?'

'Eight thirty.'

'I can't remember arriving here at all.'

'Only the walking bits woke up,' Ginny explained, still wondering what the receptionist had thought of the zombie who had been unable to write his name on the registration card.

He gazed around the room, guardedly, she thought.

'I'm next door,' she informed him.

'Oh.' His tone was deliberately noncommittal.

'I hope I brought the right clothes for you,' Ginny said, making for the door. 'Shall we meet for breakfast in half an hour? I had a quick look round the gallery and I told Sally Barnes, who runs it with her husband, that I'd be back with a colleague. I want to have a good look at the exhibits and the only honest way we can do that and keep an eye on the place for a while is to take photographs and give them to Sally for advertising material. That means we've got to go and buy a camera.'

'And lights,' Andrew said, rubbing his face tiredly. 'And a tripod.'

'Can't you hire those just for the day?'

He went in to the bathroom and there were sounds that suggested he had put his head under the cold tap. He emerged, dripping, his face hidden by a towel. 'Possibly,' he said.

'See you in half an hour,' Ginny said firmly, going away.

The long sleep, together with a shower and shave, had done him a lot of good. And after a very large breakfast and a quick look through *The Scotsman,* during which he said not a word, his gaze lighted upon Ginny as though her company wasn't such a bad thing after all.

'There's a piece missing from Murray's jigsaw effort,' she said.

'Are you sure?'

'Yes, I put it all together at the gallery last night. The bottom row has seven blocks, the next six, then five, then four. The top and bottom rows add up to eleven and so do the two middle ones. There should be two upright shapes on the very top that look like the figure eleven — I remember seeing them at the show. One is missing.'

'It probably fell off the van — the driver looked a stupid sort of bloke.'

'Either that or it's deliberately been taken somewhere else.'

'For what purpose?'

'Goodness knows. But the shapes seem to be hollow. Perhaps something's being hidden inside — drugs or whatever!'

'That's a mite fanciful, surely?'

'Nothing's too fanciful in the world of crime.'

He grimaced by way of comment. 'More coffee?'

'No thanks. Andrew, I'll rely on your experience over the camera. We can take it with us to Muirpark too and record anything interesting.'

'Okay,' he replied uninterestedly.

In the camera shop Andrew displayed the same lack of enthusiasm, mooching around with his hands in the pockets of his jeans, Ginny watching surreptitiously. This went on for quite a while.

'I'm not quite sure what you want to spend,' he called across the shop.

'Whatever I need in order to take high-quality photographs.'

'Personally I'd go for this second-hand Canon. It's the latest model and all the right lenses, filters and so forth come with it. But it's still a lot of money.'

An assistant came forward. 'It belonged to an elderly customer who bought it to take on a world cruise and then suffered a stroke. There's a remote control shutter release and tripod too. And a telephoto lens, but it's a very good one so we're selling it separately.'

Andrew whistled softly when he saw it. 'You'd get a good shot of God with that,' he murmured.

Ginny bought the lot and, although the shop did not have a hire service it knew of a local company who could lend them some lighting equipment. There was also a gift of several rolls of film.

'I might try and buy this off you when you're finished with it,' Andrew said when they had arrived at the gallery and were setting everything up.

Ginny smiled by way of reply.

If Andrew's pride would not allow him to accept the camera as a gift just at the moment, she'd play along with it – but she was determined to get her way in the end.

They had not much time to get the shots they wanted of the exhibits before the doors were opened at eleven. After this Andrew proposed to take a few pictures of the gallery from the outside, one or two of the proprietors in the attractive lobby on the ground floor and then some of any visitors studying the things on display. Meanwhile Ginny was going over everything from the MacNaughton Institute of Art with the thoroughness of MI5.

She found nothing.

When the first people came up the stairs Andrew was out in the street to take advantage of the light, the sun having just come out. So it was on Ginny that Helmut vented his bad temper.

'You have *meddled* with it!' he shouted, storming over to his display after one look.

128

Ginny, who was convinced that she had replaced every-thing as she had found it, said, 'There were cleaners up here when we arrived. Perhaps they − nudged it.'

Fuming, he pushed in one of the drawers of the filing cabinet a couple of millimetres and tweaked the sleeve of the torn T-shirt.

'Have they found the murderer?' Ginny enquired.

'That halfwit of a policeman couldn't find shit on his own backside!' Helmut yelled. 'What are you doing here with photography equipment? I utterly forbid the photographing of my work. There is such a thing as copyright, you know.'

Coolly, Ginny said, 'I think you'll find, if you read the small print of the agreement that Dr Hurrell signed with this gallery, that the proprietors are permitted to have photographs taken for their own publicity purposes, and that is what we are doing.'

Preceded by three other people, Andrew came through the door. 'Fantastic!' he said happily. 'The only bit of blue sky in the Forth Clyde valley is sitting over this building.' He saw Helmut. 'Ah, Herr Beyer. That explains it.'

Helmut said, 'I told Speir that the garden fork was yours. And that was no lie. I found it in that squalid hut you call a potting shed.'

Andrew shook his head. 'Not mine, old sunbeam. I've no doubt it was in there but − '

Before hostility could break out between them, Morag strode in. The rather secret smile on her face faded when she saw them.

Then Sally Barnes appeared. 'You'll never guess,' she said to Ginny. 'The man who delivered your work from Kinloch Ruthven has just come in and given me these. He said he found them in his van.'

She was holding a plastic carrier bag containing two of Murray's shapes, one large balsawood one, the other smaller and painted red.

'Has he gone?' Ginny asked urgently.

Without waiting for a reply Andrew ran down the stairs.

'Well, you know all about this,' Sally said, giving Ginny the bag. 'I'd be so grateful if you'd fit them in somewhere.'

Ginny was watching Morag and Helmut but neither of them showed any reaction. 'Of course,' she said.

'No sign of him,' reported Andrew, coming back.

'Very careless,' Helmut commented. 'You should not deal with that particular courier again.'

'Which company is it? Someone the institute uses regularly?' Ginny asked.

The German shrugged. 'I've no idea. I expect it's in the records somewhere.'

Ginny hoped that her hands weren't shaking as she placed the blocks on the stand. The balsawood one felt heavier than the others: the second, although in exactly the same shade of red as those already on display, was of slightly different construction, made of what appeared to be polystyrene and plywood glued together. And this was the odd one out. It did not actually slot into anything else.

'The really interesting thing,' she whispered to Andrew, who was at her side, 'is that Murray didn't bother to send a diagram, just told Sally to set it out as she wanted to.'

'It looks as though you were right.'

'But now there's one *extra* ...'

'This could all be completely on the line.'

'No, I'm convinced that they both contain something that shouldn't be there. Can you take a quick photo when no one's looking?'

This was achieved very easily, because Helmut and Morag had a blazing row of such proportions that they were both asked to leave. They departed, spitting at each other like tigers. Ginny was grateful to them − they had given her a valuable opportunity.

'There are several options open to us,' Ginny said later when she and Andrew were packing their gear. 'We can keep careful watch for the duration of the show, which I understand finishes on Wednesday, to see if anyone tries to make off with anything − or we can, in the presence of Sally and her husband, open the blocks to see what they contain and then go to the police. *Or* we can make off with the mystery pieces ourselves and then act accordingly.'

'You're forgetting something,' Andrew said. 'All this deception is fairly pointless if the stuff isn't going back to

Kinloch Ruthven. I suggest we see what's in them ourselves, substitute something else that weighs the same and see what happens.'

'That's dangerous.'

'Okay, we do that and then tell the police. But if we tell the cops now, they'll be crawling all over this place before you can say knife and ten to one frighten off the crooks.'

'I'm rather horrified that Murray seems to be involved.'

'He might not be – someone, knowing his relaxed attitude, is using his blocks as handy carriers.'

'And Jean found out about it?'

Their gaze met.

'Yes.' Andrew said. 'Could be.'

'And Hurrell?'

'That would fit too.'

'I don't like the way that Helmut and Morag are here, together. They fight like cat and dog but that might be pure pretence. I'm sure that woman's capable of murder.'

'Ginny, we've got to find out what, if anything, is in those blocks.'

'But the gallery's still full of people. We can't just tuck the things under our arms and walk off with them. I know it sounds a bit po-faced but there is such a thing as professional integrity.'

'Yours, you mean?'

'*Ours.*'

He gave her a wry smile. 'And we're due at the Mackiver place tomorrow morning. I suggest we return this lighting gear and have a wee dram before we decide what to do.'

Ginny glanced at her watch. 'We've missed lunch and I'm starving. Let's get rid of the stuff and then try that bistro round the corner.'

'I suggested a pub because there's one opposite and we can keep an eye on the gallery's front door.'

'Only on condition that you have something to eat.'

'There's nothing worse than a yatterin' woman,' he retorted. 'No, it's all right, I can manage this lot.' And with that he went away, loaded.

'Yatterin'?' Ginny said enquiringly to a woman who had overheard and was smiling at her.

'He was telling you you were nagging him, hen,' said the woman, adding comfortingly, 'But you're not to be blamed. It would give anyone a fit of the humdudgeons staying in here with this load of rubbish. I only came in because I'd missed the bus.'

Ginny resolved to buy a Scots-English dictionary.

The pub had over sixty single malts on offer, a fact that did not appear to have too devastating an effect on Andrew's mental stability. He was actually more interested in the rare roast-beef sandwiches a waitress brought from the kitchen for someone else.

'I'll only have one,' he said to Ginny, referring to the whisky. 'I don't drink when I'm really working.' He led the way to a table by the window that overlooked the street, oblivious to how happy he had just made her. But at the same time she was wishing that she hadn't 'yattered' him.

'I'm in a quandary as to what to do for the best,' Ginny admitted.

'Especially as Muirpark is unlikely to yield anything at all. Do you *really* intend to make a film with Mackiver in it?'

'I intend to make *a* film — eventually. But whether it has Mackiver in it or, for that matter, anyone in Kinloch Ruthven depends on the outcome of several ongoing situations.'

'Not least the murder investigations.'

'Quite. Oh, by the way, I got the dates of previous exhibitions from Sally.'

Andrew, who had his gaze across the road, said, 'I think our minds have been made up for us. Morag has just left the gallery and she is holding the carrier bag that the driver brought Murray's supposedly missing blocks in. Both blocks are in it all right — I can actually see the larger of the two sticking out of the top.'

Chapter Eleven

The woman walked hurriedly, occasionally casting furtive glances over her shoulder, in the direction of Sauchiehall Street. She did not see Ginny and Andrew walking on the other side of the street, and when she reached the busy shopping area their task of following her was made easier by the number of people.

Morag hurried on, heading in the direction of Charing Cross and Woodlands Road. Soon they had left the shoppers behind and, as they approached the city's art gallery and museum, there were very few pedestrians indeed. Fortunately their quarry had ceased to keep checking whether she was being followed.

'Any theories?' Ginny asked.

'Yes,' Andrew replied. 'She knows Glasgow quite well and she's making for the park where she can remove what's in the shapes.'

'But why do it here when everything's going back north on Wednesday night?'

'Because we're here and she doesn't trust us.'

'She can't be meeting anyone or surely that driver would have taken the things directly to them?'

'If he's in on it.'

'He must be − that business of finding them in his van can't be true. She came down *with* the van, don't forget.'

'You're right. I had forgotten that for a moment.'

'Any chance of a quick shot of her?'

'No, not here. I'll try to creep up on her if and when she stops.'

133

But Morag was showing no sign of stopping, not even when she had turned right into Kelvin Way and was approaching the river that gave the road its name. She was walking a little more slowly now, looking almost relaxed, but Ginny and Andrew had been forced to drop right back for fear of being spotted.

The conclusion was the last thing they had been expecting. There was a small car park by the river with room for no more than twenty cars. Morag went to a light-green 2CV, got into it on the passenger side and it drove off.

'I couldn't even get the number,' Andrew panted, having run in an effort to get closer. 'The vehicle was incredibly dirty and the rear plate was no exception.'

'A crony,' Ginny said with a groan, leaning on a tree in her disappointment.

'Perhaps she's with Special Branch,' Andrew said with a grin.

'Well, I'm glad *you're* so cheerful,' she retorted grumpily.

'And we didn't stop for our sandwiches either,' he added, still grinning.

'Did you get a glimpse of the driver?'

'No, the windows were filthy too. Shall we take the high road and see what returns to the institute on Wednesday?'

Ginny was not really listening. 'We should have grabbed her — I think that's the last we'll see of Morag Galloway.'

There were people Ginny needed to talk to and she decided that the best way one conversation could be achieved, seeing as it was Sunday morning, was to go to church. There was plenty of time; she had arranged with Andrew that they would set off for Muirpark at eleven thirty and take a picnic lunch. Having got permission to visit the estate, it seemed a good idea to take full advantage of it.

'Nice to see you, Miss Somerville,' said John Laird after the service. 'I hope you're all right after having been caught up in that disgraceful set-to at the games and the ghastly death of Dr Hurrell. I took my wife home as soon as the trouble started.'

'I was hoping to bend your professional ear on a few matters in connection with that.'

134

He smiled. 'But it's not the sort of thing that you want to make an appointment to see me about in my office?'

'No. Would you like to come home for coffee?'

'Alas, I'm terribly sorry but no. We've visitors and if I'm not at home to entertain them before lunch, then my wife will be really upset with me. But we can talk in my car for a few minutes.'

'What can you tell me about Kevin Mackiver?' Ginny said, wasting no time. 'And of course I'm not suggesting that you should breach any profession confidentialities.'

'Well, that's easy,' Laird said, 'because my firm does not represent him in any way and I have no inkling about his private affairs. All I can tell you really is that he is a local boy made good, a man of humble beginnings who has worked hard for everything he owns. And as sometimes happens in such cases he has not kept many friends in the district, call it envy or what you will.'

'Such as unscrupulous business practices?'

'Yes, I've heard as much.'

'He was once in partnership with a man called Rory McQuade. Do you know anything about that?'

'I'm afraid not. But he lived on Islay for years when he was first in the whisky business − he didn't buy Muirpark until about five years ago.'

'I understand there was some kind of swindle and a small distillery was burned down.'

'Mackiver was involved with *that?* Yes, of course I'd heard about it − it rocked the entire whisky industry. He must have been very clever to keep his name out of the papers.' He opened the car door for her. 'Miss Somerville, I feel duty bound to ask you this; are you making some kind of private investigation?'

'Yes,' Ginny answered. 'But anything I find out I shall take to the police.'

'Chief Inspector Speir is very good at his job.'

'I've no doubt that he is. But two people have been killed already and − '

'So you think there's a connection? And that Mackiver's involved? I really wish you'd leave all this to the police.'

'What did my father think of him? Did he ever mention him to you in any way?'

'Ah,' Laird said sadly. 'Well, the truth is that they loathed one another.'

'Why?'

'It's simple, really — Mackiver shot his dog.'

'But that's absolutely dreadful!'

Hastily Laird said, 'There was no proof, you understand. But the two had had an exchange of words when Mackiver accused Alastair of not having the dog under proper control when he was walking her near where Mackiver had some pheasant-rearing pens. Apparently a dog frightened some of the young birds and they panicked and flew into the wire mesh. A few were injured and had to be destroyed. Mackiver always maintained that he had recognised the dog, a black Labrador by the name of Bess, and told your father that if he saw it on his property again he would shoot it. The problem was that a path used by local people runs right alongside a fence that forms a boundary of the property and it is in poor condition. And of course, people being what they are, the fence is broken down in places.'

'But Muirpark's miles from the village.'

'Yes, but Mackiver owns a lot of land in this area too. In fact, the pheasant pens in question adjoin the keeper's cottage that is in the woodland above the Old Manse — only a matter of yards from the top of your garden.'

'Is this the same keeper who said he saw Andrew McQuade making off with the deer?'

'Yes.'

'And the dog was shot?'

'Yes, Alastair found her in the copse near the lane. There was a trail of blood as though she had dragged herself back through a hole in the fence.'

'When did this happen?'

'About a fortnight before he died.'

'But he must have been devastated! And very, very angry. It must have — '

Laird interrupted, but gently. 'He was an extremely sick man. Even if that hadn't happened, I can assure you he would not be alive now. He told me himself a few days after it occurred that it only was a matter of weeks for him.'

The utterance of a depressed and desperately unhappy man, Ginny thought, aching inside. 'Did he accuse Mackiver of it?'

'Yes, they had quite a confrontation. Mackiver didn't actually admit to being responsible, but he didn't deny it either. But this sort of thing does happen in country districts, I'm afraid. The farmers are always shooting stray dogs that worry sheep.'

'I've been meaning to ask you this for ages; were you at the institute on the open day? It's just that I wondered if you might have seen anything suspicious.'

'Yes, I usually drop in for a while during the evening. As a matter of fact, I quite enjoy that kind of thing. But I didn't see anything out of the ordinary. Now, please, take my advice and stop investigating this yourself. It would be dreadful if you got hurt.'

'You didn't tell me that Mackiver shot my father's dog,' Ginny said to Andrew later.

They were bouncing along a rutted lane in Andrew's Land Rover, the scenic route to Muirpark across the moorland at the foot of the hills.

'There was no proof,' he replied easing it into four-wheel drive to cross a stream.

'I still wish you'd mentioned it.'

'Perhaps I should have done but there didn't seem much point in upsetting you over something that no one really knows the truth about. Personally I think it far more likely that the gamekeeper shot the animal.'

'On Mackiver's orders, though.'

'Only in so far as he has orders to shoot all vermin. That includes feral cats and stray dogs.'

'But you don't just blast away at something that might be someone's pet!'

'Round here they do,' Andrew said grimly. 'Now, tell me what you think of the view.'

Having forded the stream, they had topped a rise in the track, cresting a hill that had its lowest slopes thickly wooded along the shores of Loch Linnhe. Up here, away from the deep cold shade cast by the conifers, the sun was bright and warm, the scent of summer wafting through the open windows as they pulled off the track and parked.

'Below is Mamore Forest,' Andrew said. 'And the three peaks are Ben Nevis on the left, Sgurra Mhaim in the centre and Binnein Mor on the right. You can't quite see it from here but Loch Eilde Mor is farther round on the right.'

She wanted to ask if he had climbed them but refrained, saying instead, 'We could have our picnic here.'

'We've only just started out.'

'I know. But it's so lovely here. That sort of spiky stump on the hill over there — is it the tower above the loch at Muirpark?'

He handed her some binoculars from the shelf on the dashboard. 'You've good eyes. Yes, but it's a folly built to look like a ruin. There are stairs inside that lead to an observation platform at the top.'

Again Ginny bit her tongue and did not voice the wish to climb up it.

'I've already planned where we'll have the picnic,' Andrew said, turning the keys in the ignition. 'A public place.' He added, obviously feeling that an explanation was needed, 'By that I mean it's not on Mackiver's property.'

'I wonder if Morag came back.'

'No, not yet. I went up to the institute first thing to check. There's no sign of her — or Helmut, for that matter. I had more success with the van that took the stuff to the gallery, though. One of Speir's bright young things remembered to take the number and the vehicle's been traced to a hire firm in Glasgow. But the paperwork seems to have gone missing.'

'And the police told you all this?'

'Let's just say that I used to go climbing with someone who works for the CID.'

They drove steeply downhill and over a cattle grid. Andrew took a sharp left turn into a track that wove, still downhill, through glades of silver and river birch and, as they approached the stream that could be glimpsed through the trees, the woodland changed to stands of tall beeches and oaks.

138

'The locals call it the Lost Glen,' Andrew said when he had parked the Land Rover on the riverbank and switched off the engine. 'You can only reach it down that narrow lane and superstition has it that sometimes the lane's there and sometimes it isn't.'

'All depending on the number of drams consumed?' Ginny asked with a laugh. She saw instantly that she had offended him. 'No, I'm sorry. Perhaps the people who say that those who work in television have no soul are right.'

He smiled, forgiving her. 'I have been this way in the mist and not been able to find the lane myself.'

They walked downstream, not speaking, both with their own thoughts. There was a silence and peace about the place that seemed almost magical, the tiny burn clear as glass as it rippled and bubbled over the mossy stones. Long strands of trailing mosses, like green fluffy wool, hung from the trees, stirred in the warm air and the movement of their passing.

They came to a pool created by a small dam of rocks and Ginny bent down to trail a hand through the water. It was ice cold.

'Fancy a dip?' Andrew asked jokingly. 'It's as warm as melted snow.'

Ginny sat down on the bank, hugging her knees. 'I hate to even mention his name in this place but Mackiver *must* have been lying when he said he went home before the tug-of-war started. He had a thousand-pound bet on the result with Ninian Effric.'

'We should have asked Fiona.'

'Or one of his lady friends?'

'It's not like that. When he wants a bit on the side he pays for it.'

'So he might have gone with Jean after the party.'

'Possibly. Especially if he'd had a bit too much to drink — enough to make him not care a damn if anyone saw him.' He gave her a shy sort of look. 'May I take your photograph?'

'I'm honoured. How do you want me to be?'

'Just like that, gazing down into the water.'

It seemed to her that he rattled off half a film.

They ate their picnic — sandwiches and some fruit — and

then drove the few miles to the Muirpark estate. There was no sign of life either in the grounds or around the house. They left the Land Rover parked right in front of it, to announce that they had arrived, and then set to work. Ginny almost had to drag Andrew away from photographing a day-old Highland calf before he used up the entire stock of film or was impaled on the horns of its overprotective mother.

'I could actually get interested in working on this,' Ginny said. 'The entire glen is enormously photogenic. But what I really want to do before we go is to take a look at Mackiver's boat.'

Not knowing whether they were being watched, they approached an old barn at the rear of the house, a building of such antiquity that it had probably been built during the time that the original house had stood on the site.

'The walls are at least four feet thick in places,' Ginny said, wandering in. 'And look, here are the remains of the original oak doors.'

The inside of the barn was like a small church, the massive roof beams also of oak, the vaulted roof lined with wood. The doors, lying among straw, tangled piles of brightly coloured baling twine and lengths of filthy plastic sheeting, were carved and still in possession of their hinges and locks. One of them looked as though it had been used to mix cement on.

'It just about sums the guy up,' said Andrew disgustedly after taking a look. He kicked at the rubbish on the floor. 'One dropped match and this whole building would go up like a torch.'

'What's that?'

'What? Where?'

Ginny dropped onto all fours and burrowed in the straw. Hauling out her find, she brushed the straw and dust from it.

It was one of Murray's balsawood shapes.

The pair of them delved like badgers and found four more, one painted black with red edges. The last one was damaged and beneath it were the splintered remnants of what must have been at least a dozen, now little more that matchwood.

'So Mackiver doesn't appreciate art either,' Andrew muttered, taking several shots of the hoard. 'Are you thinking the same as me — that the sale of this was merely a way of giving Murray money?'

'Either that or it was smashed up accidentally.'

Andrew was examining the pieces. 'I think it was just chucked in here and then someone drove a car over it before burying it in the rubbish.'

'But why?'

'It's possible that if they'd been used to conceal something they were smashed to obliterate that fact.' He covered it all up again and changed the film in the camera. 'Let's go and take a look at the boat.'

'Discreetly, of course,' Ginny said.

He took her hand and pulled her up from her crouching position on the floor.

'You've a very strong grip,' she commented, rubbing her fingers.

'Sorry.' He grinned ruefully. 'I didn't break my hands or arms, just my legs, ankles, collar bones and a few ribs here and there.'

She wanted to tell him that he was a different person since he had cut down on drinking and started to eat properly — she had made a large pot of soup on the Aga and given him most of it, telling him that she could not possibly eat it all herself. Again she held back, not feeling that they were on those terms yet. Perhaps they never would be.

Making a play of discussing this and that, pausing to point to various things and make notes, they made their way back to the Land Rover, Ginny again having to drag her companion away from the calf, which had curled up and gone to sleep. Andrew then spotted a buzzard circling above the pastureland and had to set up the camera and tripod to try out the telephoto lens. Ginny, happy for him but in a fever of impatience, sat in the driver's seat of the Land Rover and wondered if it merely *looked* too brutal for women to drive.

'Got it when it swooped on a rabbit!' he announced delightedly, coming back in a hurry. 'D'you want to drive? These things are extremely user-friendly — don't mind going off in third, leave the road only with the greatest persuasion, and if you hit someone the major crumple zone is always the other vehicle.'

'Perhaps I'd better try it out on nice solid tarmac first,' Ginny said, relinquishing the driver's seat with only a moment's hesitation.

He seemed keen to demonstrate. 'As long as you remember that reverse is situated a long way west by northwest,' he said. 'Somewhere in the vicinity of your front seat passenger's kneecaps.'

'Female passengers might get the wrong impression.'

'Quite. That's why I'm telling you.'

They drove down the main access road for a short distance and then struck off over the open moorland. The mingled smells of crushed grass, pine trees and the scent that Ginny had come to think of as that of the Highlands assailed her nostrils; sun-warmed moss and stones, sheep, wet peat and cattle.

The top of the tower came into view before they reached the crest of the hill. Close up it was rather an ugly edifice, built of a dark grey rock that looked almost black even with the sun on it. It reared into the sky like a jagged, pointing finger, there was something slightly obscene about it.

'You're frowning,' Andrew said. 'Yes, you've guessed it — it's known as Knoydart's Willy. Only of course Knoydart is a place, not a person, and you can't see it from here even from the top on a clear day. Polite people call it the Lighthouse and it isn't that either.'

'Sort of Gothic,' Ginny commented. 'Gargoyles and dragon's-head water spouts to take the rainwater away from the platform around the top. And the sides have a sort of pineapple effect where the stone has been left in bumps and chunks.'

'The man who built it was supposed to be cuckoo.'

They bumped down to a narrow road, one that Andrew explained took a circuitous route from the stable yard at the rear of the house. This became even narrower and twisted in a series of hairpin bends down the steep hill towards the jetty.

The *Seawitch* bobbed gently at her mooring. She was

pure white but for the wheelhouse, which was varnished, and the rubbing strakes, painted dark blue, along each side of the vessel. Although the yacht was fully rigged there was no sign of furled sails, and Ginny wondered whether they were securely stowed in lockers or Mackiver did not engage in that kind of seamanship. When she voiced her thoughts, Andrew snorted.

'Twin diesels,' he said derisively. 'Real sailing slops the gin from the glasses.' He ventured onto the gangway.

'There are bound to be alarms,' Ginny warned, oblivious of the sun sparkling on the blue water and hundreds of seabirds.

'He didn't say we couldn't go aboard.'

'If he had, it would have looked as though he had something to hide.'

'I thought you said you wanted to have a look round.'

'I do but I just think you ought to be *careful.*'

The door to the wheelhouse was not locked, a fact that seemed rather surprising, and they went in. No security alarm bells greeted their arrival.

The interior was both practical and opulent; satellite-navigation equipment, an inlaid chart table, Italian wall lights with silk shades, heavy, costly fabrics covering the bench seating and draped across the windows.

From the wheelhouse a companionway led down into the main salon. They were standing at the top of it, preparing to descend, when Andrew tensed, smelling the air like a gun dog. Then he went down.

'Are you alone?' he asked the man sprawled comfortably on a huge leather sofa, smoking.

'Of course. Why shouldn't I be?' was the reply. 'Won't you introduce me to your young lady?'

Andrew turned. 'Certainly. Ginny, this is Rory McQuade, my father.'

Chapter Twelve

'Virginia?' asked Rory, the emphasis firmly on the first two syllables, when Andrew had finished making the introductions.

'Not to my real friends,' she replied, too flabbergasted to ask questions.

Andrew said, 'You've absolutely no business to smoke those filthy French cigarettes while you're breaking and entering. Sherlock Holmes would have nabbed you in a flash.'

'And don't I ask all the saints every night why no policeman alive today has his perception, stamina and intellect?' Rory retorted. 'I broke nothing. The entire boat is wide open to whoever wants to look her over.'

'Yes, but *we* have permission,' said his son smugly. 'Sort of, anyway.'

Rory McQuade was about sixty years of age, tall and thin with a wild mane of wavy grey hair. His eyes were blue, the complexion surprisingly weather-beaten, the sort of face that was as Irish as the King of the Leprechauns.

'Take a look,' he said with an expansive wave of an arm.

The sofa, together with a couple of matching chairs, was the only furniture in the salon, all three pushed right to the sides. The empty space in the centre, an expanse of parquet floor with a high gloss, was lit by adjustable spot lamps, one group of which someone, presumably Rory, had switched on. The circles of light, bright discs on the floor, illuminated everything and yet nothing.

'What do you make of it?' Rory asked with a shrug.

Ginny examined the floor closely near the light cast by the lamps and then went to one of the lockers that lined the hull, built to the shape of the boat. Inside were sections of thin timber, polished on one side, untreated on the reverse.

'Easy,' she said. 'It's a floating art gallery. There are small brass fittings flush with the deck that the stands, packed in sections in the lockers, are screwed into.'

'Is this woman a genius?' Rory demanded to know of the heavens.

Ginny marched up to him. 'You know more about this than you're making out. And frankly, I'd love to know what you're doing here. Suppose we have a bit less of the blarney and some straight talking?'

With a sideways look at Andrew, he said, 'You look a whole lot better without all that hair.'

'She means what she says,' Andrew said darkly.

'Have you seen the *Glasgow Herald* this morning?' Rory asked in conversational tones, rummaging in a small rucksack on the sofa. 'It appears that there was an explosion up on the Gleniffer Braes near Paisley late yesterday afternoon. A small Citroen car was blown to kingdom come together with the two people in it.' He found what he was looking for and held it out. 'It was the mention of balsawood that caught my eye — Andrew told me young Murray used it.'

Andrew took the newspaper and quickly scanned the article. 'Bloody hell!' he breathed. 'The vehicle was in a car park — the hill's a well-known lookout point, apparently — and it blew up. The Anti-Terrorist Branch have been called in because the police think it might have been an IRA bomb that exploded prematurely. The bodies of the two occupants of the car haven't been identified — too badly damaged, I'd imagine. What they *have* found is small pieces of balsawood that are thought to be the remains of a box containing the explosives.' He looked up. 'We almost made off with those things ourselves.'

Ginny sat down, feeling a little faint.

'So,' Rory said, 'it isn't just a coincidence that you're sniffing around here.'

145

'How did you know we were coming?' Ginny enquired.

'Kevin told Fiona, Fiona told Kirsten, Kirsten told me.'

'But I thought the two of you weren't talking,' Andrew said.

'She was worried about you. And so am I. Now, are you going to sit down and tell me everything you've found out?'

And, to Ginny's extreme annoyance, that is what Andrew did.

When he had finished, Rory said, 'One wonders if many exhibits from the institute are sent by sea to other venues.'

'I've no idea,' Andrew said. 'As you know, I've only been there since early April.'

Ginny said, 'It's perfectly possible that they are when the official season's over. But Hurrell didn't mention anything about it to me when I spoke to him.'

'No, well, he wouldn't, would he?' Rory said. 'Especially if something illegal was going on.'

'But not the smuggling of explosives,' Ginny murmured.

'No, my dear. That was to kill both of you.'

There was a long silence while at least two of those present thought deeply about it.

Then, quietly, Rory said, 'And with a view to keeping the pair of you in full possession of your limbs, I insist that you finish with your amateur sleuthing here and now, and also that you give me your word on it.'

Ginny and Andrew exchanged glances; there was a faint whiff of mutiny in the air.

Rory broke the ensuing silence. 'This Galloway woman — do you think she was suspicious of the courier finding a couple more pieces in his van so she just decided to — ' He stopped speaking.

The *Seawitch* had rocked very, very slightly. It was a different movement entirely from the gentle sway of a boat moored to a jetty. Moments later Kevin Mackiver came down into the salon followed by two other men, the second of these carrying a double-barrelled shotgun. When he saw the nature of the company, Mackiver took it from him.

Rory and Andrew did not wait for any past threats to be

carried out, acting on the principle – Ginny realised later – that the man would be reluctant to fire the weapon inside his own boat. Andrew, who was nearest took a wild swing at him, which did not connect but caused Mackiver to duck, stagger and fall foul of a deft kick to the rear that sent him skimming across the highly polished floor. Rory meanwhile grabbed the first of the duo, whose slow wits had not yet caught up with what was happening, and sent him pell-mell after his employer. The man who had been carrying the shotgun, the one whom Ginny had seen with the dogs at Muirpark on the night of the ball, was a different proposition. There was a short but ugly brawl, ending when Rory disappeared up the companionway three stairs at a time, leaving Andrew semiconscious on the deck, Ginny huddled protectively over him.

They still didn't stop kicking him.

Ginny heard a motorboat's engine roar into noisy life, then fade into the distance, and everything became confused. Someone had kicked her on the head and for a while life was a grey blur. Voices seemed to whisper right in her ears, but they were oddly muffled and she could not make out what they were saying. She had the sensation of being lifted and carried, and one foot came into jarring contact with something hard. Then fresh air, a breeze, blew her hair off her face and hard grassy ground seemed to come from nowhere and hit her. The next thing she was aware of was sitting up, her chin propped on her raised knees, the headache almost too much to bear.

Mackiver was shouting. He did not seem to be addressing anyone in particular, just ranting and raving, mostly obscenities. Ginny put her hands over her ears; she did not want to listen. Some indefinable time later she was suddenly yanked to her feet.

'I asked you a question!' Mackiver yelled in her face, giving her a shake.

Ginny had no choice but to be sick all down the front of his Pringle sweater. She was thrown down onto the ground again.

A little later – it might have been minutes or hours – she was hauled up again.

'Walk, damn you!' someone else shouted.

There was a short journey over the grass and then steps. The steps went round and round, up and up, for ever. They were slippery and once she tripped and almost fell but was caught and shoved on upwards. There was then some kind of arrival at a level place and Ginny gripped hold of what felt like an iron balustrade and tried to focus her eyes. Sky, trees and grass swung in a sickening whirl.

She was at the top of the tower.

'This is a warning to you,' Mackiver said. He was right at her side. 'One word of anything that happens here today and I'll find you and kill you.' He went on talking in a low, deathly whisper. 'This is a *family* matter. Nothing to do with the police or your television mob in London. Nothing! Do you understand?'

Andrew was there too, his face bruised and bleeding. Dazed, he uttered an exclamation of alarm when he was dragged in the direction of the balustrade. It was only a few seconds' work for the three men to heft him right over. He clung on to the top but Mackiver clubbed his hands with the butt of the shotgun. Desperately, Andrew transferred his hold to the iron uprights, slithering down and down and finally letting go altogether when Mackiver kicked at his fingers with the toes of his boots.

'You bastard!' Ginny cried, leaning out and expecting to see a broken body lying on the ground. Then she realised that she was standing on a grating and she could see Andrew through it, hanging on to the metal supports. As she watched, numbed with horror, he transferred one hand to the thick copper wire of a lightning conductor, his toes feeling for holds on the rough surface of the stone, inching his way downwards towards one of the several narrow slits of windows that let light into the interior.

Mackiver swore and dived off down the stairs.

Ginny was never sure afterwards how she managed to stay right behind him all the way down without slipping or falling. She still could not see properly and her head hurt as though it might burst.

Andrew had made good progress, working his way down and around the tower as he followed the line of windows

148

on the spiral staircase, using them as hand and footholds, and was now almost a quarter of the way down.

Mackiver went to his Range Rover, parked close by, placed the shotgun inside and came back with a hunting rifle. Assessing his target carefully for a moment or two, he took aim.

The bullet whined off the stonework about a foot above Andrew's head, bombarding him with splinters.

'Oh, I'm a good shot,' Mackiver said contentedly and in no real hurry. He strolled off, Andrew having frantically placed as much of the tower between himself and his tormentor as possible.

Ginny tried to stop it, sprinting after Mackiver and actually succeeding in shoulder-charging him to the ground. But he cuffed her away and shouted at his men to hold her, giving her a triumphant smile before again taking careful aim.

This time the bullet ricocheted off the stone just to Andrew's left and both feet slipped. But he regained his footing, although only toeholds, and swung sideways into the comparative security of one of the window embrasures. Unfortunately they were all too small for him to climb through.

It was a race between them, for in order not to leave the kind of evidence that would result in a charge of murder, Mackiver would have to make Andrew fall. No one was more aware of this than Andrew, of course, and he was descending more quickly than seemed humanly possible, so much closer to the ground now that Ginny could see the way he was wedging his fingers and the sides of his hands into crevices in the stones.

Mackiver fired again and this time a large sliver of stone cut Andrew's head like a knife. He hung motionless for a moment, a thick red line of blood trickling from his temple. Then, releasing one hand to wipe it from his eyes on his sleeve, he carried on climbing down.

Arms pinioned to her sides, Ginny could only watch this cat-and-mouse game of murder. It was not to go on for much longer. The next shot hit the tower's wall only a matter of inches from Andrew's left hand and he lost his hold just as he was transferring his other hand to a new position.

And he fell.

There was no elation on Mackiver's part. He merely ordered his men to throw Andrew into the back of the Land Rover, like so much carrion, and then came over to where Ginny was sitting weakly on the grass.

'Remember what I said,' he warned in a low voice. 'I never want to see you round here again. Now get out.'

She was shaking so much when she climbed into the driving seat that for a couple of minutes she just sat there. During this time the three men got into the Range Rover and drove off. Twisting round in her seat she tried to see if Andrew was breathing but could detect no movement of his chest. Finally, she got out, opened the rear door, knelt on the floor of the vehicle and felt for a pulse. It was there, very fast.

The car had been parked with its bumper almost touching a large boulder. And in gear, she discovered moments later after a jerk and a loud clang. Ginny took a deep breath, put it into neutral and tried again. The engine roared into reassuring life.

'West by northwest,' she muttered. 'No, that was *first,* you stupid cow,' she berated herself, having moved the boulder several inches in the direction of the loch. 'Aim for your front-seat passenger's kneecaps.'

The journey, when she had succeeded in manoeuvring the Land Rover onto the road, was hazy in her memory ever afterwards. She knew that she ought not to follow the road all the way back to the house – dreading the possibility that Mackiver would try to finish off the pair of them – so she went across country, finding her way with a kind of sixth sense that she had never known she possessed. And at the back of her mind was another dread – that all the bouncing around was killing her passenger, who made no sound. She would rather, in a way, that he had groaned or screamed; at least she would have known that he still drew breath.

She soon learned to trust her sixth sense and also the vehicle and there was only one really bad moment when she grounded it trying to cross a stream with steep banks and, in her panic, stalled the engine. She started it again

150

and the wheels spun. She took another deep breath and put it into four-wheel-drive the way she remembered Andrew doing, and the vehicle stolidly climbed out of the hole it was in, shedding dollops of thick mud, heather stems and small stones.

Bridge of Corran Infirmary was situated at the junction of the main road and the turning for Muirpark. Because of the popularity of mountaineering in the locality, it had a casualty department.

'I can't imagine why you didn't call an ambulance,' a nurse said reprovingly, after another hazy period of time had elapsed, well after Andrew had been wheeled away.

Ginny just shook her head.

'But you must have been near the big house.'

Ginny wiped away a tear that had trickled down her nose. 'How do you know where we were?' She was sure now that he had broken his back.

'He mumbled something about Knoydart's Willy. That's up on the cliff on the Muirpark estate, isn't it?'

The tone did not invite argument. Ginny got up to leave.

'There's a contusion on your head that ought to be looked at.'

'Then perhaps you'd be so good as to arrange for someone to look at it and stop shouting at me.'

She finally got home at six thirty, took two of the painkilling tablets she had been given and curled up on the settee in the large living room under a blanket. She had tried to find out about Andrew's condition but all they had been able to tell her was that he was having X-rays. No one had known how seriously he was hurt, or whether he was conscious or not; no one had known *anything*.

Ginny must have slept, for the next thing she knew was that it was dark and someone was knocking on the front door. After blundering into a few things, she found a light switch in the hall and opened the door.

It was Murray. He looked extremely worried.

'Gee, Ginny, is everything okay? Only Andy's old bus is sort of parked in the hedge and I can't raise him.'

'Oh, God!' she wailed. 'I can't have put on the hand-brake.' That she might be in the company of a murderer was of absolutely no consequence right now.

He was staring at her in horror. 'You're *hurt!* Now just you sit down and don't worry about a thing. Give me the keys and I'll shift it for you.'

They were still in the pocket of her jeans.

'I was just passing,' Murray said when he returned, starting to talk even before he had crossed the threshold. 'And there it was. No problem, though – there's not a mark on it. It seems to have trundled over a couple of small bushes on its way down the slope but I guess they'll pick themselves up again by the morning.'

Ginny was back under her blanket by this time, shivering, so had only heard the last dozen words or so.

He sat by her side. 'Can I get you something? God, I feel awful about this, you here and with no one to look after you. Pete and I went out to look for some dead trees and stuff for his giants and we've only just got back. Where *is* Andy?'

'In hospital. And it's all my fault. I thought I was being so clever, playing God with his life. And now he's paid for it. You have no idea how guilty and wretched I feel about this. Nothing else matters – I don't care a damn about the rest!'

What Murray made of this was uncertain and he went away. But he was soon back with a plate of smoked salmon with brown bread and butter, even a slice of lemon and black pepper.

'Here, I raided your fridge. You must eat something. Which hospital? Bridge of Corran?'

'Yes.'

'I'll phone right away. What happened to the guy?'

She told him what she would have told anyone just then. 'He fell off a tower on the Mackiver estate.'

'Jeez,' Murray groaned and went away again.

Ginny found that she was ravenously devouring the smoked salmon. The food made her feel less dizzy and faint but did nothing to alleviate the sense of guilt and black despair.

'There was a bit of an emergency on,' Murray reported a couple of minutes later. 'The woman said to ring back in the morning. He's been admitted — that's all she knew.'

'What sort of an emergency?' Ginny demanded to know.

'Oh, nothing to do with Andy. A bad car crash.'

'Didn't she say anything about his condition?'

'Only that he was in a ward — not in intensive care. Shall I make you some coffee?' He made them both some, bringing two large mugs of it and a packet of biscuits he had found in the kitchen cupboard. 'Hope you don't mind if I dive into the cookies. I don't know how many bits of dead tree we heaved into that trailer. And Pete's a great guy but when he's working or thinking about working he seems to live on fresh air.'

'Let me cook you something,' Ginny offered.

'No, you stay right there. These are fine. Hell, I still feel bad about not being around when the pair of you were in trouble. Problem is, I owed Pete at least one favour as he's been making a lot of my jigsaw shapes for me — wood just seems to fashion itself into art forms in his hands. I sometimes think that he's the only real artist up at the institute.'

'One whom Miss MacNaughton would have approved of.'

'Yes, you're right, Ginny. She sounds like the sort of woman who would have had one of his giants in the bathroom.'

'Definitely.'

'Did you and Andy go to the show in Glasgow?'

'Yes. Helmut and Morag were there too. Murray, does Morag have a boyfriend?'

His good-natured features darkened. 'I really couldn't say. That creature doesn't seem to hold with other people at all.'

Someone pounded on the front door.

'Shall I go?' Murray asked.

'Please,' Ginny replied, wondering if it was the police to tell her that her next-door neighbour had died.

Pete's voice said, unusually loudly for him, 'How long does it take you to get fish and chips? If I'd known you

153

were going to slip in a little socialising I'd have fetched them myself.'

Murray shushed him and there was a short muttered conversation. They then both came into the living room, Pete on tiptoe as though a large noisy presence might upset the patient.

Sitting up straight but with the blanket wrapped around her, Ginny said, 'Well, as the two of you are here and it seems that you've both been involved with making wooden shapes, perhaps you can tell me why Murray's jigsaw arrangement arrived in Glasgow one piece short and then the driver of the van turned up with two, making one too many? Another thing I'd like to know is what was in them. I asked Murray whether Morag had a boyfriend because she went off with the odd shapes and got into a car driven by someone we couldn't see. Now it looks as though Morag, her friend and the car have been blown to bits. Well, gentlemen, what was it? Semtex?'

There was absolute silence.

'It's perfectly possible,' Ginny continued, 'that the explosive device was intended for Andrew and me because someone thinks we've been doing too much private sleuthing.'

In strangled tones Pete said, 'Someone's been using Murray's work to make bombs with?'

'So it would appear.'

'Look, I don't know anything about this,' Murray said. 'I'll admit straight away that I'm not dedicated like Helmut. And I've discovered that I'm not good enough to make a career out of art. But if someone's illegally using what I'm doing, then I want to know about it. I'd rather take the next flight home than make life easy for hoodlums.'

'The same goes for me,' Pete whispered. 'But what do the cops make of all this?'

'They don't,' Ginny said shortly. 'My next question is about Kevin Mackiver's boat, the *Seawitch*. How long has it been fitted out as a floating art gallery? Does it take exhibits abroad from the institute and if so, where?'

Both men looked at her blankly.

'I don't know about that either,' Pete said. 'This is the

154

first time I've been over to Scotland.'

Ginny looked at Murray. *'You've* been before, though.'

'Yes, but no one's ever said anything about *foreign* exhibitions. The students go home in September, don't forget — we never have time to send stuff farther afield than Glasgow.'

'What happens to the things you've made?'

'If we don't have them shipped home I reckon they're put out with the garbage.'

Pete muttered, 'Or, in Morag's case, dug into the pumpkin patch as fertiliser.'

'She may be dead,' Murray reminded him.

'Yeah. Sorry,' Pete responded heavily.

'Did you have the same sort of shapes last year?' Ginny asked Murray.

He nodded glumly. 'I'm not very imaginative after all.'

'And were they your very own idea?'

He gazed at her with a pained expression. 'Ma'am, you really do cross-question.'

'I'm sorry. It's probably something to do with the bang on the head,' Ginny said humbly. 'And I think I'm trying not to worry about Andy being crippled for the rest of his life and it being my fault.'

Murray sat staring into thin air for a moment. 'No,' he said. 'I had shapes but they were two-dimensional and I hung them by the corners. It was Hurrell who suggested I make them three-dimensional so they could be stood up and slotted together to make free-standing structures.'

A bell rang in the hall.

'Fancy that,' Ginny said. 'I didn't know I had a doorbell.'

'I'll go,' Murray offered. 'I'm getting quite good at it.'

Moments later John Laird strode into the room.

'My dear!' he exclaimed. 'I've just had an anonymous phone call to the effect that you and Andrew McQuade have been hurt in an accident. And looking at you it would seem that whoever it was was quite correct.'

He was out of breath and slightly dishevelled as though he had run from his home.

'Yes, foolish and irresponsible of us,' Ginny said. 'But why should anyone feel obliged to tell you about it?'

155

Laird sat down. 'I simply have no idea. What on earth happened to the pair of you?'

Before she could reply, the phone rang.

'My turn,' Ginny said.

'It's me,' said a weak voice. 'Can you come and fetch me?'

After thanking John Laird for his concern, Ginny asked assistance from both Pete and Murray to collect Andrew from the hospital, since it appeared he was discharging himself. She expected that he would have to be carried to the car, but he was mobile, albeit with a slight limp. They found him waiting for them in the reception, brushing aside all offers of help from the Americans. His mood was almost elated — Ginny wondered what drugs he had been given to facilitate his departure.

'I heard them talking,' Andrew said. 'Some laddie with two broken legs was going to have to spend the night in the mortuary, they were that short of beds. So I told them I'd take my bruised backside somewhere else.'

Pete guffawed with laughter.

'Did I bust the camera?' Andrew asked Ginny, not smiling now.

'No. We didn't have it with us up the tower,' she replied. 'It was still in the Land Rover.' In fact, they had forgotten to take it on the boat with them. She was praying that he would keep quiet about what had happened in front of their companions, mostly because her head hurt too much to concentrate. The past couple of hours had been interesting, though, very interesting.

'Are you *sure* you're all right?' Murray said for the second time after he had delivered them both to the Coach House.

'Perfectly,' Ginny answered.

'I'll call on you guys in the morning,' he promised. 'See if I can do any chores or anything.'

No one had mentioned bombs, Morag or balsawood jigsaw shapes.

Ginny let the two out and when she went back into the kitchen — for they had had to enter the house through the

back way, even though Murray had parked at the front —
Andrew had already found a bottle of whisky.

'I really wish you wouldn't,' Ginny said.

He poured himself out a generous measure. 'Do you want
some? You said you were getting a taste for it.'

'I don't think it would help me right now.' She turned
to go. 'Perhaps we can have a talk when you're sober
again.'

'I'm drunk now,' he said under his breath, taking a large
swallow of his drink. He closed his eyes and took a deep
breath. 'God, that's better.'

'Are you really just bruised?'

'Yes, they were only wanting to keep me in overnight for
observation. I landed in a thick clump of heather.'

'I thought I'd crippled you, driving you to Bridge of
Corran like that.'

He took another large mouthful of whisky. 'I must
have passed out.' Then, sitting down at the kitchen table,
wincing, he said, 'So did you for a while. I was quite glad
in a way.'

'Why?'

He moved his shoulders carefully, cradling the glass in
both hands. 'Climbers always have plenty of rope, he said.
I got plenty. He thrashed me with a length of it he had in
the car. It had a couple of knots in it and he made it nice
and wet in a burn first. Trying to get me to say what my old
man was doing on the boat. I didn't tell him anything.'

At the mention of one of the reasons for her burning
anger, Ginny cried, 'Rory was a bloody *coward* to run off
and leave you like that.'

Andrew shook his head. 'No, never that. I don't blame
him — he's not as young as he was.'

She sat down opposite and took a sip of his drink as
a peace offering. 'I'm sorry you were hurt, really sorry,
and I feel that it's all my fault. But we can't talk about
it tonight.'

Very gently he touched her hair near the injury to her head.
'I'm sorry too. But let's not start blaming ourselves.'

Ginny, rising and on her way towards the door, was in
no mood to argue. 'Goodnight, Andrew.'

157

He did not seem to hear, sitting with his head in his hands, quite still.

Ginny went back again. 'Look, I can't leave you like this. At least let me help you up to bed.'

He looked up and his eyes reminded her of the secret, limpid pools in the Lost Glen.

'Don't tempt a man,' he said softly.

In the event he did need a helping hand in getting to his feet and ascending the stairs; exhaustion, alcohol, the beating he had been given and the painkilling injection at the hospital combined to make him stagger slightly, giggle and not remember the way around his own living quarters. Once upstairs, though, Andrew McQuade became very serious indeed, rendered powerless by the scent of warm womankind in his nostrils and the touch of her hands unbuttoning his shirt.

Ginny, who was ready to make all kinds of allowances for him on account of the livid marks that were revealed all over his body, was not prepared for the impassioned and vivacious way she was taken in hand; nor, for that matter later, having been kissed in a fashion she had hardly dared hope for, to hear him chuckle. Then, his body warm and hard, he tumbled into her embrace.

'Sorry I laughed,' he said when he could speak afterwards. 'Somehow I never imagined you getting so randy.'

Moments later he was sound asleep.

Chapter Thirteen

Ginny was sitting in her own kitchen, clasping her second mug of tea, when the back door opened. She was not expecting visitors for it was only six thirty in the morning, a beautiful summer's morning, the sound of birdsong and a long shaft of sunlight also gaining entry.

The reason for everything being different now walked in. It was perfectly obvious that it was only his sheer stubbornness that was making this possible, because it was equally clear that Andrew McQuade could hardly put one foot in front of the other.

Ginny gave him some tea, or rather placed it on the table, ladled in two spoonfuls of sugar and stirred it for him. It was not pleasant watching his face as he sat down.

It was Tuesday morning. The previous day they had stayed in bed; this had had nothing to do with intimacy or friendship and certainly not lust. They had remained where they were for the simple reason that they both felt too ill to go anywhere else, too ill even to talk; Andrew rapidly becoming black and blue all over, Ginny suffering distressing after effects of the blow on the head. When she had suddenly woken, experiencing acute nausea, he had helped her to the bathroom and held her while she was very sick indeed. Her contribution to his recovery had been a consoling squeeze of his hand, an arm around his shoulder, when some kind of delayed shock reaction had hit him later. There is not a lot more women can do when men cry.

Andrew drank half the tea together with the two tablets she had also given him — they were sharing her painkillers,

Andrew having left the hospital before they could give him any – placed the mug back on the table and uttered a strange laugh, almost a snort, nearly a sob. Then he said, 'I'm beginning to wish I'd stayed in bed.'

'I had three visitors on Sunday night,' Ginny said.

'Well, obviously Murray and Pete. Who else?'

'John Laird. He said he'd had an anonymous phone call about us. D'you think Mackiver had a twinge of conscience and rang him in case we were in a ditch somewhere?'

'No, not a chance.'

'Andrew, you can't just dismiss the idea out of hand like that. My hotel booking was cancelled by a mystery man, if you remember.'

There were waves in the tea mug as it was slammed back onto the table. 'Look, I might have been flogged silly but I do *know* the guy. He doesn't possess a conscience, never has.'

'Who did it, then? One of the men with him?'

'If it had been their turn for the brain cell. Is there anything to eat?'

'Not a lot until I've been shopping. I can do you some toast.'

'As you can't make porridge I suppose that'll have to do.' She had put two slices of bread in the toaster, her back to him, when he said, 'Sorry. I'm not on a high like I was on Sunday night.'

A drug-induced high, Ginny thought, not at all sure of his present frame of mind. Well, perhaps their love making had had something to do with it, that half-hour or so of exhilaration and pleasure before the consequences of the day had fully taken their toll.

'We have to do as Rory suggested,' Andrew said into the quietness.

'Give up?'

Ginny badly wanted to ask what Rory had been doing there at all, how he was so closely acquainted with the facts of the case – but if Andrew didn't want to discuss it, she sensed it would be better to keep quiet.

'Yes.'

There was a long silence broken by Andrew saying, 'It's not because of what happened to me on Sunday. You were there too and I heard him threaten to kill you. He's quite

160

capable of it and also patient − perfectly happy to wait years if necessary until everyone has forgotten all about it. Even if you're given police protection they can't watch over you for ever.'

The toast popped up and, automatically, Ginny buttered it and spread it thickly with marmalade. Cutting each slice in half, she put it before him.

'Does Rory have a boat?'

'Yes, a ketch. It's much older than *Seawitch*. I suppose you could say that it's the ruling passion in his life. Ginny . . .'

'So it must have been anchored in the loch somewhere and he'd tied a small boat with an outboard motor to − '

'You're not listening,' Andrew interrupted.

She put two more slices into the toaster. 'You've never spoken about the fall you had in the mountains.'

Angrily he said, 'Don't you believe me? I've just said that it's nothing to do with that.'

'I do believe you.'

'But you're wondering why I didn't shit myself and burst into tears when I saw what they were about to do with me. Well, perhaps I exaggerated when I said I was too scared to climb onto the roof these days. Knoydart's Willy isn't difficult under normal circumstances. In fact *you* could get up it without much bother, provided you were roped to someone at the top and took your time. Having to climb down with no ropes and some maniac using you for target practice isn't much fun, though. That's why I decided to let go − before he could put a bullet in me just for the hell of it.'

'You *let go?*'

He touched the side of his head where the gash had had two stitches put in it. 'I reckoned the heather would break my fall. But I was a bit higher up than I thought − knocked myself out for a bit.'

Her toast was ready but Ginny sat still.

'Buachaille Etive Mor is different,' Andrew continued, but speaking more quietly. 'It's at the eastern end of Glencoe, a sort of sentinel, if you like, where Glen Etive branches off to the south. That's a bit simplistic but it'll do. In winter it's a beautiful big white hell and where we were climbing, Raven's Gully, can be hell plus. It was January and at about three thousand feet up it seemed as cold as a mountain in the Antarctic. A lot of ice, too much snow. It wasn't a filming job, I was taking still photographs of a guy and his friend who were writing a book together about ice techniques. I was responsible for all the illustrations except for a few drawings and diagrams that an artist was commissioned to do later. Most of mine were in the can and we were working on the last but one climb that the author had planned to do. And that afternoon there was a sudden thaw.

'It was the sort of murderous thing that a mountain like that can throw at you — sometimes you really do get the feeling that there's a malevolent something just waiting. And the little breeze that suddenly sprang up from the west was a real freak. All at once the temperature was ten degrees warmer and going up. The wall of ice we were on started to drip, then to trickle and before we could do much about it we were in a minor waterfall. The pitons I'd fixed myself securely with seemed to come out as though someone was pushing them from the other side. It was because the ice I'd hammered them into was melting. I started to do something about it but was distracted and made a mistake — there was a snowfall or something, I'm not sure exactly what happened. Someone shouted and then I was falling.'

'I shouldn't have asked,' Ginny whispered when he stopped speaking.

Andrew did not seem to hear. 'I bounced off something, mostly snow, and can distinctly remember feeling my legs break. Then I hit again and rolled for what seemed to be miles before another fall, a longer one. I just prayed for death to be quick. But it wasn't. I must have bounced at least twice more and each time I knew something else broke. It was like being battered to bits. I didn't pass out, not even after the last landing on my back in snow-covered heather surrounded by some bloody big boulders. If I ever have a daughter I think I'll call her Erica.'

'The others must have thought you were dead.'

'Most certainly they did. So they didn't rush down the mountain. I don't blame them — one slip and they'd have followed me down by the fastest route. And the best guy in the world was the one who filled me up with morphine when the rescue chopper arrived.'

'So was it luck that you survived?'

'What else? I saw someone fall half that distance and his shin bones came out through his shoulder blades. That's all I could think of when I woke up in hospital — that here was some kind of parcel of bits and pieces that would soon need a square coffin. It's always a joke, isn't it, the bloke totally encased in plaster?'

'It would have made a wonderful film,' Ginny said dreamily. 'Your rehabilitation.'

'The first faltering steps,' Andrew said derisively. 'Physiotherapy and exercises followed by our hero skipping up Everest wearing a Bog Filmorama sweatshirt. No, thanks. That sort of thing makes me want to throw up. Your toast is cold.'

'Were you good in bed before you fell off the mountain?'

The glower remained in place, 'Probably not. And that's a very odd question to ask a man at breakfast.' And when she carried on gazing at him, 'Woman, I can't even *walk,* never mind ...'

But he could and did, and Ginny, whose instincts were sound as far as things like rehabilitation were concerned, closed her mind to murder for a while, abandoning herself to what she regarded as the fruits of a good theory. She also tried to forget that soon he would probably think of her as no more than the girl he had met and made love to while he was getting better. Her own dreams of a future together were simply that — dreams.

London was in the throes of a thunderstorm of gigantic, almost tropical proportions; roads awash, the slow-moving traffic sending huge plumes of spray over hapless pedestrians, the incessant thunder succeeding in drowning out the sound of planes coming in to land at Heathrow Airport. It had, the taxi driver informed Ginny, been 'goin' 'ammer and tongs for over one and an arf hours'.

There was a pile of post behind the front door of her flat, mostly final demands or lucky numbers for bumper prize draws, the latter being immediately consigned to the waste bin in the kitchen. The remaining items consisted of a postcard from a friend on holiday in California, a letter from a woman whom her mother had known in Torquay wondering if Ginny was now in possession of what she referred to as a historic collection of knitting patterns, and a terse note from Jake containing expressions like 'in view of your present contract being almost at an end' and 'regretfully, failure to keep to agreed schedules ...'

At New Scotland Yard the guard on the security desk looked at her card without interest. 'They've gone home, luv.'

'They?' enquired Ginny, who had asked to speak to Commander Fielding.

'Nimrod. Your lot. They've gone home. The thunder was buggerin' up the soundtrack.'

As if to emphasise this, there was a great crump overhead and the lights dipped and flickered.

Ginny leaned on the desk. 'Just ask him if he'll see me.'

Dubiously, the man picked up the phone.

'I'm afraid I have to go out shortly,' Fielding said, drawing up a chair. He gave her a long, steady look. 'I see you've been hurt. I hope it was nothing serious.'

'Kicked in the head and threatened with death,' Ginny told him. 'I think I need a little advice. But what, commander, have you done with your Scottish accent?'

Demonstrating his level-headedness, Fielding answered the question first. 'It tends to be brought from the cupboard and dusted off sometimes.' He smiled. 'Perhaps when people are taking pictures of me and I want to promote my country a little.'

'And it amuses you.'

Again the same lazy smile. 'Och, aye.'

'Have you heard of a man called Rory McQuade?'

The smile remained in place but the blue-grey eyes became flinty. 'I think you ought to tell me the whole story.'

He remained passively listening while Ginny did so, making no notes, not interrupting, and when she had finished he sat frowning thoughtfully for a few moments.

Ginny said, 'It was probably a mistake on my part to confront the two Americans with what I knew — I was very angry at the time.'

Fielding pressed a button on his desk intercom and told someone he would be a little late for his next appointment. Then he said, 'Well, I can put your mind at rest about one thing, Miss Somerville. Rory McQuade is not implicated in this at all. No one by that name is connected with any known terrorist organisation.'

'Implicated!' Ginny gasped in amazement. 'Of course he's not implicated! I'd assumed that he was either working for you or Special Branch.'

The commander gazed at the ceiling and then out of the window. 'You're a very astute young woman. But I can't deny or confirm anything.'

'You already knew most of it.'

'Yes. But not the aftermath, not what they did to McQuade's son.'

'And the father I suppose was in the right place at the right time and having had dealings with Mackiver in the past, has been approached to help put him behind bars this time?'

'Mr McQuade is a bona fide businessman — any other interests he may have are not for me to reveal. As to this affair of the wooden shapes, you will appreciate I have some *very* good links with members of the Strathclyde Police. They contacted me as soon as they had the preliminary findings concerning the explosion. People who make bombs, as I'm sure you know already, no matter how careful they are, leave clues to their identity in the manner the devices are constructed. Minute clues, things that can only be spotted under a microscope. The one that killed Morag Galloway and her friend was made by the same man who was responsible for a parcel bomb here in London that blew off a woman's hands and severely injured her five-year-old daughter. Can you give me any clue to the identity of the man with Miss Galloway?'

Ginny shook her head. 'Sorry, no. Has no one been reported as missing?'

'In Glasgow? Several. All we know is that he was white, between twenty and thirty years old and with dark-brown hair. As far as this particular investigation is concerned, I don't think this person's identity, when it's established, will provide vital clues, because like you, I think the woman took the shapes because she wanted to see what, if anything, was in them. Their late arrival at the gallery was fairly public, after all.'

'They were meant to kill Andrew and me.'

'Yes, I think it's fairly safe to assume that you were the intended targets.'

'So what *might* have been in them? I take it that whatever it is is very valuable and ends up as funds for terrorists.'

'I've said too much already,' Fielding said. 'I simply can't jeopardise the operation to catch these people – and we still have a murderer on the loose.'

'The art works are being returned tomorrow,' Ginny pointed out in challenging fashion.

'Stay away from the institute,' Fielding warned. 'It's thanks to you that we have a lot of background information and for you to do more would be to put your life seriously at risk. I can't allow that.'

Ginny picked up her bag from the floor. 'Even nice policemen have a way of talking like lists of rules and regulations.'

The merest crack appeared in the commander's composure. 'Lassie, do you think I would relish seeing them collecting pieces of your body from the gutter like they did with that other unfortunate woman?'

'No, obviously not,' Ginny said. 'And I'm sorry that people have been killed. But if she had shared her suspicions instead of doing what she did, she would be alive today. Good afternoon, commander.'

'I can't give you a role in this,' he said when her hand was on the doorknob. 'It's more than my job's worth.'

'I know that. I think my motives in this have a lot to do with wanting to clear my father's name and find out who hid a body in his house.'

'I really don't know how I can help you,' Fielding observed gently.

'Just tell me where I can find Rory McQuade. I want to ask him a few questions.'

'You must appreciate that this man isn't on our payroll and we don't have personal details about him as we would with an employee. For most of the time he goes his own way, working primarily from his home in Ireland and I'm not going to give you the address. It's obvious that by doing so I would be endangering you both. You asked me for my advice and it's this: take some time off to enable yourself to recover. Go somewhere quiet, well away from Kinloch Ruthven.'

That was all rather disappointing, of course. Despite her choice of words Ginny had arrived at her conviction that Rory McQuade was using his eyes and ears for the benefit of the police only moments before Commander Fielding had confirmed it. The fact that he was already in possession of almost all the information she had gone on to give him, third-hand, it now appeared, was a bit of a shock.

Ginny felt it important to stay away from Andrew. For one thing it seemed that all roads led to Kevin Mackiver and she did not want to give him an excuse to vent more anger on his one-time business partner's son. That he harboured an enormous and vicious resentment was not in doubt. Andrew himself would stay at home, still hurting too much to do anything else.

Oddly, Fielding's advice had not touched on whether they ought to press charges against the landowner for assault or even attempted murder. Perhaps he expected her to realise that such a premature move, involving crimes to which there were no independent witnesses, would only throw the police investigation into disarray.

Nimrod Productions was unaccountably thronging with people; journalists, one or two assistant heads of programming from UK television networks, the chief executive of a cable company and several others, foreigners whom Ginny did not know at all. Once on the second floor she was immediately buttonholed by a tall, broad man whose accent suggested he was from the American Midwest.

'Say, honey, if you don't mind my saying so, that is one *hell* of a bruise you have on your head.'

In a clear, carrying sort of voice Ginny said, 'A penalty

of the job, I'm afraid. We at Nimrod tend to tackle subjects that larger, better-known companies find too controversial. But of course the compensation is knowing you're working for the cream of the industry — being right there as history is being made.'

He nodded sagely. 'Let me get you a drink.' And with that he made his way through the crowd in Jake's office like an icebreaker.

Ginny followed. Conversation faltered and most heads turned.

'My dear!' Jake crowed, having heard her voice. 'Ladies and gentlemen, allow me to introduce our youngest producer, Ginny Somerville, a rising star indeed.'

The Texan, with proprietorial tenderness, pressed upon Ginny a glass of sparkling wine — Jake was too parsimonious to buy champagne for such gatherings — and a plate of minute cocktail sandwiches. 'I hope, Jake old buddy, that you don't make life too dangerous for Ginny here. Investigative producers where I come from tend to be big men who pack some mean-looking hardware.'

Jake's face assumed a jolly man-to-man expression and he opened his mouth to speak. But Ginny spoke first.

'What do you think,' she asked the Texan, 'of a story about murder, feuding and kinky works of art set in the Highlands of Scotland?'

'Great! Who's writing it?'

'No one. It isn't fiction. It's happening now.' Ginny was aware that Jake's eyes were popping slightly.

'And I take it you have insider knowledge about this.'

Ginny smiled enigmatically. 'Oh, yes.'

'How many murders? Have there been any arrests? Do you need funding?'

'Four, no and yes.'

'Hey, wait a minute ...' Jake began.

'Don't cramp the lady's style,' the Texan told him. To Ginny he said, 'Give me a date and time when you're free to talk about this. I'm over here until the day after tomorrow for this awards ceremony most of us are attending.'

They had been speaking quietly but the hush that had descended upon the room at Ginny's entry — for it really

168

was a most spectacular bruise – had been maintained and half the room had been unashamedly eavesdropping. Then the protests started.

'Why should he get preferential treatment?'

'Surely a British company should get to hear of this first?'

'British? Why not a Scottish one?'

'The Yanks always shove their noses in.'

Barry Chichester pushed his way to the front. 'This is better, Jake. Just now you were talking about the history of shipbuilding in the West Country and the lives of famous trade-unionists.' He kissed Ginny's cheek. 'Hi, kid. Someone hit you on the head with Ailsa Craig?'

Jake was looking at Ginny pleadingly. 'Look, that letter I sent you ...'

'I tore it up,' she said.

Barry winked at Ginny. 'Not the letter offering you a new contract for the programmes about the Mounted Branch while I tackle my new project?'

'Yes, I've had a re-think,' Jake yelped. 'Six months' work at least. And a trip to Ireland where they buy the horses.'

'Now it seems to me,' said the Texan slowly, frowning with ferocious concentration at the teddy bear mascot on Jake's desk that he usually hid when there were visitors, 'that a lady can sometimes be a bit too independent.'

'No,' Ginny said. 'I'd prefer to have an office in Edinburgh and concentrate on making the highest-quality programmes, both fact and fiction, about Scotland, the Borders and the north of England. With the broadest possible subject matter, naturally, but an overall emphasis on wildlife and environmental issues.'

'There's no demand for that kind of thing – ' Jake started to say but was interrupted by a voice outside shouting down the stairwell to the receptionist.

'Hey, miss, did you say the *second* floor?'

'Oh, brother,' whispered the Texan moments later. 'Doesn't he stir the blood of a man whose forebears fought at Culloden?'

'Sorry to butt in,' Andrew McQuade said apologetically.

169

He saw Ginny. 'Ah, found you. There are developments that you ought to know about.'

Even though he was dressed in a plain green sweater with his best kilt, he still looked as though he was straight off the set of *Rob Roy*.

Chapter Fourteen

Ginny was forced to contain her impatience with regard to their escape from the social gathering – what Alvis always referred to as 'Jake's at homes' – for their flight was by no means immediate. In fact, she found her urgent need for information that had warranted a journey of several hundred miles overshadowed by the fear that his nerve would break in the company of this pack of commercial wolves. But within five minutes he had proved that he could say no to hazardous undertakings, turning down involvement in a film about climbing the Old Man of Hoy, and rebuffing a couple of other similar suggestions.

Finally, when most of the guests were on their way to pre-dinner drinks somewhere else, she gave Jake his answer.

'I've promised Andrew he can work for me,' she said quietly. 'So, as much as I'd like to carry on with such prestigious work, I'm afraid I must decline.'

'But – '

'It's your own fault, Jake, and you know it. You shouldn't try to mix business with what you'd call pleasure.'

He took a fierce swig from his wineglass and almost choked. 'Well, er . . . I suppose . . . You say he's a wildlife cameraman. Animals, that kind of thing?'

'Fresh-air subjects,' Ginny said. 'You know, the stuff you never go out in.'

He gave her a sickly smile. 'Barry's waved the magic wand since he got back to work. Landed a job with Yorkshire Televison about public schools – he's doing it with Alvis.

It'll mean we can expand a bit. If this Andrew McQuade can work with horses ...'

'Why don't you ask him?'

'Ginny ... Look, right, I was a bit of a bastard. But you're a mite young to branch out on your own yet. Can't we talk about this?'

'The gentleman from Texas was interested in what I had to say. *He* didn't seem to think my age was an obstacle.'

Barry and Andrew joined them, the former dragging up chairs so they could all be seated. By this time they were the only ones present.

'Take an old man's advice, Ginny, and stick with us for a bit,' Barry said. 'Your Scottish horror story might be just the thing for a true-crime series I'm planning − several companies have expressed an interest. That's if you give me your permission, of course.'

Andrew turned to Ginny. 'Barry's offered me a job − a short contract − for a film about the Mounted Branch. What do you think? It would mean filming in Ireland ...'

'But she's − ' Jake began.

'I think it's a wonderful idea,' Ginny said quickly.

Andrew promised to let him know by the following morning and he and Ginny left, the former leading the way to a pub in Lamb's Conduit Street.

'Two things really,' he began, after taking an uncharacteristically small sip of single malt. 'We hadn't checked the camera. They must have seen it in the Land Rover because they'd removed the film. I'm really only mad about that because of the shots of you and the calf. And the camera's damaged − they must have chucked it back in the Land Rover overarm. I posted it back to the shop where you bought it with a request for a quote for repair − I told them it had been vandalised. The second thing is that I got a phone call from the institute asking me to call in. The trustees have sent someone to take charge until another director's appointed. A real creep of a mannie he was, who looked at me over his glasses as though I was something the dog had just sicked up. And he said − and I'll try to get it just right, "Weel no be needin' ye noo, laddie, as the garden's going to be grassed. No more neeps and tatties." Then he gave me the wages owed to me plus a hundred pounds, "severance money" he called it. If I hadn't been flat broke I'd have thrown it back in his face.' Realising that his listener was merely blinking at him solemnly in response to this, he exploded with, 'The man's a *phoney!* His accent was theatre Scots, straight out of some crap so-called comedy turn where Sassenach shits put on kilts and − ' He broke off, downed the rest of his drink in one and went to the bar for another. When he returned he was off the boil. 'I'm not saying he's *not* Scottish, just that his way of speaking wasn't natural.'

'But why? Why should he wish to disguise the way he spoke?'

'No idea. He might have done it for a laugh − the normally cultured man addressing the hairy gardener. But the thing is − I'm sure I've seen him somewhere before.'

'Really? Did you ever find out who the trustees are?'

'No. And the police still have all the files.'

'I think it's important that we do. I could ask John Laird.'

'Murray was there, sort of hanging about.'

'I confronted him and Pete with what had happened to Morag. I wish I hadn't now because if they're not involved I might have unwittingly put them in danger.'

'You mean they might start asking questions?'

'Yes. Murray was convincingly angry that his shapes were being used to kill people. Andrew, I'll be honest with you. This morning I went to see a very senior policeman I know and told him everything.'

'I see,' Andrew said evenly. 'Did he know any of it already?'

'Just about everything.'

He shouted with laughter.

'How do you get in touch with Rory?'

Eyes still sparkling with mirth Andrew said, 'Ah, you really are a genius. I don't − he gets in touch with me.'

Furiously Ginny said, 'I think your father's quite capable of telling the police only half the story if it suited him. I assume he's watching Mackiver and has been for quite a long time.'

'Only now and then. Most of the time he watches far

173

more dangerous men — on the other side of the Irish Sea. Mackiver is a pot that is bubbling gently, more of a personal thing. He'll wait until he's ready.'

'Does he know what happened to you?'

'Yes, he rang me last night. He'll probably sink the *Seawitch* with all hands.'

'And as I said to Commander Fielding, the stuff is being returned from the gallery tomorrow — ' She saw that he was grinning. 'I suppose you'd laugh like hell if he *did* sink it. I wish you'd take this more seriously.'

'I found myself getting a bit serious about it all when they were thrashing the shit out of me.' He stood up. 'Shall we go? I'm going to take you out to dinner because I'm rolling in cash.'

'But how did you — ' Ginny pushed up the left cuff of his sweater. 'You've sold your watch,' she said in dismay.

'Why not? It's only a chunk of metal that tells the time. It was the first thing I did when I hit town.'

'So is it to be decided on the toss of a coin?' Ginny said later that night. 'Heads we obey all the commands, requests, and threats and from now on mind our own business; tails, we carry on sleuthing.'

Andrew loaded his coffee cup with brown sugar. 'Spoken like a true Brit film producer.'

'Okay, that was a bit of a corny thing to say. Perhaps I've had a drop too much wine. What do you think?'

'Me? I just want to lie down and sleep until all my aches and pains have gone away. But instinct tells me to fly home and follow that courier's van all the way back to Kinloch Ruthven. We don't know what the police are going to do, if anything, because they declined to tell us. They might even screw it up — that's not unknown. And I agree with you about Pete and Murray. The pair of them seem a bit naive, though, too trusting, and that makes me want to keep an eye on them.'

'Murray liked Malcolm Hurrell, didn't he?'

'Yes, Hurrell gave him a lot of help.'

'This man who's temporarily running the institute — what's his name?'

'Bloxton. I think he said he was a solicitor. He may even be one of the trustees for all I know.'

They drank their coffee in silence for a moment or two, Ginny covertly watching him. There was no doubt that the stamina and resilience he had once relied upon in the mountains were now being put to use in order to keep him functioning in the most basic fashion. How long would his strength last?

There were just two spare seats on the first shuttle the next morning. It seemed auspicious. Once in Glasgow, they did not make the mistake of going directly to the gallery. Ginny phoned Sally Barnes as soon as it opened at nine thirty. Sally reported that the courier was supposed to be coming at ten and that he would not be long in loading up as she and her husband had packed everything the night before into the boxes the exhibits had arrived in. She did not question Ginny's enquiry, no doubt assuming that, being connected with the Institute of Art in some vague way, she was wondering what time the van would arrive in Kinloch Ruthven.

'Your vehicle is a positive danger,' she told Andrew, returning to the table in the small café where they were having coffee. 'It sticks out like a sore thumb — everyone'll know you're in the area. We ought to just take my car.'

'Well I'm not leaving the Land Rover here,' he said. 'It's my only asset right now.'

'Don't you have a friend you could leave it with?'

'No, and all the car parks are around five pounds a minute. You keep close to the van and I'll stay well back.'

The van was so prompt that it almost took them unawares, the driver racing into the gallery and loading up like a man possessed. Unfortunately he also drove in such a fashion, heading for the motorway as though the challenge was to go through as many red lights as possible. Grimly, Ginny followed, expecting to hear the sirens of traffic police in her wake at any moment.

There had been no sign of any police surveillance near the gallery, not even undercover watchfulness in the shape of men digging up the road or repairing telephone cables. There was no sign now; cars in front of her and behind

175

turned off at various junctions and others joined, no vehicle staying close to the white van that was now doing a steady seventy-five miles an hour.

Ginny was not expecting to see Andrew and had an idea that he was not trying to keep up this speed. No thirteen-year-old Land Rover in dire need of maintenance should be asked to perform such heroics. It was probably parked somewhere on the hard shoulder right now, smoking like a traction engine, she concluded unhappily.

She had never felt so lonely in her life.

When they left the motorway, Ginny had to be far more careful, making sure that several cars were between her own and the van. Very unexpectedly it stopped in Luss outside a small store that sold hot food and she had no choice but to drive right past and wait in the car park of a craft shop farther along the road, praying that she would not be noticed. The man took his time and when he emerged from the shop he was carrying what looked like a couple of cans of soft drink and an unidentified something in a paper bag, which he proceeded to eat hungrily, leaning against the side of the van. Then he lit a cigarette, climbed aboard and drove off. Ginny buried her face in a road map as he went past, then threw it aside and set off after him.

A few miles farther on, before they reached Tarbet, the van slowed and stopped again, this time in a lay-by overlooking Loch Lomond. Ginny overtook and was forced to drive right out of sight of it until she came to another parking place where she could pull off the road. What the hell was the man doing?

She was wondering whether to risk going back on foot, ten minutes having elapsed, when Andrew's Land Rover roared past, braked hard and reversed back into the lay-by. He left the engine running and hurried over to her.

'There's no time to change it now — you'll have to leave it here and come with me.'

Ginny stared at him uncomprehendingly.

'You've got a flat tyre. Isn't that why you stopped?'

'No. I hadn't noticed. I stopped because the van did.'

'He's topping up the radiator with water from the loch. It must be overheating.'

176

At that moment the van went by.

The tyre wasn't absolutely flat but quite useless to drive on, so Ginny had no choice but to do as Andrew suggested. She was sure the vehicle would be broken into and everything of value stolen before she saw it again.

They began the long climb into the mountains and soon their quarry was right out of sight, Andrew cursing the Land Rover as it struggled up every steep incline and crooning to it on the more level sections when it picked up speed.

'If the cylinder-head gasket blows we've had it,' he said by way of explanation for not pushing it to its limit up a particularly severe gradient.

'What exactly are you expecting to happen?' Ginny asked.

'I'm not sure. But if the police rig a road block with a view to searching the van for whatever, it's possible that the ungodly might turn up with larger forces. I mean, surely we're talking about organised crime here − only real criminals and terrorists plant bombs.'

'Quite. Otherwise Commander Fielding wouldn't have become involved.'

'I feel bad about Morag. We should have called out, stopped her. If we had, she and her friend wouldn't have died.'

'It makes it even more important to catch whoever killed her,' Ginny muttered.

But the van was miles ahead of them now. They lapsed into silence which was broken only once, by Andrew as they drove through Glencoe.

'That one − on your left. No, the highest peak. Buachaille Etive Mor. It looks quite innocent at this time of year.' He averted his gaze from the mountain and concentrated on driving.

There was hardly any traffic and in the wild vastness of the glen it seemed as though they were the only living beings in the world; just two people and a Land Rover wending their way through the emptiness.

'What does a green light mean?' Ginny asked.

'It means that unless I stop at the next filling station, which is quite a long way from here, and give this rust bucket about three pints of oil, the engine'll seize solid. But don't worry — it won't happen.'

'No?' Ginny said dubiously.

'No. We've just past the highest point so it's all downhill from here. With a bit of luck and a prayer and if I keep an eye on the temperature gauge ... She's okay, though, running cool as a cucumber.'

Ginny said a small prayer right then, just to be on the safe side.

'There's about a pint of petrol left too,' he added.

The fuel ran out a good mile from the filling station but it was all gently downhill and minutes later they rolled serenely into the forecourt.

'We're in luck,' Andrew reported when he returned from paying the attendant. 'He's still having problems with the van and stopped for more water. A leaking hose, apparently. He's only a few minutes in front of us.'

Ginny said, 'It's all a bit strange. We haven't seen anyone. No one's monitoring the van at all.'

Andrew thrust some packets of sandwiches at her. 'No, it's probably a red herring and we've been chasing after several empty crates.'

The sense of anticlimax increased with every mile that brought them closer to Kinloch Ruthven. Then, at the top of a rise as they approached the shores of Loch Linnhe, they saw a small white dot in the distance just in front of two large lorries. Andrew sent the Land Rover down the hill like a charging warhorse.

It proved impossible to overtake the lorries, which were heavily loaded with concrete pipes, and when they reached the village the main street was as quiet as a Sunday afternoon, with no sign of the vehicle they were following.

'Well, where *is* the bloody thing?' Andrew exploded when he had pulled up on the top of the hill near the church, which afforded a good view of the road that now continued in the direction of Bridge of Corran. For as far as the eye could see there was no traffic at all.

'Go back and try the track up to the institute,' Ginny suggested.

'But you can see the front of the building from way back

there. There were cars parked but no white ones.'

'Isn't there any way it could have gone round the back?'

'No, not unless he drove through a hedge and several bushes.' With a groan he turned the vehicle round.

As they reached the road junction a car emerged from it, driven at great speed, the back wheels slewing on the rough ground and sending small stones rattling against the side of a bus shelter. It accelerated away in the direction from which Andrew and Ginny had just come, narrowly missing them as it did so.

'That was Murray's car!' Andrew shouted, preparing to give chase.

Ginny grabbed his arm. 'There's the van!'

It was stationary, parked at an angle across the track, the windscreen smashed, the rear doors gaping wide. The driver, recognisable by his bright-red sweater, lay face down on the ground. Another man was flat on his back just in front of the gates to the Old Manse. The vehicle's load, or part of it, was scattered on the verge.

'Take care!' Andrew warned as Ginny ran over to the man by the gates. Then he swore and also got out, tired, all the adrenaline gone.

Ginny was checking the other man. 'They're both out cold,' she said.

'I think I'd worked that out all by myself,' Andrew said acidly. 'It must have been Murray, with Pete probably, he'd never have overpowered them both by himself. Take a look at the size of the stone that was thrown through the windscreen. It's like a bloody cromlech. That has to be Pete. I can't believe it. Murray, yes, but not that nice-guy friend of his. And they've taken the crate with Murray's shapes.'

'So we phone for an ambulance,' Ginny said, opening one of the gates. Incidentally, this chap here is armed. He's wearing a shoulder harness under his sweater with what looks very much to me like a police-issue revolver in it.'

'Where the hell's their backup then?' Andrew raged.

'Arriving shortly,' Ginny said, hearing the sound of sirens in the distance.

'So who's *this* bloke then?'

179

'A colleague, probably, who was inside the van all the time.'

'God help me,' Andrew muttered. 'I'm going to be arrested again.'

'I doubt it,' said a voice. 'Not with the police in their chopper watching you all the way from Glasgow.'

Rory was leaning on a gate on the opposite side of the track.

'You're unreal, you know that?' Andrew yelled at him. 'I suppose you lurked here waiting for the ambush.'

'Something like that,' Rory acknowledged. 'The question is, are you going to hang around and help the boys in blue with their enquiries?' He gazed at his son coolly. 'You're a big boy now, Andy.'

The driver of the van sat up and groaned.

Ginny glanced towards him; when she turned back, Rory had gone. In the next moment Andrew had taken her hand and was bustling her over the gate and, at a run, across a field. There was another gate on the far side of it that opened into a lane, a narrow, winding way with high banks on either side that led up to the farm near the institute. That was the way they went, after Ginny, protesting, had been virtually pushed by Andrew into Rory's car: a black Range Rover, very expensively appointed.

'All I hope,' she said heatedly, 'is that everyone's not chasing another little parcel of Semtex and Murray and Pete aren't a smoking hole in the road right now.'

'Ah, no,' Rory answered caressingly. 'It's diamonds, *mo ghaiol,* diamonds.'

Chapter Fifteen

A prolonged, somewhat brittle silence was broken by Rory. He cleared his throat and said, 'It would appear that Jean Kirkpatrick didn't have an auntie.'

Ginny said, 'And she didn't have that watch either?'

'No. The only one in her possession was a cheap one that had broken some three weeks before her death.'

'And no one at the institute noticed?'

'The absence of the one from the mythical aunt? No, the husband's story was that she only wore it on special occasions – the party at the institute being one of those times. He was lying. It was bought second-hand from a jeweller's in Glasgow the morning after she disappeared – and I'm assuming she was murdered on the night of that party.'

'Did he tell you all this?'

'After I offered to break his neck if he didn't come up with the truth. No woman living with him would have in her possession for long so much as a brass curtain ring, according to local feeling in the village. It's the sort of house, I was assured, where the social workers wipe their feet on the way *out*. That was probably a cruel exaggeration while the poor soul was alive, but now she's dead ...'

'So he lied to the police?'

'He was paid to do so. By a man in a pub, according to him – and I should imagine he's been threatened with a fate worse even than a broken neck if he names names. As far as the jewellery shop's concerned, the trail's gone cold there too – which is not surprising. It's quite a while ago now and people forget.'

181

The lane had petered out in the farmyard but by opening a gate and bouncing across a small paddock used solely for dumping hardcore they had gained access to the open moorland and the track over Ruthven Loan. Behind them they could still hear the frenzied barking of several half-starved collies, chained in the yard.

'I shouldn't imagine that the watch was hidden in the Coach House until quite a while afterwards,' Rory said. 'Almost certainly they had already decided who was going to be framed for the killing — the local ragamuffin odd-job man who spent most of the time sozzled at the Dog and Drover.'

Andrew said nothing, his whole body taut with anger.

'And now you've come along, my dear,' Rory continued, 'and no doubt restored his self-esteem in at least one direction.'

'You're a callous bastard,' Ginny said quietly.

'Perhaps I am. But what do you do when your own flesh and blood spurns all offers of help, tells you to go to hell, in fact? What you *don't* do is give him what he really wants — money — so he can drink himself to death. If his stupid mother hadn't paid the rent on the house he'd have come to his senses a lot earlier, for the simple reason that he'd have been skint.'

They were skimming over the open moor, not on the track itself but an ancient drove road, little more now than a gently curving turfy smoothness among heather and boulders, Rory driving as though familiar with every inch of it.

He said, 'I must admit to being taken slightly by surprise by the attack on the van. The police didn't think anything would happen to it, but I reasoned that if an attack *were* mounted, that would be the place; a tight turn into an unmade road where the driver would be concentrating on what he was doing but at a stage of the journey where he would have been relaxed, no longer watchful. No, official thinking was that the exhibits would be returned to the institute where they would stay for a couple of weeks and then be quietly loaded onto the *Seawitch,* ostensibly for an art show in Belfast. That's exactly what happened last year, only that was a dummy run.'

'And it's diamonds,' Ginny said.

'Yes. Let's just say that a bunch of Irish crooks are living in Glasgow for no other purpose than to raise funds for a certain league of terrorists. In January they scooped the jackpot when they smashed their way into a large private house in Milngavie and made off with a safe. The house belonged to a diamond dealer with a business in Edinburgh. I don't know why he kept his wares at home, probably thought it safer. It was a fluke from the point of view of the burglars – insider knowledge appears to be out of the question.'

'There must be insider knowledge with regards to the gang, though,' Ginny said urbanely.

'Ah, yes. A snout, call him what you will. Otherwise everyone would have remained in sweet ignorance about what was going on. And now it looks as though a murderer – or murderers – has stepped in and thrown a small spanner in the works. I can only assume that their share of the proceeds is not to their liking.'

'It might be my fault,' Ginny confessed. 'I told Murray and Pete about Morag taking away a couple of the shapes and that one of them must have contained explosives. If either or both of them suspected that the police were on to them they might have decided to intercept the diamonds and run.'

'Well, the long arm of the law can catch up with them. I'm more interested in what will happen when the others with their fingers in the pie realise that someone's snatched the booty.'

'If that wasn't the agreed plan.'

'Do you think it was?'

'Not on reflection.'

'Do you think the Americans *are* involved?'

'Well, Murray did mention in passing that Pete had been making some of the shapes for him. And if you think along the lines of Jean noticing that the wooden and polystyrene cutouts were hollow and things could be hidden inside ... She might even have overheard them talking about it. Perhaps she tried to blackmail them, saying she'd tell Hurrell or the police if they didn't give her money. Both Pete and Murray were at the party and, as we know, Pete could strangle a woman with one hand and have absolutely no difficulty in taking the body down to the Old Manse and hiding it in the basement. A member of the gang in Glasgow could have bought the watch and posted it to Kinloch Ruthven and either of the Americans could have sneaked it into Andrew's bedroom.'

'Did you get any man-to-man feedback of what happened after the party?' Rory asked Andrew.

'Only that Jean welcomed allcomers on a pile of hay in the potting shed,' Andrew replied shortly.

'Who was she last seen with?'

'God knows. They were all too drunk, or pretended to be too drunk, to remember.'

'One has to bear in mind that Dr Hurrell was murdered too,' Ginny said. 'Everyone knows that Pete was in the main ring just then in the tug-of-war team but Murray's whereabouts are a mystery. I don't *think* we can lay that killing at Murray's door. But Kevin Mackiver was in the area − Ninian Effrick of Effrick saw him − and I think we all realise that he's somehow part of it.'

'He might not know anything about terrorism. The man charters the boat for a few weeks at the end of the summer. But go on.'

'If you really want my opinion − no, I don't think Murray and Pete are involved with murder. It's just a gut feeling − I can't explain my reasons.'

'Female intuition,' Rory muttered. 'You disappoint me. I thought you knew something that I didn't.'

'She does,' Andrew said with a hint of rancour. 'Plenty.'

According to Rory there were so many police watching *Seawitch* that the yacht would run aground on them if anyone tried to sail it out of the loch. As far as Ginny was concerned, she doubted that Mackiver would be so stupid. She also doubted, in the wake of four killings, whether the diamond shipment was still taking place, wondering how the police had successfully gained possession of the van and how an addition had been made to Murray's sculpture without anyone noticing.

From a point on the old drove road they struck out across the open moorland and then joined another track, a deeply rutted Forestry Commission access road that finally descended, heart-stoppingly steeply, into Glen Nevis. The road twisted and turned, ever going down through a long tunnel of sitka spruce. All was dead and dark beneath the trees, bright light only where a group had been felled, neat piles of sawn trunks in small clearings.

When they reached the road at the bottom Rory turned left, and only half a mile farther on he turned left again, straight up another rough road into the forest. After another journey through the trees they emerged into the open air, the road curving gently to the right. And then, bouncing over a rise, they saw a great spread of countryside opened out before them; pasture and parkland straight ahead and to the left bounded by more forest, Loch Linnhe sapphire blue and sparkling below to the right, the black tower like a broken chimney jutting up on the high ground above. In the centre of it all was Muirpark.

'The back way in,' Rory murmured. 'You will observe that Knoydart's Willy looks quite different from this direction.'

'I just hope you packed a flak jacket,' Andrew said.

'That isn't necessary. I have my own reasons for not going any closer. But I think that Murray with or without his large friend will come here – they're probably here already, in fact. According to the scatterbrained lady who used to live with me as my wife – and this little titbit of gossip is via her sister Fiona – Kevin has been cultivating the American for reasons that she does not know about. Knowing him rather well I should say it has a lot to do with wanting to look cultured. Unfortunately he wouldn't recognise culture if it hit him over the head with a leaded sock in the street. Kevin bought one of Murray's nightmare jigsaw arrangements. If Murray believes he's in some sort of danger or difficulty, he might try to put himself under the wing of someone he sees as a wealthy, powerful patron. And that might not be in his better interests at all.'

'You said that the police are following them,' Andrew reminded him.

Rory scanned the sky. 'Can you see them? Or hear a

185

helicopter, for that matter? No, I think something has gone wrong in that direction.'

'Contact the police watching the boat,' Ginny suggested.

'Not easy. It was agreed that radio silence would be kept and in any case I don't have a radio, only a phone. And I have no intention of driving down to the jetty and drawing attention to either myself or the surveillance.'

'Someone might have already spotted us from the house,' Andrew persevered.

'Only if they were looking this way through binoculars. It's unlikely – only forestry vehicles and pony trekkers come this way normally and it has the advantage that you can immediately see anyone who comes from the house in this direction.'

Ginny said, 'But because we can only see the back of the house it's impossible to tell whether Murray's car's parked at the front.'

Rory gave her a straight look. 'You of all people should know that real life is never like some concoction from Hollywood. And I am here as a private observer, not organising anything.'

'So I suppose I'd better go down there and make sure that Murray and Pete aren't having the thumbscrews used on them,' Andrew said, opening the car door.

'I was rather hoping you would,' Rory said with a grin.

'But what can he do if they are?' Ginny protested.

'Not a lot,' Rory answered. 'But the police can't be far away.'

'I'm coming too,' Ginny said, joining Andrew on the sun-warmed turf.

'I was specifically asked to keep you in one piece,' Rory told her.

Normally Ginny did not use bad language but now she informed Rory what she thought of him in words that caused him, tight-lipped, to reverse the vehicle away from them towards the cover of some trees.

'I had a notion I was brought along as cannon fodder,' Andrew said, setting off down the hill.

'Is he always like that?'

'For as long as I can remember. Once when I was a kid

and we were anchored out on the boat, my mother dropped a silk scarf over the side. He tied a length of rope around my waist and lowered me into the water so I could retrieve it for her. I was six years old and couldn't swim properly then. In January, too!'

'I'm surprised you survived childhood.'

'It's probably why I survived the fall off the mountain,' Andrew said softly. 'And I think I've accepted now that you can't live up to everyone's expectations.'

Ginny stopped walking. 'Andrew, what we're doing is rather stupid.'

'I know. But yours truly's fieldcraft isn't that bad. The old man was right when he said that we were unlikely to be seen coming from this direction. There are hardly any windows on this side of the house and the few there are have the view of this section of hillside blotted out by the big barn. If we follow this burn down the hill and walk almost in the water, the banks will screen us from anyone looking this way.' He took her hand to steady her as they circumnavigated some large rocks and then pulled her to him, put his arms around her and kissed her. Then he said, 'He was right about my self-esteem as far as *this* sort of thing's concerned.'

The burn joined another, larger one; now a shallow river, it bubbled and murmured down towards the floor of the valley between alders and shrubby willows. The water-worn stones at the sides, flat on top and in places resembling rough paving slabs, were easy to walk on. Where these were replaced by large round boulders, the two traversed the dry tops of rocks on the riverbed like stepping stones. It was hot, quiet and there were a lot of biting insects.

The riverbanks became higher and steeper until they were walking through a miniature gorge. Soon, by a tumble of rocks — a landslip where a huge beech tree had been blown down, bringing much of a section of bank with it — they scrambled out, using the branches of the tree, still living, as handholds. The leaves hid them from sight of the house, which was necessary now, for they were only fifty yards from it.

Andrew said, 'I'd feel happier in my mind if I knew

whose cars were parked out front. Murray and Pete might be halfway to Aberdeen by now for all we know.'

'Quite,' Ginny replied.

Just then a dreadful scream rang out.

'Wait!' Andrew hissed as Ginny prepared to run towards the house.

Again there was that awful hoarse cry.

'Look, we've got to − '

'It's not coming from the house,' Andrew interrupted. 'Whoever it is is out in the open somewhere.'

'Or in the barn? There are no doors on it.'

'The barn,' he decided. 'Make for the rear of it − there's an opening high up into what used to be the hayloft.'

They ran, Ginny expecting at any moment to be blasted with shotgun pellets. As soon as they reached the barn, Andrew hefted her like a sack of carrots into an ancient ivy that had its roots somewhere around the other side of the building. Its gnarled, mossy ropes had crept and fingered their way until they nearly covered the upper walls and were now in the process of lifting the roof off in slow motion.

It was not a good moment to voice utter panic when her weight tore a whole handful of stems from their grip on the wall or to react in any way when, within the barn, the man screamed again.

'Get a move on,' Andrew said under his breath, right behind her. 'The quicker you move, the less likely it will give way.' He then overtook her, climbing like a monkey to the opening and pulling himself into it. Above it, the old hoist apparatus was still in place but, together with the remains of the shutters on each side, it looked as though it might crash to the ground at any moment.

The loft, still with a few mouldy bales of hay on the floor, covered only a fraction of the roof space, most of the wooden boarding having rotted and fallen into the main area of the barn some twenty feet below. The oak beams were still sound, though, and Andrew silently indicated to Ginny that she should tread only where he did, following the row of nails he had exposed on the floor. This was practical only in certain directions, of course; crossing areas in between the beams, things became a little more difficult. In the end they crawled.

They had almost reached a position where they could see what was happening below when Kevin Mackiver spoke, his voice rough with anger.

'Ask the fool again. I'm damned if I'm letting him get away with this.'

Another voice shouted, 'I tell you I know nothing about this. All the time I'm accused of things I'm in total ignorance about. No, please ...'

There was another shriek of pain.

Andrew drew Ginny's attention to the fact that if they weren't careful when they looked over the edge of the sagging boards they would dislodge some of the thick layer of dust and other detritus and give away their presence. Carefully and soundlessly they brushed it to one side.

Those below were not directly beneath them but slightly to one side over by the doorway, the sunlight illuminating what was taking place. Ginny and Andrew were in shadow, well camouflaged by now, Ginny concluded with mixed feelings, with a thick layer of dirt and black cobwebs.

The scene below could have been a set for a film, such was the perfection of the natural lighting and the grouping of those present. Kevin Mackiver was standing nearest to the door, red of face and with all the self-assurance and arrogance of a fighting cock. Pete and Murray were a few feet from him, very uneasy, probably because of the shotgun that Mackiver had crooked over one arm, the impression being that it would first be aimed in their direction. The two estate workers who had been with him previously had hold of Helmut, one of them letting fall a hank of hair that floated down to lie with several others on the floor.

The German started to sob and this seemed to infuriate Mackiver, who stepped forward and slapped him hard.

'You were the only one *there!*' he roared in Helmut's face. 'Even the other two interfering bastards had gone home days previously and I happen to know that McQuade isn't feeling too well at the moment. You were there and insisted on packing your stuff yourself when the gallery staff had seen to the rest. It *has* to be you. Talk — or there won't be a hair left on your head.'

The blow had not improved Helmut's composure. 'No,' he sobbed, tears pouring down his cheeks. 'I always ... always ... handle my own work. I do not trust — '

Mackiver hit him again, a vicious backhander that knocked him over. When he gazed up fearfully, Mackiver kicked him.

'A little packet is missing,' the landowner said silkily. 'We've just checked to be on the safe side and it isn't where it should be or anywhere else and you're the only one who could have taken it. Tell me or I'll blow your head off.'

'No!' Murray shouted shrilly. 'The guy's a real shit but you can't do this to him. I reckon he's telling the truth. God, I wouldn't have come here if I'd known — '

'Shut up!' Mackiver shouted at him. 'Now you've interfered by hijacking the van you'll have to take the consequences.'

'You boobed,' Pete told Murray disgustedly. 'We should have gone to the police, not to this bunch of skunks. What the hell were you thinking of?'

Andrew's right hand was inching towards a rusting axe head half buried in the loose dirt on the loft floor. Before Ginny could react in any way he had raised himself to his knees and thrown it with all the verve of a fielder near the boundary aiming for the wicket.

He said afterwards that he had been aiming for Mackiver's head. As it was, it struck him on the arm, causing him to drop the shotgun with a howl of agony. Pete bent down to grab it but before he could do so one of Mackiver's men kicked him on the side of the head, retrieved the weapon and then had a handful of dust thrown in his face by Murray. Seconds later Mackiver and the two others were running and then were gone.

Moments after that, the boards under Ginny and Andrew gave way.

'No, McQuade *isn't* feeling too well just now,' Ginny heard him say. There was movement in the debris beside her and he sneezed three times. Life was a little vague for a while as she had hit her head where it was injured already. Therefore she was never sure if an exchange between Andrew and Helmut actually took place or whether she imagined it.

'Herr Sunbeam?' Andrew said, going over to touch the tightly curled-up man on the shoulder. 'Are you there, old cheerfulness?' He sat down beside him.

'You Scots are all raving mad,' came the muffled response. 'I hate you.'

Andrew sat him up and proffered his handkerchief. 'Clean this morning. Promise.'

Helmut took it and then, catching sight of the tufts of pulled-out hair, flung his arms around Andrew's neck and wept like a baby. And with the look on his face of a man who is at peace with the world, Andrew hugged him tightly.

Vehicles were arriving outside.

When Chief Inspector Speir strode into the barn some fifteen seconds later, he eyed the tableau within with great distrust. There were several others with him who fanned out, their demeanour suggesting they were hoping to arrest anyone who moved.

'This guy's hurt,' Murray said urgently, indicating Pete.

Speir ground out, 'The two you attacked in the van have headaches too. No, Mr McQuade, please stay right here. I shall need to talk to you very shortly.'

'Did you get them?' Andrew asked. 'Surely you must have done — they must have run right into your arms.'

'There was nothing we could do to stop them. They're armed and have driven off across open country. Unfortunately the helicopter had mechanical trouble and had to be withdrawn.'

'Where have they gone? Over to the north up the hill at the back? You won't have positioned people up there.'

'If you'll kindly — '

'My father's up there and he's *not* armed!'

Speir sighed heavily. 'Then I expect he'll have the good sense to stay out of their way.'

'You don't understand. If they're in a four-wheel drive

191

vehicle they'll get away — and he'll try to stop them.'

'Come back!' Speir shouted, but Andrew had gone.

Ginny, who had heard all this in a kind of daze, got to her feet. No one was taking any notice of her and when she left the barn no effort was made to stop her. She was left with the rather surreal idea that hitting her head on something had made her invisible.

Several cars were parked at the front of the barn, a couple more by the house, with one uniformed constable keeping guard by the door. She assimilated this while pondering the pile of smashed-up jigsaw shapes on the grass outside the barn. From the questioning of Helmut it was obvious that the diamonds had gone missing. Ginny could imagine Mackiver sweating with fear as he searched for the packet, the thought uppermost in his mind that a Glasgow criminal, not convinced by the scheme's efficiency, had sent along a little parcel of death instead.

It was quite possible that the diamonds had not been there in the first place, that someone had been watching and had spirited them away, security arrangements at the gallery notwithstanding.

Rory, for instance.

Ginny went round to the rear of the barn. She could see Andrew setting off doggedly up the hill, his clothes filthy, his shirt torn, limping slightly. Once again, she went after him.

Chapter Sixteen

Up on the high moorland a strange duel was taking place between two Range Rovers, one red, the other black. The latter, looking highly intimidating with its gleaming stainless-steel bullbars, was being driven to great effect, ensuring that those in the red vehicle could not reach the forestry road while avoiding becoming a target itself. This involved making runs at the other vehicle from an angle, preventing the shotgun being fired from the front passenger window.

Ginny started to run but had no breath to call out to Andrew. She was not even sure if he would hear her. She had to admit she was terrified that Rory did indeed possess the missing packet, and that it might contain his annihilation. If the two vehicles collided ... She was quite glad when Andrew tripped, fell flat and stayed down. Her legs leaden, she made a supreme effort and caught up with him.

Up on the hill, some fifty yards away, a shotgun roared.

'He said he had his reasons for not coming closer,' Ginny panted, on her knees at Andrew's side, shaking him. 'Andrew, don't you see? He's got it with him. He took it from the gallery. What the hell are we going to do?'

But Andrew was too exhausted to speak, let alone move.

As Ginny stood up, she saw the vehicles almost collide head-on in a war of nerves that, clearly, Rory was winning. Judging by the jerky way the red Range Rover was being driven Mackiver's injured arm was giving him trouble. All the while it was being harried and shepherded back down the hill.

Suddenly, catching Rory unawares, Mackiver wrenched the car round and made a run for the top of the hill. Rory, careful to stay on the driver's side, overtook, spun round and braked hard. Mackiver, blinded by the unexpected blaze of the sun as it caught the front of the other vehicle, also braked and then pulled away to the right. The man in the passenger seat made full use of the opportunity and fired again.

There was a kind of muted clang as of a collision between two knights at a jousting tournament, and the black vehicle rocked wildly. On the wind came the sound of a jeering cheer uttered by throats hoarse with fear. It resembled the howling of wild animals.

Ginny could only watch as the car came towards them. There was nowhere to hide or take shelter; they were in the middle of the open hillside. Behind them somewhere men were shouting: policemen started up the slope on foot. But they would be too late.

Rory was moving too, accelerating in a wide arc to head the other car off. His speed was impossible for the terrain and Ginny expected him at any moment to overturn. There was no time to run, no time to do anything but fling herself across Andrew and shut her eyes.

Wheels passed very close. Behind them. I'll look death in the face, thought Ginny and did so, gazing instead upon a scene that she never forgot. Rory had turned to drive directly at Mackiver, who again lost his nerve and veered off. But now the black car was in a highly vulnerable position.

'I've got the bastard!' Mackiver's man yelled.

The yell died in his throat as he was hurtled forward. His vehicle's front offside wheel had hit a rock and the tyre had burst. The gun still fired but harmlessly downwards, as the man holding it progressed inexorably forwards and upwards towards the windscreen.

Mackiver had not thought to fasten his seatbelt either and was flung on that same relentless and deadly journey, the car tilting now, right on the edge of the steep bank of the stream. It was helped on its way by the bullbars of Rory's vehicle tucking snugly into the rear of it. Seconds later it was all over, the red car seeming to balance perfectly for a

194

moment on two wheels before tipping over into the burn.

There was a pause, only long enough for Rory to reverse quickly some twenty yards away from the edge, and then the thing that Ginny had been dreading happened. It seemed half a lifetime before the explosion ceased to echo around the mountains and her body felt scorched by the blast, a huge burst of flame that was still burning, acrid smoke and steam rising from the water.

Rory, it must be said, appeared as shocked by what had happened as anyone. If he was also angry that the rear of his Lichfield conversion − cream leather seats to match the Italian hand-made steering wheel − had taken the full force of the shotgun blast, he kept it to himself. After a long reflective gaze at the fiercely burning car, the interior of which was a crackling inferno, he brought out a hip flask, turned Andrew over with a noticeable lack of finesse, raised his head and coaxed a little golden fluid between his lips.

'It's not a good idea to try to make unconscious people drink anything,' Ginny said, 'let alone alcohol.'

Rory gave her a mischievous, if wan, smile. 'He isn't, *mo ghaiol,* and it's not. This is a reviving elixir that can be bought in all herbal chemists. Here, take some yourself. You most certainly need it.' He again scanned the burning car. 'Well, now, isn't that a horrible way to go?'

Andrew sat up with a groan and put his head in his hands. In a twinkling, despite his own slight build, Rory had yanked him to his feet.

'There,' Rory said soothingly. 'Now pretend that you have just landed from your fall off the mountain. You are quite unhurt and here is your woman waiting to take you somewhere quiet where she will make much of you and tell you she loves you dearly. Now, if you'll excuse me I have to go and talk to those policemen.' And with that he went to his car, got in it and drove off down the hill.

'He's mad,' Ginny stated.

'Hates it when people get mawkish,' Andrew murmured, leaning on her rather heavily. 'But he might have given us a lift back.'

'He saved our lives!'

'Yes. Quite. That's why he was afraid you'd burst into

tears and thank him and things like that.'

'And I just nagged him for giving you what I thought was whisky!' Ginny sighed.

'Nagging was far preferable to sentiment in Rory's eyes — and so would whisky have been in mine. Now, I think I can walk downhill if you take charge of any tendency on my part to go sideways.'

When they had gone a few yards, he said, 'Take no notice of what he said. He doesn't understand about the sort of relationship people have when they're working together in this day and age. That a man and woman can work closely, even go to bed together and — ' He stopped dead and swung round in horror. 'What's that bloody great *fire?*'

'I didn't think you were really *compos mentis*,' Ginny said, then told him.

'Do you think Mackiver had it all along? And yet he made a play of ...'

'No,' Ginny said when Andrew stopped speaking. 'He wasn't a man who could act — not like that.'

'Greed gives people all kinds of talents.'

'Yes, I know. But I still don't think he had the package, be it diamonds or booby traps. That explosion was something else entirely — I've never seen anything like it.'

'The old man knows a lot of folk,' Andrew said grimly. 'Some of them aren't exactly legal.' He subsided onto the ground. 'I'm sorry, I simply can't go any farther.'

Ginny went down on her own and asked a couple of policemen to help him.

Despite what he had said, Rory was refusing to answer any questions and complied only when a car swept into the drive, bringing a top-ranking member of Glasgow CID. By this time everyone was in the house. Rory immediately handed a small packet to him, the recipient's lack of profuse thanks possibly indicating disenchantment with the giver. The two men disappeared into a room together for quite some time. When Rory emerged at last, two pairs of eyes surveyed him quizzically.

'You can go now,' Rory said to Andrew. 'Both of you. I've obtained permission for you to give your statements when you're feeling better.'

'We have no transport,' Andrew said.

'My motor's outside,' Murray said quickly.

Andrew said, 'Yes, but you'll be here a while yet, being charged with assaulting police officers.'

'We didn't *know* they were cops,' Pete agonised. He had a lump like a bantam's egg on the side of his head. 'After what Ginny told us, we thought we'd *do* something.'

'You didn't exactly give them a chance to show you their identification.'

'I'm sure the good commander isn't thirsting for your blood,' Rory assured them. 'No one, I think expected it would end the way it has. If the art exhibits had been returned to the institute as planned and Mackiver had taken charge of Murray's, there would have been a highly dangerous situation. The explosive device might have gone off at any time, even right in the centre of the village, and many innocent people could have been killed or injured.'

Ginny said, 'But you had already removed an extra shape that had been added to Murray's exhibit at the gallery.'

'For which far-sightedness and prudence my ears are still burning,' Rory countered. 'I'll give you a lift home.'

Andrew sat unmoving. 'And Herr Joyfulness? He's been interviewed already. A victim of circumstances, wouldn't you say, and not feeling too good either?'

'I have my own car,' Helmut said stiffly. 'Thank you, but I shall make my own way back. Slowly.'

'How come he was here?' Ginny wanted to know on the way out.

Rory said, 'It appears that he had been down into the village on foot and was almost back at the institute when Murray and Pete — bless their sweet souls — literally took the law into their own hands. From that distance he didn't know it was them — all he could see was men ransacking the van. By the time he had reached the place — and I can have missed seeing him only by seconds — the two had gone. Helmut thought one of his crates had been stolen — it's probably in a ditch at the scene of the crime — ran back up the hill to his car and gave chase.'

'While Mackiver was waiting up at the institute.'

'So it appears. Helmut arrived, shouting to the world

what had happened, so Mackiver quietly left for home by the off-road route, the track that joins the one we were on. Only, of course, he would have left it where it crosses the main road and turned into his private drive. We went a much longer way round in order to go round the back.'

'But I thought that this business of sea-borne art exhibitions was to take place at the end of the season?'

'That was the original arrangement with Malcolm Hurrell. Now the poor man is no longer around to oversee the running of the place ...' Rory shook his head sadly. 'Perhaps we'll never know the truth of it but I should imagine the man was terrorised into cooperating. We shall remain in ignorance of a lot of things now that an important witness is dead.'

'There's Bloxton, though,' Andrew said.

'He is one of the trustees and, according to the commander, without reproach,' Rory replied in tones that suggested he did not intend to talk about it further.

Ginny, however, felt that a lot more questions needed answering. She could understand how Rory felt; his professional duty was to prevent money from reaching terrorists. The fact that he had also settled certain personal and long-outstanding matters must be a source of deep satisfaction, despite the tragic outcome.

He took them home, refused all offers of hospitality and left.

'That isn't the end of it,' she said to Andrew in his living room.

'No, but it's the end of *me,*' he muttered, folding up like something suddenly deflated on the sofa.

She covered him with the quilt from his bed and went home.

There was to be no peace. First Ginny had a phone call from John Laird to ask how she and Andrew were, to which she replied that neither of them was thinking of dancing the night away, adding that Andrew was actually in pretty poor shape, suffering from utter exhaustion. Glad of his good sense and reassuring manner, she then went on to share a few of her fears with him, the greatest of these being that the murderer had not yet been caught. He tutted gravely and made her

198

promise that she would make sure that all her doors were securely locked before she went to bed.

Feminine fear was not what she had meant to convey at all.

The phone rang again. This time it was Flinders Cochran, the cameraman who had filmed at the Highland Games, saying that he was in the area and could he drop the reels off as the police had released them to him? Andrew had given him both phone numbers but he could get no reply from him. Heavy-hearted, for she was ready to drop, Ginny agreed, and he said he would be in Kinloch Ruthven in about twenty minutes.

She knew nothing about Flinders Cochran, except that he was of Scots-Canadian parentage and more than a little eccentric. She did not welcome him with her usual enthusiasm.

'The cops said you were right there for the kill!' he said gleefully when he arrived, crashing a large metal box down on the bare boards of the hall floor. 'But look, if the entire thing's up the spout for you because it's sub judice, then forget it. I got a bloody fortune for the footage of the warfare from Scottish Television.'

'Come in,' Ginny said. 'Can I offer you a drink?'

He was a bit like a well-dressed scarecrow; long flailing arms and a mop of unruly fair hair that badly needed a trim. 'Just a Coke or something — I'm driving and the cops always have it in for me.'

'I'm sorry, I've only got whisky or white wine — I haven't really moved in yet.'

'The grape!' he cried, hurling himself into a chair. 'Why not? It brings me luck, always has. Someone gave me a glass of bubbly at that show and then look what happened. Just as well I made the bucks on the riot, though; it was a dead loss as an advert for the Highlands. Come to bonny Scotland and get a skene dhu rammed up your arse. I can't see that in the travel brochures, can you?'

'Is that what you were doing — filming for the tourist industry?' Ginny asked as she gave him his drink.

'Bread and butter. Yes. It's humble stuff but who am I

199

to turn it down? Feel free to keep the stuff for a bit — I don't actually need it right now.'

'I shall have to take it down to London to see it.'

'Phooey! I can arrange for you to take a look in either Glasgow or Edinburgh any time you like. Just give me the word. A lot of it's crap, mind. The mood those folk were in when the hassle started ... I got out of the way. Cameras don't come cheap. A big hairy guy threw a punch at me — thought I was filming him half throttling an even bigger guy. And two guys who were walking into a tent didn't see me and knocked the whole caboodle over. That was before the trouble really got going.'

'Which tent?'

'God above knows. Yeah, I know, something to do with an art show. Say, wasn't that — ?'

'Yes. Please try to remember. Did you get them on film?'

'No. Not a chance. They came at me from sort of sideways, having a hell of an argument. Didn't even apologise, either, just looked at me as though I shouldn't be there.'

'Can you remember what they looked like?'

'No. Not really. But they weren't like the lot that started slugging it out. Middle-class, middle-aged bods. Yeah, I seem to think that one was wearing a green Barbour jacket — country-gentleman sort of clothes. New-looking too. The other man didn't register at all. I think he must have been wearing something pretty nondescript.'

Malcolm Hurrell had been wearing a dark-grey lightweight anorak and matching trousers.

'And they went into the tent?'

'Perhaps. I was too busy picking my equipment up to notice.'

'Did you overhear what they were saying?'

'No, the PA was drowning it out — the tug-of-war had started. All I know is that they were having the mother of all rows.'

'So what happened next?'

'I wandered over to the tug-of-war. But after the guy threw a punch at me, I set up shop in the back of someone's pick-up. That's where I got the best footage.'

200

'Are you sure there's nothing else you remember about the man wearing the waxed jacket?'

Cochran chewed his lips, frowning deeply. 'He was about as tall as me. About my build.'

'What about his hair?'

'Short,' he replied. 'But I've no idea of the colour.'

He left soon afterwards, saying that he had to get home to Edinburgh. Ginny carefully bolted and barred the front door when she had let him out, then, after some thought, she made two phone calls.

Some time later she opened the door to a grim-faced Laird.

'So you know who the murderer is?' Laird said after Ginny had settled him in a chair with some coffee. 'Have you told the police?'

'I've mentioned no names,' Ginny told him, cradling her mug of coffee in both hands.

'But surely the police aren't looking for anyone else after what happened earlier today?'

'You heard about that?'

'Murray Kenning came to see me for some legal advice. He and his friend are to be charged in connection with an offence involving a van — I suppose you know about that.'

'Yes.'

'And Harry Bloxton rang me. He's one of the trustees of the institute and an acquaintance of mine; we did our legal training together and meet very occasionally for a round of golf. He said that Helmut Beyer had returned in a very emotional state, complaining that he'd been assaulted. He's going back to Germany — as soon as possible, according to Harry.'

'He'll have to return at some point — he's an important witness.'

'He found Hurrell's body, I understand.'

'That's right.'

'I'm rather surprised the police released him so quickly after they questioned him. After all, the murder weapon *was* his property.'

'And by his own admission he was in the tent all the time. But there was no motive to kill Hurrell — the two men got on quite well. He had every reason to hate Jean Kirkpatrick, however; she refused to have sex with him, called him a dirty Jew.'

'Oh, dear,' Laird murmured, 'how unfortunate. The poor girl wasn't very bright, I'm afraid.'

'No. I think she was killed by someone she liked and trusted, someone to whom she went with her worries when she discovered that some of Murray's jigsaw shapes could be opened and packages concealed inside.'

'That's *very* unlikely, surely?'

'And there's the business of the watch – the one she didn't own, that was planted in Andrew McQuade's bedroom. Her husband was bribed to say it had belonged to her aunt – . Only she didn't have an aunt.'

'I'm staggered by what you've discovered,' Laird said.

'Then there's these mysterious anonymous phone calls. Firstly there was the one to the Glen Hotel to cancel my booking. Only one person besides Maggie Mossblown and the hotel receptionist knew I was returning to Kinloch Ruthven. Then there was the call to you last Sunday night to say Andrew and I had been hurt.'

'I've since thought that sounded like Mackiver's voice.'

'I'm sure it was. And you might be interested to know that a short while ago I had a visit from a cameraman who was filming at the Highland Games. The police have given him back all his material now – it doesn't look as though he captured anything on film that will lead to finding Hurrell's killer. But his camera equipment was knocked over by two men who were arguing as they went in the direction of the Art Institute's tent, just as the tug-of-war was starting. The description of both of them is vague, but one might have been Hurrell. Now, Andrew and I left Hurrell *inside* the tent but it's possible that he was waiting to speak to someone and, when that person did not appear, went outside to look for him. While he was gone away Helmut must have arrived – if his account is to be believed – and gone straight into the little curtained-off office, where he listened to music on his personal stereo and remained in utter ignorance of everything that was happening, both in the tent and in the show ground generally. I think I *can* believe that. He doesn't care a damn

202

about anything except his work.'

'If Mackiver was the killer, he must have been there too.'

'Yes, he was there when the fighting started. He was seen by Ninian Effrick of Effrick who was on his way back from buying a shotgun from someone. Wisely, Effrick didn't hang around. So Mackiver was in the vicinity. And Hurrell had just returned to the tent with another man and nearly fallen over Flinders Cochran's camera. That other man was wearing a green Barbour jacket. Similar to the one you have on now.'

'It won't be easy to trace him from that! There are literally thousands of them round here.'

'But there aren't many of those candlesticks,' Ginny said, pointing to the mantelpiece. 'The murderer used it to see what he was doing down in the cellar here when he dragged Jean Kirkpatrick's body in through the coal hatch. It had come from the institute – Hurrell's office, actually. I'm fairly sure that it was taken by Hurrell to cast a little light when he and several other men went out with Jean to the potting shed when the party was drawing to a close and everyone had had far more to drink than has, so far, been admitted. No one saw them. There was a power cut and either those concerned were genuinely too drunk to remember names and faces or there's been the sort of conspiracy of silence that men tend to operate on such occasions. But *you* weren't drunk. You remember everything.'

Laird stared at her, wordless.

'Solicitors meet all sorts of criminals,' Ginny continued. 'I think your friend Bloxton got involved with a few Irish godfathers in Glasgow and eventually, because the offer was so lucrative, so did – '

Deep down in the basement there was a heavy thump, the sound seeming to reverberate through the entire house; then footfalls, as though someone was slowly coming up the stairs.

Despite a firm refusal to believe in ghosts, Ginny felt the blood drain from her face.

'I thought you were alone,' Laird said.

'I am.'

'Who else have you shared your suspicions with?'

Ginny had locked the door at the top of the stairs but it now yielded with the kind of sound that suggested it had crashed off its hinges.

Visibly alarmed, Laird got to his feet. 'Well, I'm not going to – '

'Stay around while the female sleuth is finished off?' Ginny said. 'I don't think I'm in danger from outside this room, do you?'

'*She* was down there,' Laird whispered, eyes glassy. 'Now she's ...' His voice trailed away. 'You'll have to go down there too. When I've – ' He came towards her. 'I'll be quick if you don't try to stop me. Please, don't struggle. *She* struggled. That was very hard and I hadn't done it before.'

He didn't say any more, just moved inexorably in Ginny's direction with an earnest, pleading look on his face. She side-stepped around an armchair hoping to use it as a barrier between them, but he was too quick for her. She could not take her eyes off that pale, imploring face, begging her not to make a fuss, to make it easy for him. Then his hands were around her throat.

'Andrew! Where the hell are you?' Ginny shrieked.

A dishevelled figure fell in through the door. 'I couldn't get the damned thing off the wall,' it pointed out reproachfully, before prodding Laird between the shoulder blades.

Laird caught a glimpse of what he had been prodded with and fainted.

'You've killed him!' Ginny gasped.

Andrew viewed the point of the Red Graham's sword with clinical interest. 'No. There's not enough blood on it for that.'

'I knew it was you as soon as the door fell in,' Ginny said later, the police having departed with a murder suspect who needed a couple of stitches in a superficial flesh wound.

'I couldn't sleep so I had a wee dram,' Andrew reported. 'Only a wee one, you understand. That must have done the trick, for I woke up all at once when the phone rang. It was Rory calling to see how I was – I was talking to him when

204

I saw the lights of a car turn in here. I rang off and went to the window, where I saw by the light in your porch that it was Laird. Then I suddenly remembered where I'd seen that Bloxton character before — up on the golf course with him, as thick as thieves.'

'But why didn't you come in through the front door? I'd left it unlocked in case I had to make a run for it.'

'You set this up on your own? Are you mad, woman?'

'You haven't answered my question,' Ginny told him calmly.

He had been standing and now sort of crumpled into a chair. 'Well, for all I knew it might have been above board, you and him. You might have asked him round for a drink, a friendly chat. So I thought I'd sneak in and ...' Abashed, he ran his hands through his already tousled hair, shedding an appreciable amount of coal dust.

The thought of him creeping about and then falling headlong through the coal hatch was too much for Ginny.

'Go on, laugh,' he said, with an injured air.

'I didn't even have time to confront him with the only real piece of evidence I had — that he and Maggie were the only people I had told I was coming back to the village.'

'Maggie's a terrible gossip, so that probably won't stand up in court.'

'No. But he'll have to explain why he was about to strangle me.'

Andrew looked as though he was on the point of going to sleep. Then he said, 'Rory told me that there were only two bodies in the Range Rover; Mackiver's and the bloke who seemed to be his number-one thug. There was no trace of the other, the stupid-looking one.'

'And he could hide in the hills for ever.'

'That wasn't quite Rory's point. I'd not thought to ask myself why that explosive device concealed under Mackiver's car didn't go off when they were driving to Muirpark across the moor or anywhere else for that matter. The answer, surely, must be that it hadn't been planted then. That occurred when the vehicle was parked near the barn.'

'Rory can't have done it. He was up on the hill.'

'He didn't. And we know it can't have been the Glasgow

205

gang, or they would have risked losing the diamonds.'

'The stupid-looking man? But why?'

'Rory reckons he might not have been so stupid. In short, he might work for MI5 — or something along those lines. But he's not asking and he said he'd skin me alive if I told you and *you* started asking.'

'Heaven forbid that you should come to such a messy end,' Ginny murmured.

Chapter Seventeen

The odd affair of the sheep butchered in McQuade's kitchen was finally explained when Mackiver's gamekeeper was questioned by police in connection with his employer's involvement in murder and handling stolen property. It was nothing more than bizarre personal revenge − the estate worker in question being the man whom McQuade had been fighting with in the Dog and Drover and who had had his head rapped smartly on the floor. Andrew, who had not been able to remember the event afterwards, had launched himself at the man, accusing him of killing Alastair Somerville's dog. No charges were pressed against either for this affray but the gamekeeper finally found himself accused of being an accessory to murder. On the night of Jean Kirkpatrick's death he had wilfully damaged electrical power lines by sawing through a pole, causing the wires to fall into a tree on Mackiver's orders.

Kenneth Kirkpatrick, Jean's husband, admitted that he had been paid by Kevin Mackiver to say, in the event of the discovery of his wife's body, that her watch was missing. Kirkpatrick had received through the post a photograph and detailed description of a silver and gilt lady's watch, some fifty years old, with instructions to memorise the information before destroying it.

Mackiver and Laird had already decided McQuade would be implicated if and when the body was found. The watch had been planted in his house only twenty minutes before it was found by the police, the news of the body's discovery at the Manse having been in the early editions of the *Corran*

Record. The man who planted it died with Mackiver in the Range Rover.

There was no real evidence against John Laird until Harry Bloxton was arrested at Glasgow airport. At first Bloxton denied all knowledge of the crimes and he did not confess until he was confronted with a ten-pound note − part of the money with which he had paid off the institute's gardener. The serial numbers were in sequence with other notes found in a cash box in Malcolm Hurrell's office. The money, all new notes, had been stolen in a bank raid in Stirling six months previously.

For some years, money, the proceeds of organised crime centred in Glasgow, had been carried across the Irish Sea, usually by ferry from Stranraer to Larne, sometimes by air. Latterly, with increased vigilance by police and customs officers, the traffic had become hazardous. The idea of a private boat had been dreamed up by Bloxton himself. The archetypal bent solicitor, his involvement with the gang had begun when he had acted for one of its members, a man whom Bloxton managed to rescue from charges of burglary and assault amid allegations of intimidation of witnesses. And this man, who had worked for Kevin Mackiver in the past, had suggested using the *Seawitch*.

According to Bloxton, Mackiver had agreed immediately, his financial circumstances at that time being somewhat straitened. At first stolen property was hidden in boxes of frozen salmon from the Mackiver fish farm. After three trips this had been felt to be too risky and other hiding places had been sought. Mackiver, after a duty visit to an open day at the MacNaughton Institute of Art, put forward the idea.

Had it not been for Bloxton's liking for a drink, John Laird would never have known what was going on, and would never have been drawn into the series of calamities which eventually saw him standing trial for murder. Bloxton, made reckless by alcohol, had boasted one evening at the golf club that he was something of a master criminal. Laird, more than curious, had persuaded him to reveal a great deal more than was wise. The next morning, a sober and regretful Bloxton had resorted to threats and even bribes to ensure his friend's silence. But Laird, weighted down with a second mortgage on his home after injudicious dabbling on the stock exchange, wanted a slice of the cake. And, like Mackiver, he was ensnared.

Laird, law-abiding for so many years, surprised himself with his ingenuity. He discovered it was very easy indeed to take money for helping Bloxton to keep the Glasgow gang out of prison. It was child's play to befriend Malcolm Hurrell, who was delighted with the novel idea of a floating exhibition, conveying his student's work on a pleasure cruise between Scotland and Ireland – delighted until Jean Kirkpatrick whispered in his ear that Mackiver was no art lover and that local rumour favoured something strange afoot. For Mackiver's men had been gossiping. Hurrell did not live long enough to act on his newly acquired knowledge. His urgent demand for the truth, as he confronted first Laird and then Bloxton, was his death warrant. In the institute tent, his increasingly frantic questions were finally answered.

Under police questioning, Laird insisted that it was Mackiver who had wielded the pitchfork. Certainly, Ninian Effric remembered seeing Mackiver leave the tent at the appropriate time – but he wouldn't have recognised Laird, who was unknown to him, so it was possible that Laird's exit had gone unnoticed. Laird did, however, confess to strangling Jean – after the scene at Ginny's house he had little choice. Hurrell had disclosed the source of the rumours; bizarrely, Jean herself had also been seen speaking to Laird, her face earnest and anxious, on the night of the institute party. With hindsight, the police assumed that she had been denying her involvement, pleading for her life. Only much later did Laird reveal the pitiful truth: she had been desperately exonerating Hurrell, begging that he should not be dragged into anything 'wrongous'. For Hurrell had been kind to her, had been one of the few men who treated her like a human being.

And Laird had been the last man who had gone with her into the shed at the bottom of the garden. But he hadn't gone for sex.

The involvement of Morag and her friend – who was only ever identified as Tim – turned out to be a red herring, as Ginny and Commander Fielding had suspected. No one knew how Morag had stumbled upon some vestige of the truth. Had Jean Kirkpatrick, turning instinctively for reassurance to the only other female at the institute, made her an unlikely confidante? Or had Morag overheard Jean talking to Laird or Hurrell — perhaps on the night of the party? However it had happened, it was clear that she had then phoned the man she loved, the only person she trusted, and made him her partner in crime. Police investigations led to a semiderelict building in Glasgow, occupied by a group of young squatters. Tim had been one of them. They had no idea where he had come from, no idea even of his surname. The squatters told the police, albeit reluctantly, that Tim had been bragging that he'd spoken to an old girlfriend, been told how he could make some money. They had assumed he was referring to drugs. The ancient Citroën car, untaxed and uninsured, had been the joint property of the group. The squatters didn't read the papers or watch TV, so news of the bomb explosion had passed them by.

It was Chief Inspector Speir who told all this to Ginny. He was clearly moved by the thought of the two young people, unmissed and unmourned, who had set off together in the beat-up car, believing they had got away with something of value, something that would perhaps help them start a new life together. Speir said he liked to think they died happy. His faith made him look for glimmers of goodness in people.

With the Chief Inspector's words echoing in her mind, Ginny went for a walk up on the quiet hill at the end of the village. She took with her a large bunch of yellow roses from the garden at the Manse. It was a warm, overcast afternoon; the flowers seemed to glow with an inner light as she arranged them on the grave.

'Andrew's gone to London,' she whispered, 'to talk to Jake. But don't worry — I'm still looking after him.'

She yearned to achieve the impossible, to turn back the clock, find out just why her mother had denied her father's very existence, had banished him from her life. Perhaps it was simply that she was scared by her father's moods, his emotional need for something she couldn't provide. It might have had something to do with her own repressed upbringing within a very strict and teetotal Baptist family. To

Ginny's knowledge, her mother had never touched alcohol in her life.

When Andrew returned, there was only one thing clouding his horizon.

'I tried to buy back my watch,' he said, having planted a perfunctory kiss on Ginny's cheek. 'Crawthorne actually asked me if I'd like an advance − '

'I'm totally gobsmacked,' Ginny admitted. 'He must have been told exactly how good you are.'

'But someone had already bought it.'

'I found the receipt the shop gave you for it on the floor.'

He frowned. 'So?'

She had been wearing the watch and now took it off and gave it to him. 'You sold it because of me. I can't have that on my conscience.'

'I can't have owing you one and a half thousand quid on mine.'

'You don't. I paid for it with the money from the will. He'd have wanted me to do it.'

Andrew blinked quickly a few times. 'It would be very ill-mannered of me to argue with that. Thank you.'

'Perhaps, on a fine day, we could go for a walk and look at the mountains.'

'Perhaps,' he said.

'In Ireland?'

'Now there's a thought.'